The Man of Maybe Half-a-Dozen Faces

The Man of Maybe Half-a-Dozen Faces

Ray Vukcevich

St. Martin's Minotaur ✽ New York

Edited by Gordon Van Gelder
Design by Heidi Eriksen

ISBN 0-312-24652-8

First Edition: February 2000

10   9   8   7   6   5   4   3   2   1

For
Steve
&
Gladys Vukcevich

Acknowledgments

Thanks go to the people who helped with the early idea: Jerry Wolfe, Cody Wasner, Damien Filer, and Leslie What. Thanks go to the people who read later versions: Martha Bayless, Nina Kiriki Hoffman, Jerry Oltion, and Dean Wesley Smith. And special thanks go to Kate Wilhelm for reading the book and telling me what to do with it.

The
Man
of Maybe
Half-a-Dozen
Faces

one

Because she looked like something I'd make up myself, it took me a couple of blinks to convince myself she was real. Low-slung faded blue jeans and a lime-green sawed-off T-shirt. Bare midriff and (gulp) a ruby in her navel. Her eyes were brown or green or both or maybe they just handled the light well, and her reddish brown hair was stylishly windblown. Maybe early thirties—make that thirty-three for symmetry. Ice-country skin. She held a couple of trained seals on leashes. The seals balanced red-and-yellow beach balls on their noses.

No, wait a moment. I really did make up that bit about the ruby. And the seals. Kill the seals. I mean forget the seals. What was I thinking? There were no seals.

I quickly deduced that the feet leaning like drunks in their scuffed black PI shoes, alongside the remains of what may once have been tacos atop the old wooden desk, must be mine. Off to one side dragons, one right after another, were shot out of canons to fly with silent screams from one end of the computer screen to the other where they splattered and oozed down to gather at the bottom as Technicolor goo. I don't want to tell you how long it took me to jungle chop my way through the instruction manual to get the dragons shooting just the way I wanted them to shoot and splat.

I cringed at a sudden irritated honk from the street three floors below. Honking in Eugene, Oregon, is so rare that I'll bet there were people hanging out of windows all up and down the block to see what the hubbub was about.

I discovered a cigarette between the first two fingers of my right hand and sucked in a little smoke and then let it run out of my mouth and up my face to pool under the brim of my hat. Coughed.

Hey, hold the phone. Didn't I quit smoking? Yes, I definitely did quit smoking. So that was phantom smoke under my hat. I'd been sucking on a yellow number-two pencil, but the cough was real.

"So who am I?" I demanded. "And what do I want with you?"

"Skylight Howells—Private Investigator." She hooked a thumb over her shoulder at the backwards letters on the cloudy glass of the door. "You want to help me with my brother."

"Your brother?"

"Pablo."

She walked in, and as she moved, little zips and zaps of electricity fired all up and down my body. She pulled up a chair in front of my desk. I moved my feet and sat up. There was a can of Tecate next to the remains of my lunch and I picked it up and sipped. The beer was warm, but at least there weren't any soggy phantom cigarette butts floating in it.

"Look into my eyes and read my lips," she said. "You're a private investigator. You are, in fact, a world famous private investigator. You come highly recommended."

"World famous?"

"Well, okay, you're in the yellow pages."

"You found me in the yellow pages?"

"I said you came highly recommended," she said. "A foreign gentleman in whom I have the utmost trust said I should talk to you. I just looked up your address in the yellow pages."

"And you are?"

"Prudence Deerfield," she said and leaned over the desk and put her hand out for me to shake.

"Call me Sky," I said, getting into the spirit of things. When Sky comes on the scene, I have to hit the ground running. I took her hand in both of mine and separated her fingers and examined each neat bloodred nail and shivered at the cool loveliness of her skin, then turned her hand over again and gently traced the lines in her palm.

"Hey!" She snatched her hand back. "Don't get fresh, gumchew."

Had I heard her right? I waited her out with a straight face, but she gave not the slightest indication that the crack had been a joke. A slip of the tongue? Maybe English wasn't her first language, or maybe American wasn't her first culture.

"You're not from around here, are you?" I said.

"Er . . . What makes you say that?"

I decided to let it go for now. "So, what's the deal with Pablo?"

"First things first." She leaned down to dig in her bag. I could feel my neck growing up and up and as it did I could see more and more of her, but then she sat back up, and I turtled down and polished off the rest of the warm Mexican beer.

She flipped open a steno pad, slapped it down on the desk, and pushed it in my direction. There, in painfully neat handwriting, was some math.

$$f(y) = (y^2 + 1)^2 (y - 1)^5 y^3$$

"What's this?"

"Calculus," she said.

"And?"

"I want you to calculate the derivative," she said. "Use logarithmic differentiation."

"You want me to use logarithmic differentiation?"

"I want to be sure you've got the right stuff to help Pablo," she said.

"But detective work is nothing like calculus."

"So you say." She picked up the stingy yellow stub of a pencil I'd earlier been smoking and tossed it to me.

"I don't suppose you'll let me use the computer?"

"Use your noodle," she said.

"You want me to cook?"

"What?"

"My noodle?" I said.

I watched her eyes dart left and right like she was scanning her database of idioms. A few seconds later, she said, "The one on your shoulders."

I wasn't ready to give in yet, so I gave her a puzzled look.

"Your head," she said, "use your head."

She was the real puzzle. I couldn't get a handle on her. I looked long and hard into her eyes, calculating if this would even be worth the trouble. I did, after all, have a couple of other cases—a dangerous one and a ridiculously easy one. I might not have taken the dangerous one in the first place if Prudence Deerfield had showed up last week, but now that I had taken it, could I afford to be distracted? I looked so long and hard that she squirmed a little in her chair. Then she sighed and slumped back and suddenly looked so helpless and alone that I knew I was hooked. How could I not help?

Okay, it's true I didn't have to do it right in front of her face, but I did want to see her reaction, so I ripped off my mustache.

"Ouch!" she said.

I turned my back, ran a comb through my hair, put on a new nose, and Dennis, "the Math Guy," poofed into existence, but couldn't really see diddly without my glasses, so I pawed around in the top left desk drawer until I found them and put them on and took a look at a moderately interesting equation. I glanced up at the pretty woman on the other side of the desk, and she smiled at me. Nice teeth.

"Piece of cake," I said. "You want it simplified or not?"

"Your choice," she said.

I wrestled the equation to the ground and twisted its ears until it coughed up the derivative, which I then copied directly under the equation itself. No stinking scribbling around the edges.

"Here you go," I said and pushed the pad back across the desk.

She looked it over. "Not bad," she said, "not bad. Now, suppose a train leaves . . ."

So, we did a few word problems.

Then she made me straighten out a Rubik's Cube which was nooo problem.

"Next," I said.

"That's enough," she said. "Let me tell you about the case."

"Wait," I said and turned my back. I pulled off my nose and put on my mustache again. Dropped the bottle-bottom glasses back into the desk drawer. Put my hat back on. "Okay. Tell me."

She dug in her bag again and then put a thin volume on the desk and turned it so I could read the title.

ASP*+

Version 1.0

by
Gerald Moffitt and Pablo Deerfield

"Your brother?"

"We're twins."

"Is that relevant?"

She put her finger on the byline. "Gerald is dead," she said. "Murdered. Strangled with a printer cable."

"A which?"

"You know," she said, "a standard IEEE-1284 compliant parallel interface cable."

I glanced over at my own printer. "You mean the one with the little 1284-A connector on one end and a big 1284-B connector on the other end?"

"Exactly," she said. "Then the killer wrote all over the body."

"Wrote?"

"The police didn't give me the details," she said. "I don't know if it was Magic Marker or what, but there was just one word over and over again on every conceivable patch of skin."

"And the word?"

"Exceptions," she said.

"Exceptions?"

"Yes."

"So what does it mean?"

"It's a computer term," she said. "It has something to do with when things go wrong."

"Hmm," I said.

"What?"

"Just hmm," I said. "That's detective talk for the wheels are turning. Go on."

"I'm sure the police think Pablo did it."

"Oh?"

"Pablo's well . . . missing." She looked away quickly, and I decided to watch closely in the days ahead to see if she always looked away when she lied. Sure, I had no reason to believe Pablo wasn't really missing, but I had the gut feeling there was more to it.

I watched her lower lip quiver, and I thought she might cry, but she pulled herself together. "Actually," she said, "he's probably in hiding. He and Gerald were partners in GP Ink, a company that produces these manuals. If Gerald was killed because of the business, Pablo could be next!"

"And what do you want me to do about it?"

"Prove Pablo didn't kill Gerald," she said. "And find out who did!"

"Have we talked about money?"

"Money's no problem," she said.

"It's always been a problem for me."

"I can pay your fee," she said. "Whatever it is."

"I may be too busy for this," I said.

She looked around the room. The shabby couch. The dusty shelves with my collection of phone books from other cities, the bound volumes of *American PI* magazine, the silver tap trophy I'd won more years ago than I'm willing to say, the three big wall maps—Oregon state, Portland city map, and Eugene city map—the latter so covered with colored push pins you'd think I was having trouble keeping it nailed to the wall. At least the bare bulb above us wasn't swinging in a wind from nowhere.

"I can see you're up to your ears," she said.

I could understand how she might not be overwhelmed by feelings of frantic activity.

But everything depends on how you look at it.

"As it happens," I said, "I'm right in the middle of a very juicy divorce investigation. I can't wait to nail this one. You wouldn't want me to lose my focus."

"You can do this, too."

"Maybe," I said. "Why don't you get out your checkbook?"

So she got out her checkbook. I mentioned a figure and she didn't even haggle, which made me kick myself for not mentioning a higher figure.

"You know," I said, "I'll probably have to run Pablo down in the course of this investigation." I noticed the address on her check was a post office box, and she hadn't included a phone number.

"Just be careful," she said. "If he's hiding I don't want you finding him for the police."

"You know where he is," I said, and looked her right in the eye. What the hell, it was worth a shot.

"I do not!"

"Okay, but there is the possibility that he did kill Gerald Moffitt."

"He didn't."

"I have to consider it," I said.

I turned my eyes down before she could crisp my face with the glare she was beaming at me across the desk. I pulled the ASP*+ book across the desk and opened it.

"What's Asp . . . this?" I asked without looking up. "A book about snakes?"

"A computer language," she said. "A net navigation language actually. You say each letter: A and then S and then P and then Star and then Plus—ASP*+. Stands for 'A Special Protocol.' Geeks tell me it makes it a breeze to wiggle around on the Internet."

"Geeks?"

"I say that affectionately and with respect."

"I can hear the affection and respect in your voice," I said.

"So, when can I expect you to actually do something?"

I put my finger on my place in the book and looked up at her. "Why don't you go somewhere where I can get ahold of you," I had to take a couple of deep breaths to get past the thought of getting ahold of her, "and cool your heels until you hear from me? You got a phone?"

"I'll call you," she said.

"Or you'll just drop back in?" I said maybe with too much naked hope in my voice.

"One more thing," she said. "The police have locked everyone out of the GP Ink office. Is that going to be a problem for you?"

"You figure the place is full of clues?"

"Wouldn't you think?"

"I'll check it out," I told her.

She got to her feet and I watched her leave. After she'd shut the door, I sighed and bent back to the book. I turned to the index to see where I might find some talk about "exceptions," but the word didn't appear in the index. Nothing is ever straightforward.

two

I never go off half-cocked on a new case until I've run it by my therapist. Here, in Eugene, you can go out on the street and pick a pedestrian, any pedestrian, and chances are good you'll get a therapist of some kind. From photo therapy (ever notice how people change when you point a camera at them?) to guided origami and everything in between. And if you don't get a therapist, it's a good bet you can at least get a fancy massage, but I didn't do local therapy. I had trouble being myself in person. My man Roger was on-line.

Earlier someone had been covering up covert action with a phony hacking cough out in the hall, but whoever it was had moved on or at least slipped out of sight by the time I looked. I locked the door, settled back down behind my desk, peeled off my mustache and touched the tender place under my nose and winced. I tossed my hat onto the desk and pulled the keyboard over in front of me and logged on to the net. My standard browser windows divided the screen into neat squares. An e-mail window, the call-waiting alert, in case anyone had anything to say to me on the phone, and a couple of portals. Dennis called this doing many things at once "multi-tasking," and we were pretty good at it.

My animated persona for therapy looked a little like one of those *Mad* magazine spies, but with more colors available. I was blue when I popped into existence outside Roger's office. I had to wait a few minutes, and as I stood there twiddling my cyberthumbs, whistling tunes and looking right and left and up and down into cyberspace (not to mention among and through—directions not ordinarily encountered on the outside), I got sprayed in the face with purple varmint gas, and the nasties I hadn't noticed I was carrying made a dash for the hills, yapping like newspapered puppies.

Roger's door pulsed and a sign flashed on saying PLEASE COME IN, so I clicked on it. Roger sat in a simple wooden chair. He had a beard, of course, and an old-fashioned suit, and a nice smile. When he spoke his words appeared above his head: "Hello, Mr. Face (my therapeutic code name). Please sit down. How can I help you today?"

I walked my spy guy across the chat room and sat him down on the chair in front of Roger. Typing, I said, "A murder case has just been dumped in my lap."

Meanwhile, in another window, I popped on over to alt.dicks to see if maybe one of my colleagues had posted anything on the murder. It didn't take me long to discover that the case had generated enough interest to spin off a new group of its own. The new group was called alt.dead.gerald. I popped over there to see what was what.

Roger said, "And how does a murder case in your lap make you feel?"

"I'm not sure I'm up to it, Roger."

"What makes you say you're not sure you're up to it?"

"I mean, one of my other cases, for instance, is following that bozo Frank Wallace for his wife."

"Go on," Roger said.

"Well, the payoff for that one will be the look on Frank's face when he finds out it was me who made his divorce so tasty."

"Go on."

"Well, the new case is, I guess you would call it serious."

And over on alt.dead.gerald, I learned that Gerald Moffitt was a well-known figure in the tech writing world. One post referred to him as a prominent "documentalist." I liked that word so much, I began thinking of the people who burden the rest of us with instructions for computer programs as *documentalists*.

"Can you elaborate on that?" Roger asked.

"I get the feeling," I said, "that conspiracy is in the air."

"Why do you say conspiracy is in the air, Mr. Face?"

"I can feel it, Roger."

"How does it make you feel when you feel it?"

"Anxious."

In the other window I scrolled through the nasty rumble-mumble of posts about how it was an open-and-shut case. Pablo Deerfield did it, of course. Jealousy. Money problems. Something to do with GP Ink. The damning fact being that Pablo was missing. There was a lot of talk about what might have been going on behind the scenes at GP Ink—drugs, prostitution, software pirating, bad grammar.

Someone named COSMO pooh-poohed the talk as the ravings of conspiracy nuts. The weird thing about that post was the address: anon 157@4e4.com. I didn't recognize 4e4.com, but I was pretty sure I'd seen it before, and I noticed that several of the posts in alt.dead.gerald came from there. It's like once something lodges in your mind, you see it everywhere.

"Tell me more about your anxiety, Mr. Face."

I thought about it, and as I pondered, I drifted away from the experience of Roger's animated chat room and our multi-tasking and became aware of the computer screen and our conversation marching along above two animated characters, became aware of my fingers, my typing. I typed, "It's not so well defined. I'm noticing, for example, that the fact there is an x in the word anxious is making me very nervous."

"I'm listening."

"I'm getting the feeling," I said, "that everything is connected."

A beep. An answer to my query about 4e4 had arrived. It turned out 4e4.com was an anonymous remailing service based in Russia. I sat back and took a couple of deep breaths. If there was a conspiracy afoot, who better to be involved than the Russians?

"Do you see the fact that everything is connected as a bad thing?"

"Not necessarily."

"You may be avoiding the main issue," Roger said.

Maybe he was right. "I think I may be losing myself in my disguises," I said.

"What would it mean if you lost yourself in your disguises?"

"I sometimes have trouble telling who the real me is. And I'm having trouble remembering some things."

Hot on the heels of the Russians, I popped over to alt.anon. There I learned that 4e4 was a recently established company in the new Russia that provided absolute security on the Internet. They claimed they would never ever reveal the identity or location of any client. They didn't come right out and say it, but the implication was that the Russian government supported and protected the enterprise. This looked like yet another creative answer to ham-handed attempts to restrict freedom of expression in cyberspace, but I had to wonder what the Russian Mob thought about it.

"Can you give me an example?" Roger asked.

"Well, I have the feeling I may have been a cop once," I said. "On the other hand maybe I just read a lot about it. Or maybe I played one on TV."

"Go on."

"Lately, I've begun to suspect that the Sky disguise is the real me."

"Tell me more about being Sky."

"At first it was another level of misdirection," I said. "Peel away the disguise and you find another disguise. A matter of protection. A tool."

A call came in, and I flipped on the speakerphone. "Skylight Howells," I said.

"This is Ms. Divey. Please hold for Lucas Betty." I suppose it could have been Ms. "Davie" with an accent.

"My other case," I told Roger. "The embarrassing one."

"What's the story on Dennis?" Lucas asked as soon as he came on the line.

"I'm closing in," I told him. I always told him I was closing in. Lucas Betty, who called himself BOUNCING_BETTY on-line, wanted to hook up with Dennis and start a software consulting firm. Dennis figured we could make a lot of money, and money was always nice, but that kind of business would cramp our style.

"Tell me why you say your other case is the embarrassing one," Roger said.

And over on alt.dead.gerald, some guy called SOAPY told me to check out www.deadguys.com if I wanted to see a picture of Gerald's dead body.

"We're not really cheating him," I told Roger. "Sooner or later Sky will put Dennis in touch with him."

"Go on."

"You're always closing in," Lucas said. "Look, I need him. I'm up to my eyeballs. You've got to be more than one person to make it these days. If I could clone myself, I would. Come on, Howells, get with it. Maybe I should just put an ad in the paper telling Dennis he could make a lot of money. Maybe I don't need you."

"We need the money," I told Roger.

"I'm getting close, Mr. Betty," I said. "Real close. Any day now, I promise."

"Go on," Roger said.

"That's about it," I told Roger. Lucas Betty hung up.

"Why do you say that's about it?"

"Maybe I should just put my hat back on."

"What would it mean if you put your hat back on?"

I suddenly saw what Roger was getting at. "You're right, Roger, as usual. I've got to quit feeling sorry for myself and get back to work."

"How would getting back to work make you feel?"

"Better. In fact I feel all pumped up and ready to go right now. You're a lifesaver, Roger. I'll just sign off for now." I closed Roger's window and popped over to www.deadguys.com to see if there was really a picture of Gerald Moffitt. There wasn't. I didn't know what that meant. Had I expected SOAPY to be the killer and to have posted the evidence on a Web page?

And the others hiding behind 4e4.com? You might expect that kind of secrecy on alt.sex.barnyard.animals or even alt.noises.sucking but why here? I scanned down the list of postings for other people with 4e4.com addresses. There were quite a few.

I decided it was time to do some legwork.

There was almost certainly something going on at GP Ink. Prudence Deerfield had as much as told me there was something to find there.

I got out my cheap scotch and dirty glass from the bottom left desk drawer and poured myself a couple of fingers and leaned back in my chair and put my feet back up on the desk. Legwork. I could go as Dieter, and thinking of Dieter made me curious to see if anyone had picked up on the fact that a secret ingredient had been posted in alt.conpiracy. I wandered on over there and checked out the list of new posts. The original post was still there: "I laugh in your face, SSOMFC; the secret ingredient is . . ." Well, it didn't say "dot dot dot," but I'm certainly not going to compound someone's error by writing the ingredient here.

I saw there was a flurry of posts on the subject, and as soon as I opened a few I intuited what SSOMFC's strategy was for this crisis. Every post offered a different ingredient as the secret ingredient. With so many claims and counter-claims no one would realize that someone had in fact really told the world the secret for really good Mexican food.

I had been sparring (or more correctly my disguise Dieter, "the Mexican Food Chef," had been sparring) with the Secret Society of Mexican Food Cooks for years. They knew Dieter knew the secret ingredient. He made no bones about claiming that the reason it was so hard to get good Mexican food in Oregon was that most of the cooks didn't know about the secret ingredient. He liked to say that most of the grandmothers of the cooks probably knew it, but they weren't talking.

The communication I'd had with the SSOMFC had led me to believe that violence would be the preferred solution for any problem. But now this. I had to admire the way they were handling this crisis. I wondered who in the society was in charge of the operation.

Then it hit me that this is where I'd first seen 4e4.com. I brought up the original post again. Yes, the person who had spilled the beans (so to speak) was anon77@4e4.com. That person's handle was ESCOTILLA which some hasty research revealed meant "hatchway" (could that be "trapdoor"?) in Spanish. There was also a small town in the mountains of southwestern Arizona with the same name.

So now I knew why 4e4.com had bothered me in the first place, but did that mean that the society was somehow mixed up in Gerald's murder? Well, probably not, but I couldn't discount the possibility altogether. Prudence Deerfield might think certain elementary mathematical skills were what detective work was all about, but I knew it was all about intuition. The wheels were always turning even if you couldn't see them turning. You had to trust the process. The mind of the detective was always picking over the bones of the case, endlessly moving the pieces around. Never say never. Never ignore the little voices in your head.

I tossed off my drink and got up. Legwork. Just do it. I would not go as Dieter; I would go as Scarface. I made that decision without consciously deciding to do so. Process.

I walked into the washroom to become Scarface. People turn their eyes away from a really horrible facial scar. Makes it hard for them to see or remember the person behind the scar. Setting things up so people don't look too closely is the key to a good disguise. It is incredibly difficult to change a face enough to be absolutely unrecognizable. There is always something to give you away. Recognizing faces is one thing the human brain is very good at (we are all the time concerned with faces—just look at the Man in the Moon or the Face on Mars), and fooling it usually demands misdirection.

I applied the scar and put on a baseball cap with an attached ponytail. Checked myself out in the mirror. Grabbed an electric-blue fanny pack. Putting the man with the ponytail and the fanny pack in a tie-dyed tee shirt would make him altogether invisible in Eugene. And if you did look, well, there was that scar.

I turned off my office lights and left by way of the stairs to avoid anyone on the elevator.

GP Ink had its office in the Baltimore building downtown. There was a huge neon sign atop the building. The sign said TOFU. At night you could see the pink glow from the window of my office. It only took me a couple of minutes to walk around the corner and down the block to the Baltimore.

I rode the elevator up to the third floor and walked down a dim hallway. I detected no activity behind the doors I passed on the way to 317. It was as if everyone had taken the afternoon off. I knew there were people behind all the doors but they were being very very quiet, almost like they knew I was out in the hall.

When I found the right door, I looked both ways before pulling out my tools and dropping to one knee. The lock hadn't been updated in twenty years and it took only a moment for the tumblers to fall into place. I pushed open the door and stepped inside.

Late afternoon sunlight slanted into the room from a high window above a reception desk. Three white plastic chairs for people waiting to see Gerald or Pablo. A filing cabinet. A phone and a computer monitor on the desk. A poster of people drinking red wine and laughing into a blue sky above a sidewalk café. There was a door behind and to one side of the desk, and under that door a line of daylight was suddenly broken by a shadow. Someone was in the inner office.

I eased the hall door closed behind me and stepped around the receptionist's desk. I stood very still and listened. Whoever was in there hadn't heard me. If they'd heard me, they would have been holding still and listening, too. Instead, I heard movement and finally the clatter of fingers on computer keys.

There was a chance that the person in there was with the police department. I had to take that possibility into account. On the other hand, maybe I'd gotten lucky. Maybe Pablo had been unable to resist sneaking back to his office and computer to catch up on some work.

I decided to take the chance. I put my hand on the doorknob and took a breath to fortify myself for a sudden rush inside. I looked closely at the door to make sure which way it opened (away from me so I should push). It's really embarrassing to telegraph your rush into a room by trying to open the door the wrong way.

I turned the knob and pushed and rushed inside.

A man jumped up from behind the desk and leaped at me. He looked like a whole wall of flesh coming my way. The best defense is a strong offense, I guess. He was over the desk and on top of me before I could even get a good look at him. A couple of expert judo jabs to the midsection and I went down. He scrambled over me and into the outer office. By the time I got to my feet, he'd dashed into the hall.

My cap was on backwards and the ponytail was hanging in front of my face. I pulled it back in place and rubbed my abdomen and groaned. I didn't think I'd catch him, but I took a deep breath and ran after him anyway. Maybe I could at least get a better look. By the time I got into the hall, it was empty, but I heard someone to the right, and I charged off in that direction.

If I could get even a glance at him, I could confirm my impression (over six feet tall, beard stubble, cheap gray sports jacket, skinny black tie, foreign shoes) and maybe even add a few things to this list.

I rounded the corner and ran headlong into two men coming the other way. The unreality of the situation threatened to freeze me as we all went down. One of the men I'd bowled over was Frank Wallace, my high school nemesis, the man I was watching on another case, the man whose wife (sweet Elsie) wanted me to find out who he was fooling around with. I would never have agreed to follow a lieutenant in the Eugene police department if there had been any chance whatever that I'd actually run into him.

Okay, I was motivated by revenge, pure and simple. I fantasized about the day he'd get slaughtered in divorce court—the look on his face when he realized it was me who got the goods on him! Even so, watching Frank wasn't supposed to be the kind of case where you bumped into the object of your observation. Just some subtle snooping, a few photos, and a report to the Mrs.

Now I wondered who was following who.

The other man was Frank's sidekick Sergeant Zivon. It said something about how fast I must have been going that I'd managed to knock over the mountainous Marvin Zivon.

I scrambled to my feet. I decided it would not be a good idea to stick around and explain myself to Frank and Marvin, so I took off down the hall before they could get up. Whole thing took seconds.

"Stop! Police!" Frank yelled, but I didn't even slow down.

Down the stairs but not all the way down. It would be stupid to go all the way down and run right into the arms of whoever Frank would call on his walkie-talkie. I stopped in at the second floor men's room. Ducked into a stall just in case someone was sharp and fast enough to be checking the cans already. Off with Scarface's ponytail. Off with the scar. Tie-dye not so good now. Quick, strip it off and wad it up. Short sleeve wrinkle-free white shirt from the fanny pack. Fanny pack itself shifted to the side. New hair. I didn't want to be Sky. Frank and Marvin knew Sky. I became Tag, "the Average Guy." Tag was probably my most subtle disguise. He was a guy you'd look at and never notice. If I could join a crowd or even a small group of people, I would be virtually invisible.

I stepped out of the stall and checked myself in the mirror. Looking good. Just the right touch. I'd get back to being Sky after I slipped away from the cops.

I walked out of the men's room and joined a small group of people standing around the door to the Downtown Realty office.

"You hear what all the hubbub's about?" I asked a pretty blond woman in a tan business suit and really big glasses. I love the way downtown businesswomen still wear dresses.

"Who knows what wandered in off the mall," she said.

"I heard that," I said.

A couple of uniformed policeman came by on their way to the elevator. They gave us a glance but it was hard to tell if they'd even be able to report how big our little group was, much less that they'd seen me.

After they'd gotten in the elevator, I looked at my watch and said, "Looks like quitting time to me."

Everyone else seemed to think so, too. The group broke up and went back inside. I considered following along but it turned out not to be necessary. A moment later, the woman and a man in a tie but no coat came out and walked toward the elevator. I followed along just close enough to seem to be with them if you weren't looking too closely. We took the elevator to the lobby, then walked out of the building. We walked right past Sergeant Zivon and he glanced up, checked us out but didn't make eye contact, turned away.

I saw Frank at the corner of the building apparently scanning the downtown mall for Scarface. I was nearly overcome by the need to do a little victory dance right there on the spot, but fought it off and turned away before someone spotted the huge grin on my face and maybe put two and two together.

A couple of blocks later I stopped in the men's room on the mall with its metal urinals and sour smell. I looked in all the doorless stalls to make sure I was alone and then peeled off Tag and became Sky once again. Checked myself out in the metal mirror. Rubbed my hand over my blond crewcut. Not quite thirty-eight and looking okay, maybe better than okay, maybe good enough to do a little dancing.

Push that thought out of your mind.

Once the thought arrives in that devil-may-care who gives a flying rat's ass let's go dancing, dudes, there's only one outcome, and it always comes even when it takes a few days. And I could tell this wasn't going to be one of those days when it would take a few days.

You can feel it inside like steam in a boiler. It's got to get out, got to get out, click your heels and tap your toes. When I'm about to do something stupid, it's like I'm watching myself from on high. There I go heading for the west side, not because I've got any business on the west side, but because there's this place I know, draws me back, makes me homesick for spilled beer and smoke and that old gang of mine. The music. The open floor. It's like anyone can get up on that stage and dance and anyone does, but when I do, I don't stop. If I ever get trapped in there, it'll be really really hard to get out again. I won't go in. Simple. If you don't go in, you won't have to bust out.

I outlined all the reasons why it would be stupid to get trapped in my addiction again, but I kept walking. I thought about the morning after, the embarrassment of having to go confess another fall to my home group, if I ever even got far enough back into the real light of day to make that confession. I hadn't been to a meeting in a long time. Now would be a good time to go to a meeting. Going to a meeting would be a good reason to turn aside, but I kept on walking.

Down Broadway. Took a turn south somewhere past Willamette, hit Eleventh and turned west again. I would walk on by. Maybe just peek in and see who was who and what was what.

I had cases to deal with and I couldn't afford to go off on a dancing jag. I would waltz on by, take the long way home, or maybe find a regular bar, have a few drinks, watch some TV, think about the cases, think about what Frank was doing there outside of GP Ink for me to run into him anyway. That's what really threw me. He was so out of context. It wasn't his turn. I'd planned on following him later from a very safe distance. And who was the big guy tossing the office? Pablo himself? I didn't think so.

Maybe it would rain. If it rained, I could run for shelter, could run right by the wounded sign ahead, half orange neon and half dead glass, an advertisement for doom.

GOTTA DANCE!

And in smaller painted letters:

Karaoke Tap 24 hours a day!

I kept rational thought at bay by humming. Some part of me hoped I wouldn't notice what I was up to. I got to the door of the Gotta Dance and walked right on in.

For most people, tap dancing is safe and even beneficial. It is, in fact, tai chi for western sensibilities. It's not so good for me.

I am a problem dancer. There, I've said it.

When I start dancing, I dance the night away. I lose myself.

"Hey!" Someone called from the gloom, "It's the Sky-man!"

I watched myself walk confidently up to the bar. Mick put a pair of shiny black patent leather dance shoes on the bar and grinned at me.

I raised an eyebrow at him. It wasn't standard operating procedure for the bartender to hold your spare shoes.

"Been saving them," Mick said. "I knew you'd be back. You get cold feet on the way home?"

He seemed to think that was pretty funny and spent a few minutes laughing.

I gave him a world-weary shrug, rolled my eyes. I had no idea what he was talking about. Blackout at the Gotta Dance. Nothing new. Nothing to think about. Thinking about things like that can be really depressing. "Pour me a scotch, Mick," I said. "Neat."

He poured my drink and put it down in front of me. I threw it down in a single gulp, said thanks, gave him some money, waited for him to fill my glass again and walked backstage with my shoes.

Where someone handed me my top hat.

And helped me on with my tails.

Handed me my walking stick.

Said, here's your music!

Said, okay, you're on!

Putting on the Ritz.

three

When I opened my eyes, I could see the day was pretty much over. I could pretend it was the start of a new day, but I knew it wasn't. I'd blacked out dancing too many times before to fool myself about it. I recognized the way the late afternoon sunlight looked tired after a long day on the job. The traffic was making heading-home sounds—altogether different from going-to-work sounds. I had my cheek on my desk, giving me a bug's eye view of a rainbow stain my coffee cup had left in some earlier geological era. I pushed up and my pretzel back snapped. I groaned.

I made the long painful climb to my feet. I had danced the night away. That much I could tell from the way my legs felt. One knee was torn from my pants. My wallet was in the wrong pocket.

My mustache was missing.

Meaning, I supposed, I wasn't Skylight Howells today.

Still wearing my dancing shoes, I punctuated my way to the can with guilty little heel-toe heel-toe taps. My talking shoes whispered, you'll be coming back (never again), oh, yes, you'll be coming back for more. It's just a matter of time.

I splashed water in my face. Used the electric razor. Showered. Since I was back in the office I guess it made some sense to be Sky again. I got another mustache from the top drawer of my disguise cabinet (a Goodwill chest of drawers, once blue, now mostly chipped white—the thing always made me think of an egg except that it was rectangular).

I walked back into the office and got the coffeepot and rinsed it out in the washroom. Once the coffee started dripping, the happy sound and smell made me feel a little better.

The feeling didn't last. I'd no sooner poured myself a cup and settled back down behind my desk when the door banged open and Lieutenant Frank Wallace and his burly sidekick Marvin Zivon walked right in.

These bozos made the perfect cop couple. A smoldering little guy and his muscle man. Wired and short and quick, Frank Wallace always made me think of a weasel. He wore his blond hair combed up like some kind of teen idol from an old beach movie. He'd worn it that way even as a little boy, and I figured maybe he was born with it already styled. Marvin, on the other hand, looked like a big dumb guy trying really hard not to look so dumb. Big boyish face with a scattering of freckles across his nose. Sandy hair cut short emphasizing a slight point to his head. Oddly, Marvin wasn't dumb at all. In fact, in a mental wrestling match with Frank, Marvin would probably come out on top, but that wouldn't matter. Frank had the power of will and would always win.

My first thought was that Elsie had let the cat out of the bag and told Frank she'd hired me to follow him. Since I hadn't seen him doing anything, I hoped that was not the case. One of my major goals in life was to slap one big incriminating eight-by-ten glossy after another down on a desk under his nose. I wanted to see his eyes go wide, see the horrible realization of doom blossom on his face when he figured out what the pictures meant. Unfortunately there were no photos yet. And if Elsie had confessed and Frank was in my office to hassle me, why had he brought Marvin Zivon?

This was more likely an official visit and, in their official capacity, I doubted they would rough me up, but I couldn't help thinking of all the times back in school when I'd taken the long way home to avoid them and all the times taking the long way home hadn't worked. The word around town was these former high school bad guys had become pretty good cops. Who would have believed it?

Back in school, everyone assumed Frank would end up in prison or maybe the army. Marvin would be bailed out by his mother who owned the Whisper Café on the downtown mall. The Whisper Café was the place to be seen after a concert at the Hult, for example, the place for dangerously complicated coffee drinks and fancy cakes, little dishes of spiced shrimp, quail eggs, stuff like that. No one expected Marvin to follow Frank onto the police force. Some people expected *me* to follow Frank onto the police force, but that's another story.

"Marvin," I said, "Francis. What's up?"

"Cut the crap, Brian," Frank said. His face had gone red when I called him "Francis." Back in the fifth grade, I'd taken my revenge by telling everyone "Frank" was really short for "Francis" and people believed me, and Frank couldn't get away from it. He even went around one day with his birth certificate showing kids on the playground that his name was "Franklin Wallace." Didn't help. In junior high he tried to get everyone to call him "Wally" but no one would.

He sat down in the white plastic client chair in front of my desk. "I have some questions."

Marvin stood just behind and a little to one side of Frank, showing me his repertoire of dirty looks. He was getting pretty good at it. Maybe he'd been practicing in front of his mirror.

I smiled at him, and he automatically returned the smile, realized what he'd done, and went back to giving me the evil eye. His standing there like a trained gorilla made me nervous as hell, but I tried not to show it.

"Always happy to cooperate, Lieutenant," I said.

"I'm happy to hear that, Brian," Frank said. "I want to know what you have to do with Prudence Deerfield. Did she tell you where her brother is?"

"No," I said. "She said she didn't know where he was."

"And so you're looking for him?"

"I'm looking for him."

"You don't want to be holding out on me, Brian," he said. "What is this Skylight Howells baloney anyway?"

"His folks took the sixties way too seriously," Marvin said. He walked over to my printer and bent at the waist to peer down behind it.

"What? They waited till he was in high school to name him?" Frank said. "Or maybe one day everyone started calling him Brian Dobson and it just sort of caught on?"

Confusion swamped me for a moment. "It's the name of the agency, Frank," I said.

"You must have done a lot of research to come up with something so lame."

"Hey," Marvin said, "maybe there was this secret government project and Brian was kidnapped and replaced by an alien baby and Skylight was the code name for the whole business."

"What are you talking about?" Frank twisted around to look over at Marvin.

I had to wonder. Did Marvin know something? Was the reason he seemed so suddenly agitated not that he'd just said something stupid but that he'd just let something slip?

"Nice cable you got on your printer," Marvin said.

"What?" I said. "You think I wouldn't have replaced the cable after strangling Gerald Moffitt with the old one?"

"Just checking, Brian," Marvin said. He walked back to his station behind Frank.

"Maybe you should open a Pee Eye booth at the Saturday market, Brian," Frank said. Yes, my spelling reflects just the way he said it.

The Saturday market was where our local artists and craftspeople sold their goods. If you walked down to the end of the hall outside my office, you could look out the window and see it on Saturdays.

"You could charge a nickel," Frank said.

I decided to see if I could get Frank off my ass. "How did you guys know Ms. Deerfield came to me in the first place?"

"That's not your concern," Frank said. "What I want is for you to tell me everything you know about the murders."

"Murders?" I asked. "Like more than one?" My turn to be knocked off balance.

"You don't watch the news?" Frank looked up at Marvin. "You see a TV in here, Sergeant?"

"I don't see a TV," Marvin said.

"You don't seem very well informed for a hotshot Pee Eye," Frank said.

"I've been busy," I said. "So who else was killed? And what makes you think it has anything to do with the murder of Gerald Moffitt."

That got a laugh. The two of them spent a couple of minutes chuckling. Maybe I'm a funny guy. Maybe I should go on stage. Scratch that. Forget the stage. A sudden picture of what I might have done yesterday at the Gotta Dance flooded into my mind. I took a deep breath and got myself under control.

"You crack me up, Brian," Frank said.

"Yeah," Marvin said. "You're a riot."

I looked Marvin in the eye. "Your mother uses low-fat cheese in her cheesecake," I said.

He leaped over the desk, took me by the throat with one giant hand and slapped me silly with the other. Well, no, actually he didn't. In fact, while I could tell he was really steamed, I could also see he was adrift with confusion. On the one hand low fat was healthy and therefore good, on the other hand his mother's cheesecake was known far and wide for its wickedly rich taste. He finally came down on the side of being insulted. "She does not!"

Frank ignored my little exchange with his partner. "It's the state of the bodies," he said. "The MO's the same. You know what an MO is? They teach you stuff like that in mail-order Pee Eye school?"

"You're telling me the new victim was strangled with a printer cable and had the word 'exceptions' inked all over his body?"

"No words," Frank said. "But the cable's right."

"Then what?"

"A number."

"A number?"

"Sixty-six."

"Spelled out?"

"No, not spelled out." Frank leaned in and snatched a notepad from beside my computer monitor. He wrote something and shoved the pad my way.

66!

"All over the body?" I asked.

"You got it."

"Exclamation point and all?"

"That's right," Frank said.

"So did you have the handwriting analyzed?" I asked.

"Maybe I should consult an astrologer, too?" Frank asked. "I suppose you don't know anything about it."

"No," I said. "Who was he?"

"It's interesting you know the victim was a man."

"Fifty fifty," I said.

"Tell me what you know about Dennis," Frank said.

I gulped. I know Frank saw it. Maybe my face went red. He couldn't be talking about my Dennis. He shouldn't even know about my Dennis. But maybe he was talking about the new victim.

"Dennis who?" I asked. "Is that the new dead guy?"

"No," Frank said. "The name has come up a couple of times along with a bunch of other computer freaks. Dennis is one we can't seem to get a handle on."

"So who is the dead guy?"

"He worked for a local game company," Frank said. "You ever hear of Challenger Video?"

"Sure," I said, "I've probably got a game or two of theirs on my machine."

"Randy Casey may have tested one of those games," Frank said. "He was what you call a beta tester. You know what a beta tester is?"

I ignored his question. I jotted down the name he mentioned and asked, "So Randy Casey was the victim?"

"That's him," Frank said. "I'm sure you didn't let the fact flash right over your head that he had something to do with the computer business. You being the world famous detective and all." He stood up. "You may have picked up on the fact that Gerald Moffitt had something to do with the computer business, too. Not to mention Pablo Deerfield. And this Dennis guy." He put both hands on my desk so he could lean in close. "I want you to know, Flashlight, that I don't necessarily believe you and the Deerfield woman are in the dark about where her brother is."

"I'm sorry to hear you don't believe me, Lieutenant." I got up, too, and came around the desk. Probably not the wisest move, but I was operating mostly on instinct. "So what are you calling this one? The Graffiti Killer?"

"If I see that in the papers, I'll know you've been shooting off your mouth, Brian."

"Hey! I'm the very essence of discretion."

Frank implying that I'd go to the press to pump up my own image really did hurt, but I couldn't let him see that he'd scored a point. I smiled at him; I smiled at Marvin.

"All this smiling is making you look like a goofball, Brian," Frank said.

Marvin looked like an ape scanning the ground for bugs to eat. Or maybe my feet had suddenly become fascinating. I couldn't help looking down, too. My bright black spit-polished dancing shoes. I couldn't exactly see our faces in the shiny toes, but I could see light and shadow. I looked up.

Frank poked me in the chest. "Stay out of my way," he said, "unless you're coming around to tell me where Pablo Deerfield is." He poked me in the chest again. "And remember, I've got my eye on you." He stepped back.

I didn't bother pointing out that he'd have some trouble keeping an eye on me if I was staying out of his way.

Frank nodded to Marvin, and Marvin grinned and picked up one huge foot in a scuffed black loafer and scraped it across the shine on my dancing shoes. He pushed his face in close so I'd get the point. His breath smelled like cappuccino.

He gave me a little shove, and then the two of them left. Frank never looked back, but Marvin paused at the door, glanced over his shoulder and gave me a wink.

four

The next day Prudence Deerfield came banging into my office as I put the final touches on Lulu.

"Sky?" she called. "Where are you?"

"Just a moment," I said in falsetto from the washroom.

Being Lulu made me feel lovely. Feeling lovely is all in how you look at yourself. Objectively, I guess you'd have to say Lulu wouldn't turn many heads, but she didn't look much like Sky, and since I planned on following Frank Wallace later that afternoon, and since I was now on Frank's mind, I needed my most extreme disguise. Lulu was complicated, and even after a good night's sleep, I was still pretty fuzzy from my time at the Gotta Dance. I was doing the best I could.

I hoped I could wrap up the Wallace case in a day or two. I'd considered calling Elsie Wallace and quitting, but I knew just how she'd react. She'd tell Frank the whole story, including the part about me following him. He would find that out anyway, of course, if I ever saw him doing anything incriminating.

I came out of the washroom.

"So where's Sky?" Prudence asked. She hadn't given Lulu more than a raised eyebrow and a quick head-to-toe glance. She leaned to one side to peer around me into the washroom.

I guess you'd call what she was wearing a charcoal double-breasted business suit. The outfit was all one piece like a coat and the bottom of it was mid-thigh. The way she looked was making it hard to be Lulu.

"He's behind the door," Lulu said.

Prudence stepped up to the washroom and addressed the door. "Hey, I'm here for a progress report."

"It's only been a day," Lulu said.

Prudence glanced over her shoulder and frowned, then spoke to the door again. "Randy Casey was killed," she said. "Now the police are all over me about Pablo. What are you going to do about it? Did you get into GP Ink? What did you find out?"

Sky had nothing to say.

Lulu walked over and sat down behind the desk.

Prudence stormed into the washroom. A moment later she came out again. "I thought you said he was behind the door."

"I lied," I said, no longer struggling to be Lulu. I'd get back in character after Prudence had taken her distractions out for a walk.

She picked up on what was happening without even blinking. "Now that I look close," she said, "no one would believe you're really a woman."

"No one looks close," I said. "And if they do, they still just see Lulu, so what's the difference?" She didn't say anything, and I suddenly felt compelled to justify my methods. "In fact, this ability to compartmentalize my mind is a real asset for a detective. I can look at the case from a number of different viewpoints."

"Haven't I seen you hanging around the mall?"

"I often lunch at the Whisper Café," Lulu said. "Now sit down and tell me what you know about Randy Casey."

"Randy wrote documentation, too," Prudence said.

"What? The police were here earlier. They didn't say anything about documentation. I thought he played games for Challenger Video."

"That's what he was doing when he was killed," she said. "I knew Randy. He didn't talk much. I don't see why anyone would want to kill him."

"How did you know him."

"The documentation community isn't that big," she said. "But the truth is I met him when he worked for Gerald and Pablo."

"He worked for them?"

"Gerald fired him," she said, "and Pablo let it happen."

"That doesn't look good."

"I guess not," she said. "Randy just wasn't serious enough for GP Ink. Getting fired was the best thing that could have happened to him. He really liked Challenger Video. They make games."

"I thought I just said that."

"Well, what you may not know," she said, "is that Randy had just done the game playing instructions for a new product called Seventeen Worlds. The instructions hadn't been printed yet. In fact they'd only been released on the net to a mail group."

"So, he was a documentalist, too?"

"Challenger hadn't hired him to write the docs," she said. "It was pure speculation. He was hoping the company would move him up to the documentation department when they saw what he could do. I guess no one out of the group ever got a chance to see his work."

"Do you have access to that group?"

"Yes," she said.

"So what is it?"

"It's secret," she said.

"I think you're going to have to tell me about it," I said. "I can't do my job if you're keeping things from me."

"I suppose you're right," she said. "It's not a really big secret anyway. The group is the Secret Brotherhood of Documentalists. People call it BOD."

Did she give in too quickly? I filed that question away for later consideration.

"So, that's where that word comes from," I said. "I keep running into it."

"Secret?"

"Documentalist," I said, "but speaking of the word 'secret,' shouldn't people call the group SBOD?"

"The S is silent," she said.

"And invisible?"

"Yes," she said.

"So how do you know about this secret group?"

She paused for only a moment. "I'm a member," she said.

"So, if you're a member, shouldn't the group be the Secret Brother and Sisterhood of Documentalists?"

"The Sisterhood is silent, too," she said. Was she serious? I didn't have a clue. The way she talked, the little mistakes and awkward phrasing, I couldn't get a handle on her. What did that small smile really mean? Did it reach her eyes? Was she putting me on?

"So can you bring up a list of people in the group?" I asked. "Maybe we can spot something."

"Sure," she said. "You got a place I can plug in?"

"Why not just use mine?" I twisted the monitor around to face her.

"Too crude," she said. She dipped into her bag and came out with a tiny computer, a set of datashades already dangling from the side. She put it on the desk and held out the net connection to me.

I plugged her in next to my own connection. The office might be run down, the building might be poorly maintained, but at least it was wired with the latest high bandwidth computer cables and outlets. Wireless or no wireless, no one would do business here at all if that weren't the case.

When I glanced back up at her, I saw that she'd put on the shades. She poked and wiggled just one finger like a cyberwitch in sunglasses making hocus-pocus gestures in the empty air and a moment later my printer started rattling its ancient teeth.

"What is that you're using on your finger?" I asked.

"Like a dataglove," she said, "but just one finger when you don't need so much."

"So it's a datafinger?"

"Yes," she said. "It's one of Pablo's innovations."

"So Pablo's a hardware guy, too?"

"Pablo has lots of ideas," she said. Since she was still wearing the shades, I couldn't read anything in her eyes.

"Can you download Randy's book, too?" I asked.

"No problem."

"Maybe mail it to me," I said. "So I can look at it later."

"I'll just route it to your hard drive," she said.

I opened my mouth to ask her just how the hell she was going to get access to my system, but then I changed my mind. She already *had* access. She'd just routed the BOD list to my printer.

She poked at the air a couple more times with her datafinger. Then she pulled it off and took off her shades and put them on top of her little computer. "All done," she said. She glanced at me, and then she looked away.

"What?"

"Nothing," she said. "I guess it's just the strangeness of your voice and the way you look. I mean, they don't go together."

"They don't?" Lulu said in Lulu's voice.

"You're really pretty good."

I was pleased, but a little embarrassed, too. I got up and walked over to the printer and got the BOD list. I scanned the list as I walked back to my chair and sat down behind my desk again.

It only took me a moment to find prud@gpink.com. "So how come you get these mailings and Pablo doesn't?"

"Gerald gets them," she said. "Or he got them. You know what I mean. Pablo figured one was enough."

Yes, there was Gerald, and further down the list randy@chlng.com.

"Hmm," I said. Wouldn't Pablo be on this list even if Gerald was on it? Didn't computer guys grab every opportunity to get e-mail?

I half expected to see Dennis on the list. We tried to make him keep his head down on the net; he was, after all, one of my disguises, and while we let him have an Internet account, we didn't let him spend a lot of time there. What I'm trying to say is, I didn't really think he would be on the list, but if he had been, it wouldn't have totally flabbergasted me. The beauty of my method is just letting go and allowing the process to work. The downside is that sometimes when I get out of my own way, I lose track of where I am.

I didn't see any other familiar addresses, but one thing did catch my eye. There were a bunch of addresses that ended in 4e4.com, the anonymous Russian remailing service. If the killer were on this list, surely he'd be among the anonymous.

Or maybe not. I don't remember who said it (but I think it probably is true)—naked is the best disguise. The killer could be right out in the open here.

And I hadn't crossed Pablo or even Prudence off my own list of suspects yet. It was way too early to go jumping to conclusions. I gave her a suspicious look over the top of the printout.

"Is that a suspicious look?"

"You bet," I said. "Do you know all these people?"

"More or less." She reached across the desk for the list "I haven't actually met them all. Everyone was probably from Eugene originally, or they were friends of friends or something like that. Maybe college chums. People move. I'll bet not many are still physically here in town any more."

"Do you know what four-e-four is?"

I thought I saw something cross her face. Something sudden. Had I surprised her? In any case, it was over in a flash, and she pulled herself together.

"You mean the anonymous remailing service?" she said.

"So is it secret, too?"

"No. Just not widely publicized," she said. "I'm surprised you picked up on it. Where did you hear about it?"

"I am a detective, you know."

"You think it might have something to do with the case?"

"Who knows?" I said. "It keeps popping up everywhere I look. Do you know who the people with four-e-four addresses are?"

"Well, that depends on what you mean." she said. "I've been in touch by e-mail with all of them, but I guess I don't know who any of them really are. The whole idea of anonymous is that no one's supposed to know. I mean all I have are handles."

I got up and came around the desk and stood looking over her shoulder at the list. I reached down and pointed at anon12@4e4.com. "What do you know about this one, for example?"

"Well, she signs her messages 'Cleo.' Ah . . . let me see. She's very very picky."

"You're sure she's a woman?"

"Well, sure," Prudence said. "Well, maybe not. How could I be sure?"

"Little clues," I said.

"I guess I'd have to be looking for them at the time," she said.

"I suppose so." I pointed at another 4e4.com address. "What about that one?"

"Bob, from Buffalo," she said.

"You know he's from Buffalo?"

"Yeah," she said. "Well, I guess I actually don't know that either. That's just what everyone calls him. Maybe he just came from Buffalo or something."

"Or maybe he used to be on TV."

"What?"

"Why would documentalists go to the trouble of working through an anonymous remailer? Especially a high-power one like this Russian company?"

"How did you know they were Russian?"

"I told you," I said, "I'm a detective."

"I'm impressed."

"So what about it? Why do almost a third of these guys need to hide?"

"You know how it is." she said.

"Tell me."

"For some people," she said. "It's a matter of principle. It's no one's business who you are and where you live. If you're anonymous, you're free. In a way, that's what the net is all about."

"Yeah, well one of those guys could be our killer," I said. "I want you to write down what you know about each of the names on the list. Even the ones not using the remailer."

"What kind of stuff?"

"Handles," I said, "and names and locations if you know them. Oh, and if you do know anything juicy, like time spent in prison or stuff like that, put it down."

When she'd finished I glanced over the list again. There were a lot of holes in our information. Prudence didn't know the real names or locations of any of the 4e4.coms, but she did know their handles. Of the others, most were scattered all over the world. Five (aside from the two dead men and Prudence herself) were marked "Eugene."

Leo Unger from Challenger Video, where Randy Casey, the second dead man, worked—small world.

Sadie Campbell of SplashDown Software. I thought Dennis might have met her once.

Lucas Betty (BOUNCING_BETTY)! Things just kept hooking up. This was the guy who'd hired me to find Dennis! About Lucas, Prudence had written, "Known for keeping the balls of a dozen projects in the air, all at once and fast." I figured I could string him along for another week or so, and then I would have to get Dennis to call him.

Bernie Watkins (THE_DUNGEONEER). Prudence had written "HS" by his name.

Ramona Simmons who Prudence identified as "mean."

I made a list of handles of those people using the anonymous remailer.

CLEO
BOB
THE_FLY
NANOVICH
2DIE4
THE_REAL_DOOMSTER
COSMO
ADOLESCENT_BOY

What could I deduce from the handles? Well, NANOVICH sounded at least a little Russian, and the Russians had to have something to do with this case. The Doomster would be an adolescent boy no matter how old he or she was, while ADOLESCENT_BOY would be a yuppy with an imaginary sense of humor. It was easy to see what you were supposed to think when you thought about 2DIE4. Maybe THE_FLY was really a disguised spider in the World Wide Web. Maybe COSMO was Carl Sagan doing the Web from the great beyond. Sure, and BOB would be David Letterman's dog.

So, the anonymous handles didn't help much. I still had the five for-sure locals to run down. It wasn't like I had nothing to try next.

"Okay," I told her. "I'll chase down the known locals. If nothing else maybe I can fill some of the holes in the list."

"Seems pretty thin to me," she said. She put her computer back in her bag.

"It's a place to start."

"Did you get into GP Ink?" She asked her question and then she looked away.

"Not all the way," I said. I gave her an edited version of the story ending with what I thought was the key question. "So, who do you think would be tossing the office?"

"I have no idea," she said. "So you didn't actually get to look around the office at all?"

"No."

"You seem to be pretty much lost at sea." Prudence gathered her bag and got up.

"Who, me?" I scooted to the side so I wouldn't have to be peeking around my monitor at her. "No way. It's just these things take time. I'll get into Pablo's office. You can bet on that. Hey, as it happens that's at the top of my list. Relax. You can't expect instant results."

"I guess not." She walked toward the door.

"Hey," I said, "how can I get in touch with you if I need to?"

She stopped at the door. "I'm on the list," she said. "Send me e-mail."

I watched her leave, and then I settled back in my chair. I fired up my word processor and called up Randy Casey's game instructions.

SEVENTEEN WORLDS

It must have been some game. The manual was as thick as a novel.

I looked first for chapter 66. No chapter 66. No section 66. I looked at page 66. Something to do with elves on World twelve. No clues. I counted paragraphs from the beginning of the book. Paragraph 66 didn't shed any light on the case. Ditto with word 66.

I spent a few minutes thinking about 1966.

I turned to the index and scanned down the page looking for 66. I found one right away. Devils 66. Strange I didn't remember reading about devils on page 66. I kept scanning, and near the end found Spiders 66. I turned to page 66 and read it again. Carefully. No devils. No spiders. No devil spiders. The index was wrong.

five

Lulu finally just tossed the BOD list onto my desk and left the office. Thinking was getting us nowhere.

We hoped to pick up Frank's trail downtown at Maxwell's Lunch Room. Lulu would have to forgo chocolate lime cake at the Whisper Café today. Frank wouldn't be there. After all these years, Marvin's mother still didn't like Frank. I suppose the Whisper was no place for a hardy cop lunch anyway.

Maybe Lulu's confidence was low. When she passed the big front windows of Maxwell's and saw Frank bent over his plate forking noodles into his mouth, she didn't go in and take a table where she could keep an eye on him. Instead, she just kept on walking. He didn't look up as she passed.

Once downtown Eugene had been a pedestrian mall that ran un-broken for blocks. Now the mall was crossed by reopened streets, but there were still long quiet patches. A little to the east of Maxwell's, there were two wood and iron benches and a couple of trees. Just down the block was an espresso booth. It had rusted wheels and looked like someone had knocked it together with old plywood and bent nails. The red paint screaming ESPRESSO! was chipped and you could see that the sign had once said something else, but you couldn't tell just what. Lulu got a double raspberry latte and sat down on one of the benches where she could watch Frank Wallace eat his lunch.

A man walking by gave her a head-to-toe full body scan. Then he did a double take, and his eyes went cold. He put on his attack smile, his in-your-face grin, his what-the-hell-is-this and would-you-get-a-load-of-that look. Lulu turned her face away, ignoring him, and found herself looking right into Frank's eyes. She glanced away, but not before she'd read his face, and what she read made us reassess, at least for the moment, our attitude toward Frank Wallace. The look he had beamed at Lulu said you need some help you just holler. Our hero? That was not a feeling any of us were comfortable with.

The man muttered something nasty and moved on, and when Lulu looked back at Frank, he was eating noodles again. This was pretty much what it had been like all along watching Frank. He didn't do anything exciting. He didn't spend much time away from the office, and when he did go out, he mostly had business downtown and he mostly walked everywhere. His main task seemed to be moving papers from one building to another. We'd only lost him once when he hopped into an official car at the corner of Oak and Eighth and zoomed away before we could get to our own wheels.

Because he was so predictable, Lulu was surprised when she saw him signal his server for the check. That meant he'd been at Maxwell's for some time. He'd taken an early lunch. She gathered her bag and got up quickly and walked to the waste barrel and tossed the rest of her latte. What if he stopped and spoke to her? We just didn't feel that secure in our identity. He would see right through us. Lulu walked up the block and stopped to stare through a store window.

Frank came out of the lunch room. Lulu glanced at him then went back to window-shopping, then glanced at him again. He looked both ways up and down the mall. He gave her a puzzled look, and for a moment she was sure he was going to walk up to her, but then he pulled up his sleeve to see his watch and turned and walked the other way.

What would she have said to him? Something about whatever she'd been looking at in the window? She let her eyes focus on the merchandise in the window. She gasped and took a step back. Through the window she saw many people at desks all looking back at her.

She took another step back so she could look up at the sign—SPLASHDOWN SOFTWARE. They'd taken over the old dime store that had closed several years ago. She knew that. Frank knew that, too.

Her staring into this particular window was what had puzzled him. His cop instincts.

Lulu still assumed she was being watched; she always assumed that, so she waved at the people inside as if that's what she'd been up to all along.

And she did see someone we at least recognized—Arthur Snow, the head guy at SplashDown. He had a handful of printouts, and he stopped to say something to a woman at one of the desks. We knew the woman, too, but couldn't retrieve her name. She and Snow both looked up at Lulu.

We moved away from the window.

Frank had reached the corner. That was lead enough. We hurried to follow.

Ordinarily he would just walk back to his office after lunch, but we could tell he would break his pattern today. For one thing, he already had. He'd taken that early lunch alone.

Following anyone is an art, but following a cop takes special care. Lulu turned on Olive, leaving Frank to continue down Broadway on his own. She was pretty sure she could pick him up anywhere along the mall before he reached the police station.

As long as he didn't get into a car along the way, we probably wouldn't lose him. If he used his own car, we'd be okay. The lot where we had permanent parking places was only a block from the police department's underground parking garage. Sky kept his Cherokee in that lot, and Lulu's old Ford Escort was pretty much permanently parked there. The car was registered in my mother's name. I wondered what Frank would think if he suddenly suspected Lulu was following him and had the plate checked. Would he think my mother had lost twenty years and gained fifty pounds?

Lulu passed the police station and walked around to our parking lot. She was playing a hunch. If he just went back to his office, she'd know soon enough, but if he walked through to the parking garage, she would be ready to follow him in the Escort.

Lulu unlocked the Escort, but before she climbed inside she saw a small group of mushrooms on the floor under the steering wheel. We didn't remember buying mushrooms, much less dropping them as we unloaded groceries. Lulu leaned down to pick one up. It was growing in the Escort's carpet! How long had it been since she'd used the car? She didn't remember. We hoped the battery wasn't dead. Lulu plucked the mushrooms from the carpet and tossed them to the pavement and climbed in behind the wheel.

Sometimes you win. Not only did the Escort roar to life when Lulu turned the key, but she had no more done that when Frank pulled into view on the one-way street in his own beat-up green Dodge.

Lulu gave him a moment, and then followed. Frank took Seventh Street to Franklin and for a moment we thought he would drive right out of town. Maybe he had a rendezvous in Springfield.

Fast food and motels on the left, the University of Oregon on the right. He pulled into the left turn lane at a light.

It was decision time. We could pull in behind him and risk him spotting us, or we could take a chance that he would make a legal U-turn here in order to get to the businesses on the other side of the street. That was the main purpose of a left turn here. If he really went on down the cross street we'd probably lose him. We stayed in the lane that didn't turn.

Frank made a U-turn. The light turned green and the traffic in front of us moved on. We just needed a moment more to see what Frank was up to. The traffic behind us waited patiently, but they wouldn't wait much longer. A bunch of horn honking might attract Frank's attention. We thought he might be doubling back to downtown, but before he got out of sight he turned into the parking lot of the Quack Inn. Lulu dropped the Escort into gear and zipped into the left turn lane. Got some dirty looks, but no one honked. That reticence on the part of locals to use the horn aggressively is one of the things that amazes visitors.

By the time we could make our own U-turn and get down to the Quack Inn, Frank had parked and disappeared into one of the rooms. That meant someone else had already rented the room. Or at least that Frank had done it himself some time in the past. He hadn't had time to check in while we waited at the light.

The bar at the Quack Inn was called the Tail Feathers Lounge. Both of the names had to do with the U. of O. Ducks. A lot of stuff in Eugene has a duck theme, the school's mascot being a duck and all, especially in this part of town, what with the university just across the street.

We were a little surprised Frank would pick this part of town when he was looking for a steamy love nest. There's a whole other area of town with motels catering to hanky-panky. Lulu was glad we weren't there. While Eugene has no really mean streets, there are a few decidedly grumpy ones Frank might have picked.

Part of the Tail Feathers Lounge was dark and smoky, but part of it had once been a coffee shop and was bright and filled with potted plants and little white tables with bent-wire soda fountain chairs. Lulu took a seat at a table by the window and ordered a glass of white wine. From that vantage point we could see Frank's car and a row of upper and lower motel room doors. Unless Frank parked around the corner from his room, we ought to be able to see him when he came out. More important, we ought to be able to see who he was with. Lulu opened her bag and fussed with her Nikon Auto-Everything. She pointed it out the window and snapped one shot of Frank's car. Then she dropped the camera back into the bag and took a sip of her wine.

So it was all true. Elsie had been right to suspect Frank. He was out for a nooner with some bimbo, and we would soon get the goods on him. We had begun to suspect that he was on the up-and-up which would have been disappointing.

Lulu had time for another glass of wine. It was a lazy afternoon, and she relaxed and let our mind wander. Surely Frank would have to get back to work soon, but until he did we could take it easy. The Tail Feathers had no tap dancing floor, so we were in no danger of wandering off to lala land and losing track of time and space. We could just relax all afternoon and drink wine and wait for Frank to come out with his secret squeeze so we could take his picture.

Some forty-five minutes later, he did come out of a room three doors down from his car and on the bottom floor—room 142.

Alone.

Damn. We were hoping for some hand holding. An affectionate butt squeeze. Maybe a good-bye kiss.

Frank marched to his car and dug into his front pocket for his key. Lulu snapped his picture.

Oregon clouds. They are such a part of your life you don't even see them coming and going. The Nikon thought it needed more light and flashed, and Frank jerked his head around. Lulu yelped and dropped the camera into her lap. Frank scanned the window then walked quickly toward the door of the lounge. Lulu snatched up her bag and camera and hurried into the shadowy part of the bar.

The bartender's look said, "Hey, don't barf in here," and a man at the bar twisted around to see who was running by. Lulu ducked into the ladies' room. We hoped no one would be in there. We hoped Frank wasn't so fired up he'd come in there himself. We hoped the bartender and his lone customer wouldn't mention us.

Okay, the flash was a dumb mistake, but we learn from our mistakes. When things get too automatic there's usually trouble. Put it on the to-do list—get a simpler camera. Lulu pushed open one of the stalls and went inside, closing the door behind her. Looked around. This would have to do. She didn't sit down.

We took a deep breath. We took a bunch of deep breaths. We waited ten minutes.

Lulu peeked out into the bar, but the angle of the door was wrong, so she couldn't see much. We couldn't hide in the ladies' room forever. Lulu pushed back into the bar. No Frank. She walked back to her table by the window and sat down. The server came by and Lulu ordered one more glass of white wine.

Frank's car was gone. He must have figured the flash had not been about him. We weren't off the hook. The idea of the flash had been burned into Frank's mind. Even if he didn't know it, on some level, he would be thinking about people taking his picture. Since it looked like he really was fooling around on Elsie, the subconscious awareness of being photographed coupled with his guilt could make him even more dangerous to follow. We'd need to be extra careful.

But Frank was not here now. We decided to wait and see who else might come out of room 142.

If anyone else did come out. If she hadn't already come out while Lulu had been hiding from Frank.

An hour passed and no one came out of the room. We didn't think Lulu could handle another glass of white wine, so we left.

Whoever Frank had met wouldn't know Lulu nor have any reason to suspect she wasn't telling the truth when she said, "Whoops, wrong room. Sorry!" It was possible Frank's squeeze was still in there.

Lulu walked up to the door of room 142 and knocked. No answer. Knocked again. Nothing. She put her ear to the door. Just silence from the other side. Sleeping? Lulu banged on the door. Listened again. Nothing. We were pretty sure there was no one in there.

That special someone really had left while Lulu was hiding in the can. We'd missed her!

There was still the back of the building to check. It wasn't impossible these units had back doors. That would be good to know.

They didn't. And if someone had crawled out the back window, she would have had to crawl through a lot of shrubbery. And why would anyone bother?

We could try to bribe the desk guy. Probably not a good idea. What we could learn was not enough to risk someone telling Frank about us.

There was nothing to do but go back downtown and see if Frank would do anything else today.

So, by three that afternoon, Lulu was prowling around outside the police station waiting for Frank to come out and do something his wife could be told about. We bought an Italian soda (vanilla) from a street vendor. We wandered down to the underground garage to make sure his car was still there.

We sat in the Escort for over an hour.

We wandered back to the mall and spent some time throwing quarters into the guitar case of a street musician.

Frank didn't come out until after five and then he drove straight home.

Lulu grabbed some dinner at a Thai restaurant in the Market District and then ambled on back to the office.

Stripped.

Showered.

Gargled scotch.

Brushed my teeth.

Wandered around the office making painful faces.

Brushed my teeth again.

I don't know why I let Lulu order Thai. Eating the kind she likes is like letting a live wasp go crazy in your mouth. Hours later your tongue still feels like it's sitting on a bed of nails.

The blinking pink glow from the TOFU sign across the alley on the Baltimore building taunted me. See? You should have fried up some tofu.

I was disappointed about not wrapping up the Wallace case, but it wouldn't do any good to brood about it. I decided to switch gears and spend time with the case of the Graffiti Murders.

Prudence Deerfield was hot for me to get back into GP Ink. The big guy I'd surprised had been looking for something. Putting those two facts together, I could only conclude there really was something to find there. The police had surely been all over the place, and they probably had gone over it again after I'd bowled over Frank and Marvin, but they may have missed something. I would have to go back, and I might as well do it right now while I still had some momentum going.

Maybe go as Dieter?

No, if I let Dieter go, we'd probably stop off in some secret back alley kitchen for midnight menudo. My tongue needed the night off. I'd let Dennis do it.

Dennis was an old disguise. I could put Dennis on in my sleep. Being Dennis reminded me that there would be the GP Ink computers to poke around in! He couldn't wait to get his hands on them. Who knew what neat stuff they might have squirreled away over the years?

Curbing his enthusiasm a little, I pushed our disguise down a level by disguising Dennis as a janitor in tan overalls. I looked Dennis over from head to knees in the long mirror on the washroom door. The nerdy guy who sweeps up. I gave him a big thumbs up.

I locked the office and walked down the hall to the janitor's closet and borrowed a mop and bucket. I had never seen anyone in my building use them. I only knew they were there because no matter where I am, I like to know what's behind every door. I'd found this closet the first day I rented the office back in . . . well, a long, long time ago.

I made the short walk around the corner and down the street to the Baltimore building. The night was cool and cloudy, the dark mall all echoes and whispers, shadows and night eyes.

The service entrance was locked, of course, but it didn't take me long to get inside. I wondered if the real janitorial staff would be bumping around in the building. If my building was anything to go by, janitors at the Baltimore might be purely mythical.

When I got to suite 317, I looked for light under the door, and just because I didn't see any, I didn't pick the lock right away. Instead, I put my ear to the door and spent some time listening. Nothing. So I went to work on the lock.

Once I'd gotten the door open, I walked directly to the door of the inner office to check for light under it. No light. I did some more listening. I did some sniffing. It's a fact that most bad guys would be more elusive if they showered more often.

I eased the inner office door open. Listened. Sniffed. All was quiet and everything smelled inorganic.

By the time I flipped on the lights, I was pretty sure I was alone. I put on my hey-don't-hurt-me face and held up my mop just in case, but there was no one there.

The inner office contained two desks. I'd had the impression there was only one desk when I was here so briefly last time, and that was because the desk to the left was turned sideways and pushed up against the wall. Maybe Gerald or Pablo had been trying to get a little privacy. I wondered if they had gotten along. I wondered why they'd never thought to put some kind of barrier between the two desks. The current arrangement would have driven me crazy.

I went quickly through the drawers of the desks and found nothing interesting. Address books and the like had either been taken by the police or maybe had not existed at all. The big filing cabinets back against the wall between the desks were empty.

I peeked behind the posters taped to the walls. I flipped through the books on the shelf running around the room just a foot or so from the ceiling. Nothing.

It made sense, I suppose. If there were anything to find in a place like GP Ink it would be on computer media. The police had evidently taken all the CDs, floppies, removable hard disks, and tapes that must have been everywhere in an office like this. That left only the hard drives on the computers. The police would have copied the data, but I doubted they would have erased it. My one hope was that I would see something they had missed, or maybe make some connection they hadn't made.

There were three computers—one in the outer office and two back here. Computers always made it easy to be Dennis. He decided to call the computer in the outer office computer number 1. Facing the back wall of the inner office, the machine on his left would be computer number 2 and the machine on his right would be number 3. That meant we could choose one of six (three factorial) orders of search—123, 132, 213, 231, 312, or 321.

Because we lived in this universe and not some other universe, the stuff we were looking for, if it existed at all, would be in the last place we looked.

Knowing that, Dennis figured it should be possible to fool the universe and save some time.

He turned toward the front office as if he were going to go for 123 or 132, then at the last minute he spun around and sat down behind computer number 2. At this point in the procedure, the information would be on computer 1 or 3 (it would all depend on which one Dennis chose next), so he could get up now and skip number 2.

He got up and walked over and sat down behind computer number 3. Now the information we needed would be on computer number 1.

He got up and walked out to the front office and sat down behind number 1. He switched on the computer and started in on the files.

A half an hour later, we decided the universe had not been fooled by our little game of musical chairs. There was nothing but routine day-to-day outer office stuff on the hard drive of computer number 1. Dennis turned if off and walked back into the inner office.

Just pick one, we told him, and he walked to the computer on the right (number 3) without further debate.

There was some interesting stuff on this one—Gerald Moffitt's machine as it turned out, technical stuff and personal stuff. Dennis had a lot of experience looking at the organization of information on hard drives, and it soon became clear to him that there were some holes in Gerald's stuff—sections ripped out. Hastily ripped out as if someone were scanning files, maybe copying stuff, and then erasing what they'd read. For instance, Gerald had kept a directory for important e-mail organized by date. But there were dates missing, and some of the existing subdirectories were empty.

My Sky side popped up and offered the theory that the big guy in the foreign shoes had been in the process of searching and trashing Gerald's hard drive when we'd surprised him.

So what had he missed? Well, there was no e-mail subdirectory for the day of the murder. None for the day before either. And so on back to five days before the murder. But there was a place for e-mail six days before the murder. Dennis opened it up. There were three messages. Dennis figured that meant the big guy had been here, too. Who gets just three pieces of e-mail a day? No one. So Mr. Cheap Suit may well have been poking around in that very directory when we interrupted him.

Dennis jumped into the mail program so he could see e-mail by sender address and subject line, switched over to the day in question and spotted something interesting right away.

The subject of the middle message of the three messages received six days before the murder was WARNING! The sender was anon33@4e4.com.

We opened it up.

The message read, "This is your next to last warning, Gerald Moffitt!" It was signed SOAPY.

It was from the loose screw who claimed to have posted a picture of Gerald's body on the Web.

If SOAPY had been threatening Gerald before the murder, it made his claims a lot more plausible. But there was still something screwy about the warning. Then we got it. How did SOAPY know this would be the "next to last warning?" Didn't people just say "This is your last warning!" Even if they had to say it a dozen times? Had SOAPY planned to issue a fixed number of warnings and then kill Gerald anyway? And what was he warning Gerald about? And where was his last warning? Maybe he'd killed Gerald with no last warning.

Also puzzling was the fact that if the police had this information why were they still so hot to grab Pablo? Could they have missed this? Unlikely. Another puzzle for our list of puzzles in this case.

Dennis copied the letter onto a floppy. The only other interesting thing on Gerald's machine was a file called DATAPANTS. Besides the name, of course, the neat thing about this file was that it was encrypted. Dennis loved encrypted files. He copied the DATAPANTS file onto the floppy with the warning from SOAPY and put the floppy in his shirt pocket. Then he erased both the warning from SOAPY and the DATAPANTS file. Why make things easy for Mr. Sucker Punch if he decided to come back to finish up?

Dennis turned off Gerald's computer and switched over to the one on the other desk.

We were making progress!

That sudden burst of enthusiasm was a flash in the pan. Even with this new information, I felt an old despair creeping up, and I knew I could make it go away with a little dancing, but I knew too that down that road was just more despair. The hell of it was that I knew I was already deep into relapse. I'd proved that at Gotta Dance. It's like something good happens and I've got to run off and celebrate.

At least one of us had been planning it all along.

I'd been avoiding looking, fooling myself, but once the realization hit home, there was no sense denying it. I stopped in the middle of the room and looked down at my feet. I might be Dennis disguised as a janitor, but I was wearing our shiny black dancing shoes.

Unless I made a serious life change, everything I did now was just a holding action. My weird double-think ability was all that was keeping me going. Maybe that would be enough. You needed time to make big life changes, and time was not a luxury we had right now. Right now we had cases to solve. Dennis moved on to the next computer.

Pablo's computer was filled with nifty games. He and Randy Casey must have had a lot in common. It was hard to see how Pablo had gotten any work done at all. At least that was my impression before I started in on the directory called EES.

We hit another jackpot.

There were a lot of documents written in a foreign language. There was also a file of business letters discussing the foreign language files.

The first startling thing I learned was that the language was Russian! The reason I hadn't recognized it at once (not that any of us speak Russian) was that it wasn't written in the Russian alphabet, so I hadn't been tipped off by any of those funny letters they use. Instead everything was in the regular alphabet. Maybe the words were spelled like they sounded.

But the thing that really knocked me out was that the Russian company was called Evil Empire Software!

The nerve of these guys. They put it right out in the open and dared you to make something of it.

From clues in the business letters I deduced that GP Ink had been hired by the Russians to translate Evil Empire documentation into English.

six

There were simply too many Russians in the case. EES and 4e4—it had to mean something.

I decided to call a conference. I hadn't been making excuses when I'd told Prudence Deerfield that my disguises gave me the ability to look at a problem from a number of different perspectives. Each of my disguises represented a unique world view. In the old days, getting a discussion going had been difficult (not that we didn't manage it). These days, we did it with computers. Now I could log on to a private chat room, split myself into my several pieces, and talk the problem out.

I flipped over to Pablo's telecommunication directory and logged on to the Internet using the Skylight Howells office account. I jumped over to a commercial service I knew was usually not too busy at that time of night and made arrangements for a private room.

Once inside the room, I made an animated icon for each of my aspects. Sky became Mr. Face, the *Mad Mag* spy I often used when talking to my therapist Roger. Dennis liked to appear as a red, white, and blue superhero in netland. Huge chest. No butt to speak of. Goofy cape. Scarface wore a human body with the head of a bat. Lulu liked to dress up, and in netland she had the figure for it. Dieter always dressed in black. The clothes were a sharp contrast to his blond hair and piercing blue eyes. The Average Guy (Tag) waited until everyone had a look, and then assumed the precise average of the other five.

"The Russians seem to be a factor," Sky said.

"I've been looking at the numbers," Dennis said. "It may go even deeper than you think."

"What do you mean?" Lulu asked.

The six icons moved into a circle, and their conversation appeared near the top of the screen. At first it was like looking down at the tops of their heads. That is, it was an experience from the outside, but then I let my mind drift free until I was hearing the conversation rather than typing and then reading it. I got inside the experience.

"What are the two Russian pieces we have?" Dennis asked.

"Well, there's the Russian remailing service," Sky said, "and now this software company that Gerald and Pablo were apparently doing some work for."

"Okay," Dennis said, "now let's look at the numbers involved in both of those. I mean four-e-four and EES."

"Those aren't numbers," Lulu said.

"She's right," Scarface said.

"We may be on the wrong track altogether with this Russian business," Dieter said. "There is a more obvious sinister secret group."

Dennis hurried on before Dieter could turn the discussion away from the Russians. "In fact," he said, "four-e-four is a number. It's just in hex. That is, it's in base 16. Look, it consists of 4 times 256 plus 14 times 16 plus 4 or 1252."

"And what does that tell us?" Sky wondered.

"I don't know," Dennis said. "Let's play with it and see what we get. First the prime factors."

He pulled a line out of the air and stretched it open and it became a chalkboard. We formed a semicircle around Dennis, and he put some numbers on the board.

313 times 2 times 2 equals 1252

"Here we have the parts of 1252 that can be divided no further," he said.

Lulu raised her hand.

"Yes?"

"I don't see where you're going with this."

"You're missing the point," Dennis said. "What we're doing is just poking around to see what the numbers might tell us. How do I know what we'll find until we find it? Let's go on."

"Grumble."

"Who said that? Oh, never mind. Look." Dennis wrote on his chalkboard again.

2 313 2

"I've rearranged the factors symmetrically," he said. "The other possibilities are these."

22 313

313 22

"Let's take each one in turn. What are the prime factors of 23132?" He made a calculator appear and divided 23132 by 2 and got 11566 and divided that by 2 and got 5783. "Now is 5783 prime?"

We watched his eyes roll in his head while he figured it out. The rolling eyes in his superhero head were just for show. What he was really up to (and we all knew it but were too polite to say so) was slipping back out into Pablo's system, locating a programming language (C++ was all Pablo had on hand) and writing a quick routine that would take the square root of any number and then divide that original number by successive odd numbers until it either found a number that divided the original number evenly, in which case the original number wasn't prime, or a number that was bigger than the square root, in which case the original number was prime.

Dennis used the program on 5783 and found that it was prime and brought his rolling eyes to a halt.

"So 2 times 2 times 5783 is 23132," he said.

"And that tells us exactly what?" Dieter said.

"Well, nothing, that I can see," Dennis said. "Negative results can be productive, too, you know. Let's go on."

"Sigh."

"Who said that?" Dennis glared around at us for a moment. Then he turned back to the board, and using the prime routine on 22313, produced the factors 53 and 421 both of which turned out to be prime. Then he divided 31322 by 2 and got 15661 which turned out to be prime.

"This had all better add up to something," Scarface said. He made something that looked like blood run off his bat fangs.

"Hey, that's a good idea!" Dennis said. "Let's add up one instance of each of the prime factors from all the numbers."

$$
\begin{array}{r}
313 \\
2 \\
5783 \\
15661 \\
53 \\
421 \\
\hline
22233
\end{array}
$$

"Wow, look at that. Three twos and two threes!" Dennis said. "Now if you apply three to the twos and two to the threes and multiply you get 66666."

"Or maybe two groups," Sky said.

"What."

"Like this." Sky wrote on the chalkboard.

$$666 \ 66$$

"So we have the number of the beast," Lulu said, "and a mostly defunct highway featured in an old TV show?"

"Or," Scarface said, "the number of the beast and the number inked all over Randy Casey's body."

"I think the Satan connection is barking up the wrong tree," Dieter said.

"If you want Randy's number," Dennis said, "you can just add up the three twos and get six and the two threes and get six and put them together to get 66."

"Exactly," Sky said. "That's a lot neater."

"There is a sinister secret much closer to home," Dieter said.

We ignored him.

"So, what are we saying here?" Lulu asked. "That the reason 66 was written all over Randy's body is that it is a secret number embodied in the name of the Russian remailing service four-e-four?"

"Nicely put," Sky said. "But what about EES? Is it also embedded in there?"

Dennis erased the chalkboard and wrote EES on it.

"This is not a hex number," he said.

"Maybe you could make that S be a five?" Sky said.

"We could try that," Dennis said, "but it's not very elegant. Suppose we simply pull no punches and assume this is a number in base 26. Hang on a minute. I'll do the math."

He filled the board with figures and the others waited. A moment later, Dennis turned back to the group. "It doesn't add up to anything," he said. "Not only that but I tried using 5 for that S and still got nothing."

"What if you use 19 for the S and just Hex for the rest?" Scarface asked.

"Why 19?" Lulu asked.

"Well, S is the nineteenth letter of the alphabet," Scarface said.

"But that was the idea when we did base 26," Dennis said. "And I already tried base 19, too. Nothing."

"But you didn't try thinking of EE as a hex number."

"Actually it would be EE0," Dennis said. "Here. EE0 is 3808 and that plus 19 is 3827 and the prime factors of that are 43 and 89 and 43 plus 89 gives us 132. Doesn't help much."

"Oh, no?" Scarface said. "Just what do you think half of 132 is?" He walked up to the board and wrote.

66

Everyone was quiet for a while.

We saved the calculation Dennis had made in a file. Lulu told us of her theory about Gerald's death being a crime of passion. We wondered how Randy fit into that theory and she admitted she hadn't worked that out yet.

"I think we may be onto something with the Russians," Scarface said. "Maybe Gerald and Randy were both moles. Now that the Soviet Union no longer exists, someone is cleaning up the loose ends. That would explain the Evil Empire business."

"But if Evil Empire Software really was evil," Lulu said, "they probably wouldn't call themselves the Evil Empire."

"I think it's all the doing of you know who," Dieter said. No one could think of another delaying tactic, so we let Dieter go on for a few minutes about the Secret Society of Mexican Food Cooks who, he was convinced, was the true power behind the scenes.

"It seems clear to me," he said, "that Gerald and Randy were responsible for the posting of the secret ingredient on the net."

"But no one even noticed," Sky said. "There were hundreds of posts offering other ingredients. No one would be able to pull out the real secret ingredient from that mess."

"That bombardment of other ingredients was pure genius on the part of . . . well, someone in the society," Dieter said. "But the society must have figured Gerald would just keep posting it until someone believed him and then the cat would be out of the bag."

"So to speak," Scarface said.

"But what about Randy?" Lulu asked.

"Somehow he must have been in on it," Dieter said. "Maybe when he was working for Gerald, Gerald told him the secret."

"But how did Gerald know the secret in the first place?" Sky asked.

"I don't think the Secret Society of Mexican Food Cooks has anything to do with this, Dieter. The fact that someone posted the secret ingredient is probably a coincidence."

"That won't be the case," Dieter said. "Mark my words."

"We're always marking your words, Dieter," Lulu said, "and you're almost always wrong."

"Here's what I think," Sky said. "We really *do* have Russian involvement. I don't know about the Mexican Food and the passion and the Satan angles. We need to find out more about four-e-four and Evil Empire Software. Looking at the numbers, I think the connection with four-e-four is clearer than the connection with EES. That mixing of bases seems a little shaky to me."

"You're probably right," Dennis said.

"What we probably have here is an international conspiracy," Sky said. "It obviously has something to do with advanced technologies and probably the Internet. Gerald and Pablo screwed up somehow, and Gerald was murdered for it. Pablo, fearing for his life, went into hiding. Maybe Randy learned something while he was working here, and it got him killed."

"That's nice, Sky," Lulu said, "but that doesn't tell us who the killer is nor what happened to Pablo Deerfield."

"No," Sky said, "but it's progress!"

In fact, I felt so good about our progress that I closed down the chat room and jumped over to the newsgroups. My thought was to post our theory to alt.dead.gerald and maybe mass mail it to the BOD list. Maybe include the insights we'd come to through the math Dennis had done. I thought there was a good chance the killer would see the message. Maybe we could smoke him out.

The newsgroup alt.dead.gerald had vanished. It took me a few minutes to discover that since we now had two dead computer people, alt.dead.gerald had evolved into alt.dead.nerds, and I wasted time wading though a flame war about the name change—reams of anal bickering and backstabbing and what's in a name and I'll tell you what's in a name you hereditarily challenged clown! And on and on. I was finally able to conclude that no one knew more than I already knew about the murder of Randy Casey. No one was talking about the BOD mailing list, so that at least was not common knowledge. I decided not to mention it.

I composed a message explaining our international conspiracy theory for the murder of Gerald Moffitt and Randy Casey. I spell-checked the message and read it over one more time. I was pleased. I was encouraged. I posted the message on alt.dead.nerds. I thought it ought to light some fires.

Now if there were just some way to make this explain what Frank was up to at the Quack Inn, life would be perfect.

Well, you can't always get what you want.

We spent some time congratulating ourselves, back pats for everyone. We were filled with the happy glow of accomplishment.

We left GP Ink, but we got lost on the way back to the office.

Still Dennis, still carrying the mop and bucket, we must have taken a wrong turn and ended up at a club called Twinkle Toes on the east side. We hadn't been there in a while, but everyone seemed to be happy to see us.

You don't want to be poking around in the head of an addicted tap dancer, but let me tell you that all dances are the same dance and when you come home to the dance it's as if you never left. I mean you could lift your foot for a step and be suddenly yanked away to another life—you get a job, say, and meet a woman, you get married, you have kids, you raise the kids, get them into good colleges, and then one day for no reason you can articulate, you walk back into Twinkle Toes and put your foot down, and it's the same step, and no one even notices the time that may or may not have passed from the moment you lifted your toe to the moment you tapped it down again. Dance clubs are all different; dance clubs are all the same, one club, one time.

Dance time is a train on an entirely different track.

So we had this nifty mop and bucket and the possibilities were endless. Twinkle Toes was dark and smoky, but there was a well-lighted stage. The bartender tonight was a woman I couldn't name—big blond hairdo and perpetually astonished eyes and a small frozen smile. What distinguished Twinkle Toes was mostly the glitter on the big mirror behind the bar. We got a drink and went backstage and got in line. Things got fuzzy until we came onstage and entered the crystal dance time loop.

We knocked them dead at Twinkle Toes. Improvised with the mop and bucket then got back in line to wait for the chance to perfect it. We danced and waited to dance again, and every time we danced, the routine got a little better.

People came and went. Maybe outside the sun rose and set again, I couldn't tell; I didn't care. The mop became an extremely precise instrument for expressing my place in the universe. The bucket became the focus, the anchor, the locus to dance around.

First few times through the loop, I stopped off at the bar to throw down a scotch, loosen me up some, but as I perfected the mop and bucket bit, I no longer needed loosening up. Once I think someone must have given me a sandwich as I waited in the wings for my turn onstage. Maybe it was more than once. I remember what must have been the can, slick white porcelain, and peeing, but I don't remember how I got there or how I got back to the stage.

I remember the moment I realized the perfection I was reaching for was an illusion. I suddenly knew that no matter how many times I came around, I would never get it right. I'd reached a peak, and now things could only get worse. A lot worse. The dance became not a quest for enlightenment and redemption, but a struggle for survival. The change had a lot to do with a big bad guy.

The big bad guy joins you onstage (and you wonder if you're the only one who can see him) and he's got a six-shooter and he says, "Dance, dude," and he shoots at your feet and you jump around in a goofy parody of dance in your big boots and he laughs and you can't stop dancing while the devil is shooting at your feet and it simply goes on forever.

Oddly, I still had to get back in line periodically to wait for another turn. I spent the time in line trembling and sweating (we call this jitterbugging—I have no feet and I must dance), and as bad as the time onstage was, the time in line was worse.

I noticed a man named Yuri from my support group lurking in the wings, and I figured someone had sent out a rescue party, but the face faded so quickly I decided I was hallucinating, especially since the woman with him had looked just like Prudence Deerfield. Yuri was a green card Russian guy and Russians had been on my mind lately.

I kept jumping around the stage dodging bullets, until someone threw a bag over my head and dragged me away.

I didn't care who had snatched me; I didn't care why. I went limp with surrender and let myself be led. We walked and walked and walked and then I could tell we were outside. I got folded into a car.

Once we were in motion, someone yanked away the bag (it was a big yellow pillowcase) freeing my arms and head. I looked over and saw that the driver really was Yuri Kost from the twelve-step group. I leaned my head against the window and closed my eyes.

When we got back downtown, Prudence (I wasn't all that surprised to see that it was her after all) and Yuri helped me up to my office. I stretched out on the couch and they took chairs like friends at a sickbed or maybe mourners over a deathbed. I thought I should talk to them. I closed my eyes instead.

seven

I'd been staring at a spot of sunlight reflected onto the ceiling for some time before I decided it looked like the state of Texas. I wondered how many days I'd lost.

I rolled my head to the left and saw Prudence Deerfield leaning forward in her chair with her elbows on her knees. She widened her eyes at me. She was wearing a pale purple flower-print dress and black grunge boots. Or maybe she'd been time traveling, too, and her feet just hadn't caught up with the rest of her yet.

"Let me guess," she said. "That's your what-the-cat-coughed-up disguise."

"What the cat dragged in." I swung my legs off the couch, sat up, and put my head in my hands. "You're so weird, Prudence. Everything you say is just a little off."

"But cats are always coughing stuff up, aren't they?"

"Never mind," I said. I lifted my head up out of my hands. "So where's Yuri?"

"He had to get back to work," she said. "He said he'd come by later and get you for one of your support group meetings."

"He's your foreign gentleman who recommended me, isn't he?"

"Yes."

"Another Russian in the mix," I said. "I should have thought of Yuri earlier."

"Your Russian number theory," she said.

"You read about it?"

"It's all the rage on alt-dot-dead-dot-nerds," she said.

I got up off the couch. I hoped it looked easier than it was. I was still swimming through pancake syrup, and I produced a strange echo every time I spoke. I made it across to my desk and sank down in my chair. I logged on, moved over to the newsgroups, and called up alt.dead.nerds. "So what's going on?"

Prudence came around my desk and stood looking over my shoulder at the message list.

"Go down a little," she said.

I scrolled down the list.

"There," she said. She put a hand on my shoulder and leaned in to point. I got lost in her touch and her smell. She shook me, and I came a little more awake and followed her arm down to the screen.

The message line she was pointing at said, "Jumbo Dinner Frank."

Prudence took her hand off my shoulder and backed off a little.

I took a deep breath.

My mind was like a machine in need of oil, moving slowly and painfully with a lot of noise no one else could hear.

I guessed the "Frank" in "Dinner Frank" could refer to Frank Wallace, but that was another case entirely.

"What made you think this would pertain to anything?" I asked. "Did you read everything?"

"Yes, I read everything," she said.

The subject line became clear when I read the first line of the message itself. "Skylight Howells has all the deductive power of a jumbo dinner frank! Russians! What a weenie!"

The handle for this user was becoming familiar.

SOAPY.

SOAPY went on at some length about how my numerical speculations of the night before were utter nonsense.

"It's perfectly obvious why Gerald Moffitt and Randy Casey had to die," he said. But then he didn't go on to state what he thought was so obvious. Maybe he was a mathematician. They like to do that—just say something is obvious when it's not and then leave you twisting in the wind. The thing was I couldn't admit that I was twisting in the wind. I was supposed to be some kind of hotshot detective.

"You noticed the from line?" I asked, tapping the 4e4.com address with my fingernail.

"Oh, that," she said.

"Yes, that," I said. "Isn't it strange this jerk is so down on my Russian theory when he's using the Russian anonymous remailer? I think he's trying to throw us off the track."

"You think SOAPY is a Russian?"

"Well, maybe," I said. "Why not?"

"And you think he's the killer?"

"I think he or she ought to be right up there on our list of suspects," I said.

"You got anything else?" she asked.

I remembered the threat SOAPY had sent to Gerald Moffitt, and I slapped my hand over my left shirt pocket where Dennis had put the disk. "Well, nothing definite yet," I said.

I could feel her looking down at the disk in my shirt pocket. I slowly moved my hand back to the keyboard.

"So, how do you plan on finding out who SOAPY really is?" she asked.

"Just good solid down-to-earth detective work," I said. At that moment I had no idea what I should do next, but I knew I would think of something.

I considered hitting her with the word "DATAPANTS" just to see how she'd react, but then I figured I'd save it for a time I was feeling a little more alert.

"Lots of people think you're blowing smoke up the wrong alley with that Russian business," Prudence said. "You'd better read some of the other posts if you want to know how many people think you're a weenie."

I didn't have anything to say to that, so I didn't turn around and look at her, but I was very aware of her standing there just behind me.

"Your ears are red," she said. She touched my right ear then leaned in close and touched her cheek to mine. I twisted around and pulled her down into my arms.

No, wait a minute, I was making stuff up again. Prudence wasn't even behind me anymore. She'd walked around the desk and was now sitting in the client's chair.

"So what is the connection with Evil Empire Software?" I wanted to see if she'd lie to me about the Russian company.

"If there is a connection," she said, "it's just that EES hired Gerald and Pablo to translate their manuals into English."

I was seized by a sudden realization, and I slapped my palm down on my desk. "And Yuri works for Evil Empire Software!"

"I think we may have mentioned that last night," she said. "That's how I know Yuri. And Yuri knows you from your twelve-step group and you're a detective, so when this whole nasty business came up, he told me about you. He said you were a nice guy."

"Yuri thinks I'm a nice guy?"

"Yes."

It was all very neat. "It all seems very neat to me," I said.

"Way cool," she said.

"What?"

"Neat. Like you said."

The bells from the church down the street rang, and while those bells didn't only ring on Sundays, they always reminded me of Sundays, and that reminded me that I still didn't know how many days I'd lost.

"What day is this?"

"Thursday," Prudence said.

I'd lost all of Wednesday.

Time ticked away at the top of the computer screen. Nearly noon. I could still make visiting hours.

I pushed up and walked over to the cardboard wardrobe behind the screen by the files and grabbed a change of clothes and ducked into the washroom to shave and shower.

After dressing, I took a roll of tape from the disguise cabinet and secured the disk with SOAPY's threat and the DATAPANTS file underneath the cabinet. Dennis would just have to wait to play with the encryption.

Prudence was still sitting in front of my desk when I came out.

"You look a lot better," she said.

I grabbed my coat.

"Hey, where are you going? You're supposed to wait for Yuri."

"I always visit my mother on Sundays," I said. "I'll be back later." I stopped with my hand on the doorknob and looked back over my shoulder at her. "And, hey, thanks. You guys. For, you know, rescuing me."

"But it's not Sunday!"

I ducked out before she could fire another question my way. I took the stairs in case she tried to catch up with me at the elevator. I didn't have anything else to say, but I had something to do.

Come hell or high water, I always visit my mother on Sundays. Which means I always visit at least once in any seven day period. No matter when I visit, Mom always thinks it's Sunday. Unless more than seven days have passed since my last visit. In that case, she gently chides me for missing a week. Sometimes my visit is a chore and sometimes it's a joy. Either way, I go. Today I was pretty much in a total fog, but I couldn't let that stop me. If I waited until tomorrow I would have missed a week in her mind.

My mother had once been a leading force in Eugene high society. You couldn't throw a big benefit dinner without her. You wouldn't build a bridge or reopen a street without checking to see if she was on your side or not. If she wasn't, you knew the project would take a lot longer and would cost a lot more. One of the major downtown streets is named after her great grandfather (or maybe his father, I forget which).

She married my father, Richard "Dick" Dobson, in 1954. His great grandfather (or whatever) is the Dobson after whom another major downtown street was named. On one corner of the intersection where the family streets cross is a mediocre Mexican food restaurant (which drives Dieter crazy); there's a convenience store across from the restaurant; a bead and incense shop occupies the third corner, and just recently a fancy coffee place has opened on the fourth corner. My mother spent a lot of time scheming to get that intersection. She wanted to build family houses on all four corners, but she was never able to get the properties.

Both sides of the family go way back. My grandfather, however, was the last Dobson to amount to a hill of beans (as he himself never tired of pointing out). Grandfather died when I was fourteen, seven years after my father was killed in a bar fight in San Francisco. He'd left Mom and me high and dry (as my grandfather liked to say), and I believe his leaving was the first nudge of so many nudges that finally pushed my mother over the edge. I couldn't have thought that at the time. In fact I don't remember thinking anything at the time. I don't remember my father. It's not like we were broke and hungry after he left. Grandfather still controlled the money on the Dobson side, and Mother had her own money. It was Pop who ended up in poverty. Growing up, I often thought we must have really been awful for Pop to choose a life of desperate poverty over us. Later I decided he was just a drunken jerk.

Mom went a little wacky after he left. It's easy to see that now, but it came upon her so slowly over the years that no one really noticed. Now it didn't matter much, because something the doctors said probably wasn't Alzheimers was taking the rest of her just as fast as it could. That's another reason (besides guilt, I guess, and the occasional bright moment when we laughed or I saw some of the old light in her eyes) that I drove up Bailey Hill Road and into the forest every "Sunday" to the Oak Leaves Care Center to spend some time with her.

She's still weird.

I always go as myself, but she always thinks I'm one of my disguises. I don't even know how she knows about my disguises. I don't know how she gets the details right.

Last week she thought I was Lulu and we spent the afternoon talking about flattening our tummies.

Today when I came into the lobby feeling so disconnected and demoralized, Mother sitting in one of the big flowery overstuffed chairs by the fireplace put out her hands for me to take and when I'd taken them, she said, "How nice to see you again, Dieter."

That meant we'd be talking Mexican food.

I remembered the first time I realized there really was a Secret Society of Mexican Food Cooks. Anyone can see there is a marked difference between the Mexican food you can get along our southern border (especially along the Arizona/Mexico and the New Mexico/Mexico borders, where I spent quite a few of my college days tasting, toasting, and learning the ins and outs of the local cuisine) and the Mexican food you find here in town. Most of the restaurants here tried too hard and never got it right. In Eugene you can get crab quesadillas and tofu tacos.

Home for the holidays, I discovered there was one exception. There was one restaurant in town in which the food was like the food of the Southwest. I later learned the cook was a member of SSOMFC.

In college (at Arizona State University, where Dennis had done two degrees in computer science) when I worked as a kitchen assistant in a dozen Mexican restaurants over the years, the main cook (usually a woman) would shoulder me aside at the critical moment to put the final touches on the enchilada sauce—surely, I decided, adding the secret ingredient. By careful observation over the years and one major ruse, I learned what the secret ingredient was.

But you won't be learning the ingredient from me. My revealing the fact that there is a secret ingredient and a society to protect it is a very serious matter. I thought I'd made up the secret society to add another layer to my Dieter persona until I got a phone call late one night.

The caller asked to speak to Dieter. I figured this must have something to do with a case, figured I must have talked to someone as Dieter and left the office number, so I told the caller to hang on, went into the washroom and changed and came back and picked up the phone as Dieter. The man identified himself as Señor Equis.

"Dos Equis?"

"What? Look, don't jerk me around, Dieter. I don't speak Spanish."

Señor Equis told me he represented a "certain organization." That got my attention. I have had no contact whatever with organized crime, but I've seen the movies, and I didn't want to have guys in organizations noticing me.

I think my voice squeaked when I asked him what I could do for him.

He mentioned a bunch of names, most of which Dieter recognized as Mexican food cooks we'd met during our college days. Señor Equis said that Lisa Mendoza had confessed on her deathbed that a young man had tricked her into revealing the secret ingredient many years before and she had been too ashamed (and frightened) to tell anyone until now.

Dieter remembered Lisa. Her tamales were maybe the best in the world. We were sad to hear she'd died.

"Yeah, yeah," Señor Equis said. "The point is we need to meet."

I suggested a popular Mexican food restaurant near one of the big shopping malls—my little test.

I could hear Señor Equis making spitting, gagging, and barfing sounds, so I guessed he might really know something about Mexican food. We finally agreed to meet at a noodle shop on the west side.

So, to make a long story short (and thereby hopefully not reveal anything I shouldn't reveal) Dieter met Señor Equis at the noodle shop, and Señor Equis told him about the Secret Society of Mexican Food Cooks (which we thought we'd made up).

Señor Equis questioned Dieter about the secret ingredient, made him tell the whole story of how he had teased and prodded and finally tricked Lisa Mendoza. Then he had sworn a tearful Dieter in as a member of the society with all the rights and obligations.

My mother had been delighted when she heard the story. Even in those days, she'd been confusing me and Dieter, and if Mexican food were the defining detail for Dieter in her mind, the secret society and the secret ingredient (which she never tired of trying to get out of him) were the spices that fired our conversations.

That afternoon Dieter let go of her hands and leaned down and kissed her cheek. A nurse brought her wheelchair and Dieter helped her into it. He wheeled her out to the courtyard which looked south over rolling hills of deep forest. The building was situated in such a way that you couldn't see the clear-cut to the west. You might be looking at the land the way it looked hundreds of years ago. Okay, you had to ignore the blacktopped road and the line of houses to the east but if you held your head just right . . .

Dieter receded, and I pushed Mother up to a metal patio table and pulled a chair around for myself and sat down beside her.

"How have you been, Mom?"

"It's so noisy here," she said.

I listened but could hear only the sounds of birds and insects, cut occasionally by laughter or louder talk from inside. Way back in the background I thought I could hear traffic on Bailey Hill Road. I must have seemed puzzled.

"All that crackling and popping," she explained.

"Yes," I said.

"You kids can't imagine."

You kids would be me and my disguises—or maybe just my disguises these days.

"I've been telling Louisa about the lard," she said. "I love the way it makes her face go purple when I tell her she's got to start with real lard if she wants to make good enchilada sauce."

"You can use butter," I said.

"I know it." She grinned and winked. "I just like to see her turn purple. 'Your heart! Your heart!' "

"My heart?"

"No, silly, that's what Louisa says. 'Think of your heart!' "

"Well," I said.

"The flour," she said. "The crushed chilies. The . . ."

She paused for me to fill in the secret ingredient, but I knew she really didn't expect me to do it. One of our little games.

"Nice try," I said and patted her hand, and we laughed together.

We spent some time just sitting. I loved the air on the back patio— the crisp forest smell. The place was above any auto or wood stove smog. I bet there would be a good view of the stars whenever there were stars to see (such a rare and special sight in Oregon), but then I realized there would be no one sitting out here at night.

"So what's new?" she asked.

"Sky is working on a murder case," I said.

"Has he figured it out yet?"

"No."

"Tell him to look the answer up in *The Big Book of Clues*," she said.

"I'll do that."

"I remember the way you all hated to dance," she said.

The word dance sent a chill down my back, but I'm used to running into it in odd contexts so I pulled myself together. I wondered who she was talking to. In her world had there been six little dancers and Brian, too?

"All that fuss," she said. "Do a couple of steps for me. I do so miss that."

"What?"

"I said dance for me."

As she spoke, I could see that her words no longer matched the movement of her lips. Who knew what she was really saying?

"Here?"

"Why not," she said. "They expect crazy things from me."

"But maybe not from me."

I had to clear my head. This conversation was happening on several levels for me, and it was probably happening on more than one level for her, too. On the one hand we were both talking to ourselves and missing one another altogether, but on some other level I felt we were approaching some defining moment in our relationship.

I could feel some uncontrollable dancing coming on.

"Show your mother that old soft-shoe, Brian."

Because she suddenly knew who I was, I couldn't help thinking she'd known all along. Calling me by my name took me back, made me see the kitchen table in the old house on Lincoln, Mom in an apron (or maybe that was the Beaver's mom) and me in my gleaming black tap shoes and white shirt and red crepe paper vest with the sparkling green stars. Someone had blown glitter onto the front of my outfit. White foam hat. What was that stuff they used to make your hat? You could bite a piece out of the brim of a hat like that, but you'd get in big trouble if you did.

"Don't just sit there looking so glum," she said. "Listen to the song in your heart!"

So I got up from the kitchen table and jumped around the room trying to remember the steps Mrs. Fountain had run the twelve of us through last Saturday. Boy, was she ever a tyrant. A woman of one age or another. Her face looked years older than my mom's, but she could have stolen her body from a teenager. She always wore a scarf around her neck, and I figured that was to hide the stitches that held the head and the body together.

My mother clapping time to the tap-along music on the stereo.

Mom driving the station wagon, still whistling—pick up Elsie and Peggy, pick up Ted(dy—he hates that), and Marvin, already bigger than the rest—here a kid, there a kid—maybe half the tap class.

The twelve of us in a line onstage, Marvin in the middle like a mountain peak. Mrs. Fountain in the wings looking like a bird, maybe a vulture. I could just die, Ted said. Yeah, but then she'd eat you. Curtain goes up. We look around blinking like someone's just flipped on the lights and caught us with our pants down.

The crowd rumbles like a huge empty stomach.

Dorky music.

And we dance.

Crazy hail on a tin roof. We're not exactly synchronized.

Every shadow claps anyway. Cheers and whistles.

Ted grows up as he dances and by the time he's a teenager he wanders off shaking his head and grinning sheepishly. Elsie puts on pounds but perseveres. She dances to the left getting older, bigger; she dances back to me getting smaller; we patty cake and click our heels together and she dances away to the left again getting bigger. We repeat that a couple of times, she comes, she goes, but one time she just doesn't come back, and it's just Marvin and me. Then he whaps me a good one on the back of the head and I'm dancing alone on the stage. Grandparents and parents and siblings and friends and well-wishers have all taken up smoking and no one is paying much attention to the stage anymore. Everyone is talking and rattling the ice in their glasses. You've really got to dig in your heels and put on a show to get the attention of a crowd like that, but in most ways I don't care if they're watching—I'm an artist; I dance for myself.

I am large and I am the master of tap. I am small and clumsy. I am large and sweaty and the tangy pine air blows across the patio and cools my face. I can see my mother's face, but I cannot decipher her expression. Her mouth moves but I can't read her lips. I'm afraid she looks frightened.

Then there's a guy on my left who takes my arm, and a guy on my right who takes my other arm. They make soothing sounds as they urge me from the patio and down and down and down the long hallway toward the front door of the nursing home. I've gone too far. Things have gotten out of hand. I wonder how much of that was real. How much of that did I share with my mother and how much of it did I live alone. Once I get wound up like that, I don't stop until I crash. I felt a deep sense of embarrassment. I wondered how my mother would be next "Sunday." Would she remember? The staff would pretend that nothing had happened. Except for Jennifer, the nurse at the front desk, who would give me a look that said you'd better behave yourself or else!

"I can walk," I said.

"It's okay, Mr. Dobson," the guy on my left said. "We'll just help you to your car."

It was a long walk to the front door. I felt like a fool, but I was too ripped to put up a fight.

"Do you think he can drive?" the guy on my right said.

"I'm okay," I said. I rolled my shoulders and shook them off. Okay, what really happened was we were outside so they just let me go. I held up my hands and backed away from them. "I'm okay."

I walked to my jeep. I opened the door and climbed behind the wheel and then looked back at the front of the nursing home. My escorts had gone back inside.

I rested my forehead on the steering wheel and took a couple of deep breaths. Big raindrops splattered against the windshield. Maybe I needed a meeting. Of course, I needed a meeting; I'd needed a meeting for weeks, but I knew I wouldn't make one yet.

How low can you go?

We'll have to let you know.

Apparently I was still on the way down.

eight

I'd lied to the guys in white; I was in no shape to drive, so when the rain let up a little, I left the Cherokee at the Oak Leaves Care Center and hiked down the hill to Eighteenth Avenue where I sat for fifteen minutes in a bus shelter listening to the rain hitting the roof and waiting for a bus to take me back downtown. The only good thing you could have said about me at that time was that at least I wasn't behind the wheel.

The bus driver gave me a nasty look, and nasty looks from bus drivers are not common in Eugene, so I figured I must look pretty much like I felt. I took a seat about half way back in the bus and struggled to get invisible. Maybe I was trying too hard since the driver kept looking up at me in his big mirror.

All that attention made me so nervous I got off maybe ten blocks too soon and had to walk the rest of the way. Once I hit the downtown mall, there were more people about. They slowed me down, and everyone seemed to notice me. There is an opposite for almost everything. The opposite of being invisible is that state where everyone notices you. Everyone you pass looks at you, catalogues your failings, notes your distinguishing features for a potential police line-up. It's like when you get a goofy haircut and everyone you pass looks at your head, smirks, and looks away. I put my hands in my pockets and watched my feet and hurried on down the mall to my office. Slipping into my building was like ducking into a cave. I almost never met anyone in the corridors or elevator and that evening was no different. I got to my door without seeing anyone.

Once inside, I sat down behind my desk and poured myself a big drink, drank it, and poured myself another. The scotch radiated warmth from my belly down to my knees and toes and up to the tops of my ears. I finished the second drink and then stretched out on the couch and closed my eyes. I needed to get away, but I didn't want to drink myself to sleep. My head was spinning a mile a minute (as my mother would have said), and I planned on lying there with my eyes closed pretending to be asleep or passed out until it stopped.

I was still pretending when the door opened and a couple of bumblers came whispering and shushing into the office. I recognized Prudence at once and a moment later I was sure the other one was Yuri. I didn't open my eyes.

"Put it down on the desk," Prudence whispered.

They were moving around as carefully as they could, which meant they were making a lot of noise. I could smell barbecue sauce. Suddenly hungry, I thought about sitting up and rubbing my eyes and saying, "Hey, you guys brought ribs." But then I thought that if they thought I was really out, they might say things they wouldn't ordinarily say around me.

"I may need to unplug something else," Yuri whispered.

"Later," Prudence whispered.

I heard the client chair being dragged across the floor closer to the couch. And then a puzzling squeak that I soon figured out was from my desk chair being pushed across the floor on its rollers. They were pulling up chairs around the couch. Would they put the tub of ribs on my chest? What were they up to?

I almost sat up when Yuri said, "More sleep learning?"

"Yes," Prudence said.

"He may be a lot further out than you think," Yuri said. "Post-dance. I know what this is like."

"I wonder if he found the next to last warning to Gerald?"

"You said he went back in," Yuri said.

"Sure, but maybe all he found was EES stuff."

"Tell him about the warning to Randy," Yuri said.

I heard the chair scrape and scoot a little closer to me, and then I felt Prudence's breath on my cheek. She whispered, "SOAPY sent Randy Casey an e-mail message just before he killed him. The message was like the one he sent to Gerald. It said, 'You're running out of time!' "

"Maybe you'd better tell him where to find it," Yuri said.

"He is a detective," Prudence said. "If he suspects a warning exists, he'll find it."

"Sure, but do you want him wasting his time looking?" Yuri said. "Also right now I don't think he could find his own butt with a flashlight, a detailed map, and slowly spoken directions."

Hey, watch it! I thought.

"Too bad we can't just jack his head into the net," Prudence said.

It was clear I was being played for a fool, a sucker. These two knew a lot more about the case than they'd been telling. They were stringing me along, and for all I knew they had killed Gerald Moffitt and Randy Casey. Maybe they were setting me up to pin the blame on this SOAPY character. You drop clues like bread crumbs along the garden path and Skylight Howells just follows along picking them up.

"Should I tell him about Sadie?" I could tell from the sound of her voice she had sat back up. So were they through feeding me information after just one piece? And who was Sadie?

"No," Yuri said. "We don't want him to start imagining he's got paranormal powers. Let him pick it up on the TV news."

"So what's with the vegetables?"

"He doesn't eat right," Yuri said. "One of the things you've got to watch when you're fighting the Dance is that you eat right."

He walked back to the desk. There was a sound like seeds rattling in a gourd. "Vitamin C." More rattling. "Beta carotene." He went on rattling and cataloging vitamins and minerals for some time. If you took that many, when would you have time to do anything else?

"Meanwhile let's eat the ribs," Prudence said.

"Good idea."

The barbecue smell got a lot stronger once they opened the tub. I listened to them eat for a couple of minutes, and then I groaned. It sounded pretty fake to me, so I didn't try it again. I rubbed my eyes and sat up.

Prudence sat on the edge of my desk with a dripping rib held between thumb and finger. A smear of sauce on her cheek. She still wore the sheer purple dress and black boots. Yuri had been poking around in the ribs when I came awake and he was still bending over the tub. He looked over at me and smiled.

Who would guess Yuri was a Russian working for a company called Evil Empire Software? These days he even wore American sneakers. Did he even care about the workers who made those shoes? He was maybe five-foot-nine or -ten and slender with black hair and brown eyes, the kind of guy who could easily get lost in a crowd. Until I met Yuri, I didn't know they tap-danced in Russia, much less that it would be a problem. I suppose, though, that it being a problem pretty much follows from the fact of them having it. You provide the opportunity to dance, some people are going to abuse it. Yuri once told me the Russian word for tap dancing was "chechyotka."

"You look like hell," he said. "You want some ribs?"

I sat up, then stood up and grabbed the back of my desk chair. "Why not?"

I pushed the chair back behind my desk like I was straightening things up. Actually I used the chair to support myself because I wasn't feeling all that steady on my feet.

Once behind the desk I grabbed a rib. It took me a few minutes of messy gnawing before I noticed the machine on my desk. White plastic and gleaming stainless steel. I reached over and turned the machine my way. SuperJuicer III. When I moved the machine I saw Yuri's line of vitamin bottles.

"What's all this?" I asked. What I wanted to ask was why the two of them were holding out on me, but the machine and the vitamins distracted me. Not to mention the ribs, which were warming my stomach and making me think that maybe all was not lost after all.

"Healthy body, healthy mind," Yuri said. "You know the drill. I'll bet these ribs are the most healthy things you've eaten in weeks."

Actually that wasn't true, but I didn't correct him. He dipped down below my sight and then came back up with a grocery sack. He put the sack down on the desk by the SuperJuicer III.

Prudence reached over and pulled a carrot out of the sack. "What's up, Spoc?"

Yuri rolled his eyes at her. He took the carrot out of her hand and put it back in the sack. He picked up the sack and put it in her hands. "Can you wash the fruit and vegetables, Pru? I'll plug in the machine."

Prudence hopped off the desk and took the sack of produce into the washroom. Yuri poked around beside my desk looking for the powerstrip. I had another rib.

"So," Yuri said. He was still down on the floor beside my desk and I couldn't see his face. "Prudence tells me you got into GP Ink."

"That's right." I needed time to figure out what these two were up to.

When I didn't say anything more, Yuri went back to moving around and looking for a place to plug in the juicer. A moment later he stood up again. "Got it. So what did you find?" He flipped a switch on the juicer and a little red light came on.

I decided to let him squirm. "So, why do you call your company Evil Empire Software?"

"Our little joke," Yuri said. "In the new Russia we have a sense of humor." Then his smile disappeared and he half closed his eyes and leaned across the desk invading my space, getting in my face. "Also it's part of our evil plan. Soon every child in America will have one of our computer games which display devilish messages if you play them backwards." He laughed an evil laugh.

I was in no mood to smile, so it hurt a little when I did.

"So, you found me out when you searched GP Ink," Yuri said. It was easy to see he wanted me to pick up that line of conversation and fill him in on everything I'd learned. Since he and Prudence apparently already knew all that there was to know from GP Ink, he was just trying to make sure I had found what they wanted me to find. That seemed to be the warning to Gerald from SOAPY, so they wanted me to think SOAPY was the killer. Next they wanted me to track down a warning from SOAPY to Randy Casey. I wouldn't bother, of course. The fact that the warning existed was all I needed.

I wondered if this solved my puzzle over Frank and Marvin not making noise over SOAPY's warning. Maybe they hadn't seen it! Maybe Prudence and Yuri planted it for my eyes only.

And what about the DATAPANTS file?

Prudence returned carrying wet fruit and vegetables. Someone should have painted her—Grinning Woman with Dripping Fruit and Vegetables.

Yuri pushed papers off my desk. "Put them here by the machine," he said. "Parsley. The secret is parsley."

He gathered a big bunch of parsley and poked it into the hopper at the top of the machine.

Prudence stooped and grabbed something Yuri had swept off my desk. "Here's the manual," she said.

Yuri looked at her like she'd lost her mind. I'll bet my look was pretty much the same. Yuri hadn't even tried the machine yet. This was no time for manuals.

"What?" Prudence looked from Yuri to me and then back again. "Well, I'm going to take a look." She opened the manual.

"Give me a glass," Yuri said to me.

I opened the bottom drawer and grabbed my scotch glass and handed it to him. He smelled it but didn't comment. He put the glass under the spout at one end of the machine. "We push with a carrot," he said. "I saw a guy do this on TV." He switched on the machine and pushed the parsley into the hopper with a carrot. The machine made a lot of noise. Green juice dribbled into my glass.

"Boy, that sure looks good," I said.

"You think so?"

"Green juice is in the index," Prudence said.

"More," Yuri said, "we need more." He pushed more parsley into the hopper and tamped it down with his carrot. He did that a couple more times until my scotch tumbler was about half filled with green juice.

"Page twenty-seven," Prudence said.

"Here you go." Yuri handed me the glass.

"You expect me to drink this?"

"All in one go," Yuri said. "That way it doesn't matter how it tastes. You get the pure essence of green zapped directly into your system."

"Hey, it smells pretty good," I said.

"Wait a minute," Prudence said.

I raised the glass of good smelling green stuff and chugged it down.

It was as if I'd swallowed a small, angry woodland creature—maybe a raccoon.

"It says here," Prudence said, "you should never drink straight green juice."

"Yack!" I said.

"Why not?" Yuri asked.

"It's just too strong," Prudence said.

"Too strong for a dude like Skylight? I don't believe it!"

"Youch," I said.

"His face is pretty red," Prudence said.

"So how are you supposed to serve parsley juice?"

Prudence flipped through the pages of the manual. The raccoon in my stomach had died and now its spirit was moving through my bloodstream. I felt dizzy; I felt high; I felt like maybe I should bolt for the toilet.

"You're supposed to mix it," she said. "Here's a recipe with carrots and apples."

"Okay," Yuri said, "we mix it. How much difference could it make if you mix it before or after you drink it?" He grabbed the glass and put it back under the spout and fed one carrot after another to the machine. When the glass was about half full, he handed it to me. "Drink this."

I chugged the carrot juice. Didn't help.

"He still doesn't look so good," Prudence said.

"Maybe the apples are necessary." Yuri snatched the glass from my hand and put it back under the spout. "Give me your knife."

Prudence dug into her purse and came up with a long folding knife of the kind you'd expect to see affixed to the belt of a guy in camouflage fatigues. Yuri opened the knife and cut up an apple.

"Maybe the key word was mix," Prudence said. "Maybe we should get him to jump around some."

"Good idea!" Yuri fed the machine another apple then gave me the glass.

What did I have to lose? I drank the apple juice. Yuri took one of my arms and Prudence took the other, and they guided me around the desk to the middle of the room.

"Jump," Yuri said and he and Prudence jumped. I sort of stood up on my toes.

"We need to go higher," Prudence said, and they jumped again and this time I jumped with them.

"Deep knee bends," Yuri shouted and we did a couple of those.

"Let's try some butt rotations," Prudence said.

"Can I watch?" I asked.

"No, you do it, too."

So we did some butt rotations.

"More jumping!" Yuri cried.

As we jumped around, I could feel the electric juice zinging and zapping though my system. My fingers tingled, my vision narrowed into a tunnel with sparkling light for walls. Energy flowed to my toes.

And I did a couple of steps.

"Hey! None of that!" Yuri said. "Get him back to his chair before this gets out of hand."

They guided me back to my chair and dumped me into it. I tried to uncross my eyes. I needed to focus on something, on anything but the building bundle of energy threatening to explode from me in dance.

"So what's up with Sadie?" I asked.

Yuri didn't miss a beat. "Sadie Campbell," he said, "of SplashDown Software. She was found murdered yesterday in her apartment."

"Why didn't you tell me before?"

"We just found out," Prudence said. She dug into her purse and then slapped a green book down onto my desk. I could tell from the annoying size of the thing that it was a software manual. Prudence turned it my way so I could read the title. SplashDown NodeHoofer II: Installation and Interaction Guide. Boy, it looked like it was getting harder to find new names for Internet browsers.

"Sounds exciting," I said. "Sadie Campbell?"

"Yes," Prudence said. "She gets a credit on the inside cover. Did you know her?"

"Dennis did," I said.

They exchanged looks.

"Hey, don't expect me to make sense," I said. "You just poisoned me with parsley juice."

"He must be feeling better," Yuri said.

"He looks better," Prudence said. "His face is not so red."

"That's not the way it looks from where I'm sitting," I said. "So what were the words on the body this time?"

"The words weren't on the body this time," Yuri said.

"No?"

"The killer left a note," Prudence said.

"Rolled up and stuck in her left ear," Yuri said.

" 'Would it kill you to give me one lousy example?' " Prudence said.

"What are you talking about?"

"Those are the words on the note," she said.

"But how can you know the words on the note?" I asked. The police wouldn't have released such detailed information yet. "If Sadie Campbell was murdered just yesterday, how do you two know so much already?"

"I talked to Lieutenant Wallace," Prudence said.

"Hold that thought." I put my right hand on my stomach and groaned. I stood up. I snatched Sadie's manual off my desk. "Excuse me."

I ran to the washroom, got the door closed, dropped my pants and sat down just in time.

You'd think they would make phony conversation and laugh and move around, maybe sing campfire songs, to mask all the embarrassing noise I was making, but all was quiet in my office.

"Hey, Sadie Campbell was on the BOD list," I yelled when things quieted down.

No reaction from Prudence and Yuri.

But speaking of the BOD list, it hit me then that the list wasn't a list of suspects. It was a list of victims.

"Maybe the killer is systematically knocking off people on the BOD list," I yelled.

Silence outside.

"Hey, maybe he didn't write all over the body this time because he didn't want anyone to think this was some kind of bizarre sex crime."

So, if they weren't some kind of bizarre sex crimes, what were they?

"So, what do you guys think?"

No answer. Some people just can't talk through a closed bathroom door.

It looked like I was going to be in there for some time. I opened Sadie's manual.

I felt myself slip into Dennis mode as I flipped through the pages. I found myself getting interested in the technical details in spite of myself. By the time we realized Dennis was hooked, it was too late. We didn't need to be at a computer to imagine what it would be like to install NodeHoofer II.

When you go into a computer problem you can get frustrated and throw up your hands and give up or you can go deeper; you can scream obscenities or you can go still deeper; you can jump up and kick the wall; you can sweep everything off the top of your desk onto the floor or you can go deeper. Completely focused. The sounds and smells of the outside world disappear. The porcelain ring hugging your butt fades. You forget where you are. The stuff that's always lurking in the corners of your eyes isn't lurking anymore. All the bells in your ears stop ringing.

You see the shape of the thing; you see the beauty. Sure, it's a lot better if you're working at the computer, but if you're good, you can do it all in your head. Sometimes when you get like this, your favorite computer is a Turing Machine, a paper computer, a pure mental construct.

Until you hit a bump in the road, a dead end in the tunnel, a fly in the ointment, a glitch, probably not a bug, but definitely a confusion.

Come on Sadie, for crying out loud.

If only the manual would give you one lousy example.

I almost leaped to my feet, which would have been a really big mistake.

The note!

Would it kill you to give me one lousy example?

"Eureka!" I shouted.

The killer wasn't just killing documentalists; he was killing bad documentalists!

Oh, Sadie!

Gerald hadn't mentioned the key concept 'exceptions' in his index. Randy had screwed up his index, probably throughout, but certainly on page sixty-six, and Sadie had produced garbled prose that could have been saved with an example or two at key points. Instead, hers were instructions that would turn the average computer user into a head-banging basket case.

The Russians still might have something to do with the big picture, but I was convinced the killer's main motivation was revenge upon people who had frustrated him (or her) and wasted his (or her) valuable time.

"The killer's mad as hell and not ready to take it anymore!" I yelled.

No response.

I figured it was time to stop pussyfooting around with these two. "I wasn't asleep when you guys came in," I yelled.

They had nothing to say to that.

I took a few more minutes to finish up my business. I didn't delude myself that the parsley juice was through with me, but it did seem to be taking a break. I pulled up my pants and opened the door, ready to confront Yuri and Prudence.

They, of course, were no longer in my office.

nine

It was a little after three in the morning. I sat down behind my desk and looked at the pile of produce and the juicer, which proved I hadn't made up the events of the evening. I picked up an apple. I put it down again.

I wondered if Prudence and Yuri had ducked out before they'd heard my revelation about why the killer was killing people.

I pulled up my keyboard and straightened my monitor and ambled on over to alt.dead.nerds. I posted a short note explaining my reasoning in regard to the killer killing bad documentalists.

Next, working on full automatic (maximum intuition), which is the way I work best, I tossed a question into cyberspace. People, I said, tell me if you've ever been irritated by bad documentation. Do any of you even read it? I was looking for some insight into the mind of a person who would kill over bad documentation. Sure, any one of us might feel like it, but what kind of person would really do it?

Finally, I posted a note consisting of nothing but the word DATAPANTS. I now believed that Yuri and Prudence had wanted me to find SOAPY's warning to Gerald, but maybe they hadn't expected me to find the DATAPANTS file, and they might not be the only ones who would get nervous thinking that I knew something I shouldn't. I wanted to see what I could spook out of the woodwork.

But then I wondered why I should even bother. I was pretty much at a dead end. Not to mention the fact that my client was lying to me. I told myself I should get smart; I should quit following Frank, drop the Documentalists Murders case, come clean with Lucus Betty about Dennis, and spend the next few weeks going to meetings maybe

three or four times a day—get my head screwed back on straight. But
if I were smart I'd be some other person living some other life in some
other place and time. The truth was that if I stopped being a detective,
I'd disappear. I'd simply cease to be. You ask me what I'd do if I
couldn't be a detective and I tell you I'd rock and hum.

Instead of dwelling on that, I decided to do something. Doing something is almost always better than thinking about doing something.
But what would it be?

Just then something from my middle desk drawer, the drawer
where I toss things I know I'll get around to needing sooner or later,
called out in the persistent mouse voice of memory, "Try me, try me!"

I pulled open the drawer to see what was trying to get my attention,
and it didn't take me long to find the scrap of paper containing my
list of 900 numbers for psychic services. Oddly, I'd never called any of
the numbers. I'd meant to. I'd talked to my therapist Roger about it,
wondering if my collecting these numbers might mean anything, and
he'd said it probably did mean something, and I'd asked if it were a
good idea to call one of the numbers, and he'd guided me to the
conclusion that if I thought it was okay, it probably couldn't hurt to
give them a try sometime, but I'd never gotten around to it until now.

YOUR PERSONAL PSYCHIC
UP CLOSE AND PERSONAL PSYCHICS
PSYCHIC AMIGOS
YOUR OTHER EYE
PSYCHIC SIDEKICKS
WE KNOW
AND SO ON

Go on, I told myself, just pick one and see what happens. I could
try for a Psychic Amigo, for example, and when someone answered
they'd say, "Hola" and I'd say, "No hablo . . . er . . ." and Dieter would
mutter, "Jeeze Louise, hola on the phone?", already deconstructing my
daydream and getting into a fight with my new psychic amiga, who

would say to him, "What? You expected bueno?", but who to me would simply say, "No problema!" The truth of the matter being that neither Dieter nor I really know much Spanish.

If there were conspiracies afoot (and who could doubt that there were) maybe the people to call would be the people at We Know. But if they were really the people in the know, they probably wouldn't come right out and say so.

Okay, I would leave it to the same luck that had led me to the numbers in the first place. I closed my eyes and turned the list around and around until I'd lost track of which end was up. Then I ran my finger down the numbers hoping for a little tingle to tell me I was on the right spot, but I felt nothing, so finally I just stopped and opened my eyes and looked at what I'd chosen. Psychic Sidekicks. Upside down. Well, I already had all the Watsons I needed. In fact everyone in my head took a turn being Watson, but maybe someone out of the loop altogether would bring a fresh viewpoint to the problem. I grabbed the phone and dialed the number before I could come to my senses.

Would the fact that the list was upside down influence my Psychic Sidekick? Maybe I should believe just the opposite of what I was told? How did that work with the tarot?

There was a welcoming message, then a very businesslike exchange about my credit card and then a pause and then a woman came on the line and told me her name was Greta and asked how she could help me. The voice was strangely familiar. Did she sound like my mother in the old days? No, that wasn't it.

"Are you there?" she asked, and I realized my Psychic Sidekick sounded just like the voice in my head when I was Lulu.

I took the phone away from my ear and looked at it, counted my fingers wrapped around the receiver, counted to ten, blinked my eyes a couple of times.

"Hello, hello?" Greta said when I put the phone back to my ear. She'd probably been saying that for some time. She was probably ready to hang up.

"I'm here," I said. I was no longer sure this exchange was external, and that uncertainty made me feel suddenly loose and fancy-free.

"How can I help you?" she asked.

"What are you wearing?"

"I don't think you quite have the concept here, gumchew," she said.

Show me an edge and I'll go over it, but this time I had to be hearing things. Look at my logic. I pick a number at random from a list of psychic hot lines that's been in my desk for months and I get Prudence Deerfield pretending to be Greta, my Psychic Sidekick, who is actually Lulu? I didn't think so.

"What did you call me?"

"Sir," she said. "I called you sir. Now can we get down to business?"

"Sorry," I said. "What I meant to ask before was what *will* you be wearing?"

She laughed and her laugh was nice. Just that laugh would be worth the lousy $3.99 a minute.

"So are we looking into the area of romance?"

"Probably not," I said.

"Fame and fortune?"

"Maybe," I said. "The thing is I'm a detective and I have several puzzling cases I hoped you could give me some insight on."

I was pretty sure I had the killer's motivation pinned down. My new theory explained the words on the first two bodies and the note found with Sadie Campbell, but I didn't know who he was, and I didn't know what Yuri and Prudence were up to. I didn't know what had happened to Pablo. Not to mention the fact that I didn't have a clue what Frank Wallace was up to at the Quack Inn.

"Well, I don't know," she said.

"It'll be fun," I said. "We've got the Evil Empire and the Russians and the Secret Society of Mexican Food Cooks."

"I see," she said.

"I hope so," I said. "We've got some murders, and this guy in the other case I'm following for his wife, and he goes to this motel, but for all I know he was there alone, and I need to figure out what's going on."

She didn't say anything.

"So, what do you see?" I asked.

"I see too much at once," she said. "Take it a little slower. Fill me in while I lay out the cards."

"Okay," I said, stalling for time to organize my thoughts, "let me see. Well, okay. Just the facts. The pertinent details. The very essence of things."

"Maybe you'd better take a moment to organize your thoughts," she said. The way she touched my mind and said just what I needed to hear convinced me I'd done the right thing when I called her. I could hear her slapping the big tarot cards down on a green felt surface, maybe a poker table, yes, a green felt octagon. Everything is dark outside of the cone of light that shines down on the table. There is a column of smoke to her left.

"You're smoking," I said.

"Not yet," she said. "I'll need the facts first."

Yes. The facts. So, I told her about how Prudence Deerfield came into my office and dumped the case in my lap. I told her how Gerald Moffitt was killed. I told her about Pablo. I told her about how I already had a case following a 'city official' for his wife, and another case I didn't want to talk about. I didn't tell her Frank's name. I didn't tell her he was a homicide detective. I can only be lulled so far by a woman's voice. But then I told her about Frank and Marvin bringing me the news of the second murder, and maybe I mixed the two cases up at that point. I told her about following Frank to the Quack Inn. Or actually I told her about my operative Lulu ("who by the way sounds a lot like you") following Frank to the Quack Inn.

I told her about GP Ink, and I gave her the details of Randy Casey's murder. I told her about SOAPY, and I told her about the BOD list. I brought the list up on the screen and read her the names, both known and unknown. I told her about Yuri and how I thought he and Prudence were holding out on me. I explained my theory on how the killer was killing off the creators of frustrating software documentation. I told her about Sadie.

"Oh, so that's the disturbance on the astral plane everyone is picking up on," she said. "Murders. Yes, murders out in Oregon."

"Did you figure that out from my area code?" A sudden attack of skepticism?

"From the cards," she said. "The cards are ready now. Let's do this one question at a time."

"Okay."

"So, ask your first question."

"Let's start with the obvious," I said. "Who is the Documentalist Killer?"

"I see a man," she said. "Yes, definitely a man. A white man, definitely not a boy."

"Yes?"

"Not an old man," she said. "He is filled with anger. He hates people who can't explain things properly."

"So my theory was right?"

"Yes, the killer is killing people who produce bad documentation. He must be a person for whom documentation is very important. I see him as a person who has to read those awful manuals all the time. Day after day. Hour after hour he's reading those manuals, trying to look stuff up that can't be found. Maybe someone is pressuring him to get the job done fast? Yes, that's it. He needs the information right now, and the documentation is slowing him down, it's wasting his time, and he's very very angry!"

I could hear her suck in a big breath. I could feel her trembling after that psychic two-step with the killer.

I gave her a couple of moments to recover, and then I asked, "What about this SOAPY character?"

"That's not his real name," she said. "I can see there is some deception going on with the name."

"So, are you saying even though he seems to be saying he's the killer, he's really not?"

"Not necessarily," she said. "He warned Gerald and he warned Randy. But I don't see his name on the BOD list."

"That's right," I said. "Hey, wait a minute! I see where you're going. If SOAPY is the killer, how did he know about Randy's documentation? It was only circulated among members of the BOD list. So, if SOAPY's not on that list, he would never have had an opportunity to be irritated by Randy's manual!"

There was a pause, a short burst of throat clearing, and then she said, "Exactly!"

"But what about the warning to Gerald? Prudence practically told me it was there."

"Well," she said, "let me see. Hold on, I'm getting something."

"Yes?"

"This Prudence person wants you to think Mr. SOAPY is the killer."

"Why?"

"She has her reasons."

"Yuri?"

"Yes, here it is," Greta said. "I see Yuri and Prudence making plans behind your back. You'll need to watch those two."

That sounded like good advice.

"And there was apparently a warning to Randy Casey, too," I said.

"Umm," she said.

"I wonder why Yuri and Prudence didn't tell the police about SOAPY," I said.

"Umm," she said.

"What do you think?"

"Yuri is a Russian?"

"Yes."

"Umm," she said.

"So, what are you picking up?"

"What I can tell you about Prudence and Pablo and Gerald and Yuri and Randy and Sadie and the killer and the Russians is that everything is connected to everything else," she said. "Everything has something to do with everything else. You must step back and take a look at the big picture. Keep your eyes peeled. Never stop looking for clues."

"That's what I need," I said. "More clues. I need answers to key questions. I need to know what SOAPY means."

"Can't you just look that up?"

"In my *Big Book of Clues?*"

"Do you have one of those?" she asked. "If you've got one of those, you should certainly use it."

"That's what my mother said."

"You should listen to your mother," she said.

"So I will in the end solve the case?"

"Sure," she said. "Sure you will. You will face the facts and prevail in the end."

"And I'll find Pablo?"

"Hold on, I'm picking something up in regard to Pablo," she said. "Let me see. Let me see. Yes, there it is. Are you sure Pablo's even real?"

Wow, now there was a thought. What if there were no Pablo? All I had was Prudence's word that she had a twin brother. What if the P in GP Ink stood for Prudence? Who better to have people suspect of murder than someone who doesn't exist? Which reminded me somehow of the deception Dennis and I were putting over on Lucus Betty. I didn't want to think about that.

"Maybe I should spend some time looking for people who have actually seen Pablo," I said.

"Good idea," Greta said.

"Anything else I should know?"

"Oh, let me see," she said. "Oh, here it is, the secret cooks will turn out not to be the guys pulling all the strings. That will be someone much higher up."

"Can you tell me who?"

"Everything is melting," she said.

"Melting?"

"Getting blurry," she said. "I'm losing the connection."

"Well, you've been a big help, Greta."

"Maybe you can call back? Next time you call I'm sure there'll be more to discover."

"You bet," I said.

"Oh, here's something else before you go," she said. "Frank really isn't fooling around on his wife."

I put the phone down, but I could still hear her whispering to me. She sounded more like Lulu than ever now. "Your eyelids are getting heavy," she said. "You're getting very very sleepy," she said. "You want to get up and walk across to the couch."

Yes, you do. That's right.

Put your head back.

Take a really deep breath. Another one. Another.

ten

The next day, I picked up the user's guide for the SuperJuicer III from the floor where Prudence had dropped it. Flipping through it, I could see reading it would be a frustrating experience. You couldn't just look things up; you had to follow along step-by-step from the very beginning to do even the simplest things. Whoever wrote the manual wanted you to have the full SuperJuicer experience. My irritation must have been (on a very micro level) something like what the killer felt when he picked a victim, but why was he concentrating specifically on computer documentalists? Why not something like this? Well, maybe he just hadn't gotten around to everyone yet. Sooner or later he might even pay a visit to the guy who wrote the infamous "fit the big end of Part A into Slot B," when Part A was perfectly square and none of the slots were labeled.

I finally tossed the SuperJuicer docs in the trash and juiced some cantaloupe, apples, and this weird yellow thing with bumps and tiny black spots. I washed down a selection of vitamins from the bottles lined up on my desk. The juice was pretty good. In fact, it was wonderful. In fact, it filled me with so much energy that I jumped up and shouted (I don't know—something like "whoopee" or "yahoo"). I would have burst into song but I couldn't remember all of the words. I decided not to throw Yuri's machine out the window after all.

I needed to get moving! Just do it. Make things happen. Shake the trees and see what falls out. I drank the juice and made another batch. I ducked into the washroom and cleaned up. Put on a fresh mustache.

Back at my desk I pulled up the BOD list. Now that Sadie Campbell was dead, there were only four locals I could chase down.

Leo Unger—"Challenger Video"

Lucas Betty—"the university"

Bernie Watkins—"HS"

Ramona Simmons—"mean"

It was possible one of these people was the killer, but I thought it more likely that this was a list of victims. If the killer was on the BOD list, he (or she) would probably be one of the anonymous ones. The killer might be a BOD member from out of town, but that would mean he (or she) had made trips to our city just to kill bad documentalists. It's not like there was a shortage elsewhere. Why come to Eugene?

If the killer was not on the BOD list, there was the problem of how he (or she) knew about Randy Casey's manual for Seventeen Worlds.

Lulu tapped me on the head from the inside, and played back the memory of her standing on the sidewalk looking into the offices of SplashDown Software. We watched Arthur Snow looking down at a woman working at her desk. Surely he could see whatever she was doing. Surely he could have figured out how to look at Sadie Campbell's e-mail. Not that we were saying the head of SplashDown Software was our bad guy, but whoever the killer was, he (or she) could have gained access to the BOD list without actually being on the list.

I had already decided to catch Leo Unger at work, but I pulled out the Eugene phone book and looked up his home number and address just in case I missed him at Challenger Video. He wasn't listed.

Next, I discovered Bernie Watkins wasn't in the phone book, either. I spent a few frustrating minutes being irritated at Prudence for writing nothing but "HS" by his name. Was that another software company? High Software? Hot Software? Hairy Software? No HS in the phone book.

Bernie's handle was THE_DUNGEONEER.

"The Dungeoneer," I said out loud. "The Dungeoneer."

And then the sky opened up and the sun came out; a light bulb came on over my head, and it hit me like a ton of bricks that "HS" meant High School! Bernie wasn't in the phone book because he was still a high school kid living at home. It took me less than ten minutes to track him down. It turned out Bernie Watkins was a junior at South Eugene High School.

There was a number and address for Ramona Simmons, so I would find out just how "mean" she was sooner or later.

There was no home number for Lucas Betty listed, but I knew how to get in touch with him. Now might be the time to wrap that case up. Just put him in touch with Dennis, warn him about the Documentalist Killer, collect the rest of our fee, and call it a day.

I let Dennis take over. He found the number for Lucas Betty and dialed it.

"Experimental Support Services," a woman said. "Ms. Divey speaking."

Dennis asked for Lucas Betty.

"Mr. Betty is busy," she said. "Can I take a message?"

"Tell him it's Dennis."

"Dennis who?"

"He'll know."

She put us on hold.

While he listened to the void, Dennis let his eyes roam over the top of our desk, and he spotted something sticking out from under the SuperJuicer. A card. He pulled it out and took a look. Yuri Kost, EVIL EMPIRE SOFTWARE, a phone number, and P.O. box.

"Lucas Betty." Lucas always sounded impatient.

"Dennis here," Dennis said. "A mutual friend tells me you're looking for me."

"A mutual friend? Friends don't charge friends huge fees for so little work."

"Nobody's charging me," Dennis said. Huge fees? Who did Lucas think he was kidding? "So, what's the scoop?"

"The scoop," Lucas said, "is that you have the know-how I need, and together we could make a lot of money. We need to get together and talk about it."

"You want to do lunch?" Dennis asked.

We groaned inwardly.

"Next you'll want to 'interface' with him," Lulu said.

"No time for lunch," Lucas said.

"I've come up with a couple of ideas," Dennis said, "on what we might do in regard..."

"How about coffee? Let me check my book." Lucas was the kind of guy who leaped ahead of you in conversation. It wasn't that he finished your sentences for you, but just as soon as he saw where you were going, he expected you to shut up.

He didn't bother to put Dennis on hold. He wouldn't be gone that long.

When he came back he said, "I can meet you at ten-oh-five."

"Too soon," Dennis said.

Lucas was gone again, then he was back.

"How about Starbucks at two-thirteen?"

"How about the Coffee Corner at four?" Dennis asked.

"How about Strictly Coffee at three-oh-five?"

"Which one?"

"Corner of Kent and Patterson?"

"I'll be there," Dennis said.

Lucas hung up. Oddly, we thought, he didn't seem all that hot to talk with Dennis after all.

Sky took control.

I was ready to do some legwork, but first I wanted to see if my new theory had started any fires on the net. I was especially interested to see what SOAPY had to say about it. I wondered, too, if anyone would post their documentation gripes, and I wondered what my posting of the word "DATAPANTS" would scare up. I logged on.

The newsgroup alt.dead.nerds was gone. I looked for a name change and found it. The newsgroup was called alt.dead.docs. When I checked it out, I discovered that my posting had hit home. Almost everyone seemed to think I was on the right track with my theory about why the killer was killing people. There was the usual grumbling about the name change, and there was a full-scale flame war over my question about bad documentation. Everyone had a horror story. Or a defense. They all thought their own stories were the most horrendous. There were wild accusations and more than enough blame to go around. Hurt feelings. There was so much stuff that my original plan to build a model of the killer's mind from it would have to be tabled. There was just too much.

The most interesting thing, I thought, was the fact that there were no posts from SOAPY. Had he just given up? Did that mean he really was just a nut who had been taken by a new enthusiasm and was now off bothering someone else?

It was something to think about, but my energy level was way too high to sit around thinking about it. I made a few notes and grabbed my coat and hat.

The day was clear and warm—a beautiful fall day. It would rain later of course but that would be good, too. I bet I had a goofy grin on my face. I tipped my hat at a woman just outside my building, and she smiled at me.

I was whistling a tune by the time I got to the parking lot, but I cut that out quickly when I discovered my Cherokee was gone.

What could this mean? Who would steal my car? I could take Lulu's Ford, but I would still have to spend too much time with the police dealing with my stolen vehicle. My juiced-up mood took a nose-dive, but before it hit the ground, I remembered that I left the jeep at Mom's nursing home. I'd taken the bus downtown, and now I could take it back to get my car. That would slow me down, but it wasn't a disaster. I took a couple of deep breaths. I considered going back to the office for more juice. The mixture I'd made this morning certainly had made me feel good. I walked on toward the bus stop instead.

In less than an hour, I'd picked up the jeep and was on my way to Challenger Video on West Eleventh.

Challenger Video was pretty low-key. No security badges. I could probably just wander on in and no one would care. The company occupied what used to be an auto repair and tire shop just up the street from one of our favorite tropical fish stores—Scarface is the fish fancier. We don't actually have any fish, but he's always lobbying for us to get some. We let him look. Anyway you see the fish store and you slow way down because you've got to make a tricky left turn to get into the parking lot of Challenger Video.

The bays for auto repair had been boarded over, but you could still tell what the building once was. I imagined I could still smell old oil and hot tires and gasoline. There were no windows on this side of the building. There was a door with a small crude sign that told you the name of the enterprise inside.

Challenger had been around a long time, and while they didn't make a lot of money, they made money consistently. Years ago I heard they nearly changed their name after the shuttle disaster. But they hadn't and it hadn't seemed to hurt them much.

I pulled open the door and walked on in.

The place was bright with cloudy light through huge skylights along the backside of the roof. The inside of the building had been completely gutted and was now one big room with desks scattered in what seemed a random arrangement. On each desk was at least one computer monitor, most had more; cables snaked around on the floor between the desks and around the walls, and I wondered how the propeller heads avoided tripping and shorting out the whole operation. There was a bank of soft drink and snack machines along one wall and a table holding a huge silver coffee machine and a microwave. Three refrigerators.

Of the two dozen or so people hard at work, not even one looked up when I came in. I stood by the desk of a woman who was sitting very close to her monitor. I mean her nose was about three inches from the screen. I cleared my throat. No response. Everyone here would be in a world of their own. The level of concentration was so high you could almost hear the brain electricity buzzing like busy bees.

"Excuse me," I said, and the woman yelped, banged her nose against her screen, and jumped up out of her chair.

"Jesus," she said. "Who are you? And why are you sneaking up on me? Ouch." She rubbed her nose. She ran a hand through her hair. She sat back down, forgetting or maybe just ignoring me.

"Can you tell me which one of you is Leo Unger?" I asked before she drifted off the planet again.

"What?"

"Leo."

"Who?"

"Leo Unger." I made a sweeping gesture meant to indicate all the other people in the room. There was no way to tell if she was even aware there were other people in the room, but she must have figured it out.

She pointed to her left and said, "Over there."

I went through the whole routine again twice more before the creature I startled up from its hiding place turned out to be Leo Unger.

"I'm looking into the death of Randy Casey," I said. I paid some close attention to the look on Leo's face when I said the name, but the reaction I saw was not so easy to interpret.

"Randy was a good guy," Leo said.

"Did you hear about Sadie Campbell?"

"Her, too," he said. "What's going on?"

Leo was a small man with very red hair tied back in a ponytail that ran down to the middle of his back. He hadn't shaved for a while, but I couldn't decide if it was that half-shaved look so popular a few years ago, or if he just hadn't been home for a while. Maybe the latter if his smell was anything to go by. Computer folks are often the most fragrant among us.

"So, what do you think got Randy killed?" I asked.

"How would I know," Leo said. "There's a guy on-line saying the killer is knocking off people who make mistakes in documentation."

"That's a polite way of putting it," I said. "What do you think?"

"People think this is so easy," Leo said. I could see he was getting steamed over the thought that people didn't know how hard he worked. "I mean, they think you can just tell the user how to use the software, just say what buttons to push and what's supposed to happen when you push them. No one appreciates how hard it is to say just what a person needs to know just when he needs it. Especially in a linear form like a book!" He tapped a fingernail on his screen. "This is going to change everything."

"Oh? What is it?"

"Hypertext," Leo said. "No more paper. Everything is on the screen. Each concept is linked up. What you need to know when you need to know it! You control everything."

"So if Randy had written his stuff as a hypertext document he would have been safe?"

"Well, I don't know about that," Leo said. "Randy thought he was some kind of hotshot artist when it came to documentation. The truth is he made a better game player. You know, someone who can really get into the games and live there."

"So the thing he posted to you guys isn't very good?"

"No," Leo said, "it's not very good."

"So, why didn't he do it in hypertext?"

"I wouldn't let him," Leo said. "This stuff is going to save us from that printed garbage, and I just wasn't ready to let Randy screw it up. All the good stuff is hypertext."

Leo was still pretty red in the face. Looking at him I could believe he could work himself into a killing rage. This was a guy who belonged on my suspect list.

He must have seen something in my expression. He narrowed his eyes. Maybe it was occurring to him at last that I hadn't actually said I was with the police. Since I still had questions, I decided I'd better get to them quickly.

"What about Ramona Simmons?" I asked.

Leo gave me a grin. "You know Ramona?"

"Never had the pleasure," I said. "I thought maybe you could fill me in. What's her story?"

"She's mean," Leo said. "Really really mean."

"So, she slaps you around a lot or what?"

"Actually, I've never seen her," Leo said. "But no matter what you say on-line, she'll come jumping down your throat for it. And the thing is you can't ignore her because what she says is designed just for you. I mean it's perfectly structured to get your goat no matter who you are. She finds your weak spots and pokes them."

"I can't believe you guys," I said. "Don't any of you ever do anything in the flesh?"

"Sure we do," he said. "We do lots of stuff in the flesh." He looked away like he was worried I might ask him to name one.

"Make sure your insurance policy is paid up before you drop in on Ramona." Leo glanced at his screen then back up at me. He rearranged his ass in his chair. I could see it was time for me to get on down the road.

"Watch yourself, Leo," I said. "All the dead guys were on the BOD list."

After I left Leo I swung on by South High School and checked out the yearbook. The secretary in the main office got the idea that I represented a company that printed these things. She kept telling me that Mr. Adams the journalism teacher would be free to talk with me at three. I thanked her for her time, but I didn't stick around to talk to Mr. Adams. I photocopied the page with Bernie's picture on it, and took down his address. Talking to a high school kid was pretty low on my list of priorities, but I would get around to it if nothing else came up.

On the way back to the office, I got to thinking about juice again. I thought how nice it would be to have some of that juice right now. I couldn't carry Yuri's machine around with me, but I could mix up a batch and carry it around in a big Thermos bottle. If I had such a bottle, which I didn't. I love problems with easy solutions. I dropped in at one of those everything-anyone-could-possibly-want warehouse stores and bought a Thermos bottle.

I drove back downtown and parked the jeep next to Lulu's Escort. Took my new Thermos upstairs.

My door was closed but not locked. I knew I'd locked it. I froze with my hand on the knob. Yuri and Prudence could have returned. They didn't seem to have any trouble with my door. Maybe they'd lifted a key when I was out of it. On the other hand, if there was someone in my office, it might be someone waiting to do me harm. There could even be a burglar in there who had nothing to do with anything else in my life. That would be the worst, I thought, to be killed by a bad guy who didn't have anything to do with your cases, who didn't even know who you were.

I could just charge into the office, but that would probably be a dumb move. I eased my hand off the knob. I'd sneak on down the hall and call the police from one of the neighboring offices. If I could catch anyone in. The Magazines-by-Phone woman sometimes worked afternoons. I'd seen her come and go. Maybe I could use her phone. Or I could just leave the building and use a pay phone on the mall. I turned to move quietly away.

The door behind me flew open and someone grabbed me.

I saw the side of his face as he spun me around, and I saw the gun. In one motion he was going to snatch me back into my office, spin me around, and shoot me.

I swung my own right hand up, the one with my new gray Thermos bottle. My arch was a little shorter, or I was a little faster, or maybe a little more desperate. My Thermos crunched into the man's nose before he could bring his gun around. He stepped back and crashed into the door. I grabbed his hand with the gun and hit him in the face with my Thermos again.

This was the guy who had jumped me at GP Ink. He was way too big for me to handle ordinarily. And he had a gun. All I had going for me was that he hadn't expected me to be carrying something I could hit him in the face with. I hit him again and jerked at the gun in his hand. He didn't let go of it. I raised a knee for his crotch but he twisted away and pushed me, and I stumbled back, tripped over one of the white plastic client chairs and scrambled on my hands and knees around behind the desk.

All the drawers were open, the contents scattered around on the floor. It was times like these that I wished I had the nerve to defy Frank Wallace and all the people who had decided I shouldn't be allowed to carry a gun under my coat. If I had just done it anyway, I could be squeezing off shots at this very moment.

I'd hit him hard, so blood might be running into his eyes. I could roll to the side and come up at the side of the desk with my gun in hand and yell, "Freeze."

I did it anyway.

Yes, the blood was running into his eyes, and he squinted at me crouched there pointing my six-shooter finger at him. I had time for only a quick mental snapshot of him running one hand over his damaged face, trying to see me through the blood and his fingers, the other hand with the gun coming up for a shot, before he ducked out the door and slammed it behind him.

I scrambled to my feet. It would hit him any minute that I hadn't really had a gun when I'd shouted "Freeze!" Once he realized that, he'd pop right back inside, and I'd be a sitting duck. I rushed to the window and pulled it open.

The alley was three stories down. There was a ledge about five feet below my window. I climbed out over the sill and lowered myself onto the ledge. I turned my back to the building and shuffled off to my right toward the street.

One really scary thing about standing on a narrow ledge, with a building keeping your back straight and an alley three stories below, is the way the building seems to tip you forward. It seems the building will tilt just a little and you'll be windmilling your arms as you make the big plunge. Or you'll get dizzy. Lose yourself for a second, and you'll get to see how well you fly. I took another couple of shuffling steps toward the street. I really wanted to be around the corner before the bad guy poked his head out of my office window.

Down below in the alley, a guy in a dirty white apron came out of the building next door. He dumped his trash in the dumpster and on the way back just happened to look up and see me standing on the ledge.

He did a double take you could see even from where I was standing. "Don't jump!" he shouted and ran back into his building.

"Quiet," I whispered, but he was gone anyway.

A couple of people stopped at the mouth of the alley and looked up at me. Moments later a crowd had gathered. I heard a siren not too far off in the distance. The guy in the apron came back with his coworkers. At least now if the bad guy leaned out of my office window and shot me, there would be quite a few witnesses.

Uniformed police officers scattered the crowd. Another siren approached. Just after the fire truck pulled up, a man did poke his head out of my office window, and I jerked around to look and almost fell.

But then I saw it wasn't the big guy with the gun. This man had a serene smile. He looked like everybody's grandfather. "You want to talk about it, Son?"

"Jesus," I said. "I'm not out here to jump!"

I looked down at the firemen below. They had one of those round things they used to catch falling people, but they were having some trouble deploying it in the alley. I shuffled back toward the window.

"That's the ticket," the suicide negotiator said. "Just take it easy and keep coming."

Greta, my Psychic Sidekick, would probably tell me that I'd had a premonition of all of this earlier when I thought I would have to deal with the police over my stolen jeep. The reason I'd forgotten I'd left the jeep at Mom's nursing home was just so I'd think of the police, which would warn me about the police experience I'd have after someone broke into my office and chased me out on the ledge.

My office was full of uniformed police officers. The guy who had "talked me in" turned me over to them at once and left. I was handcuffed behind my back. We took a little trip down to the police station, and I spent the rest of the day sitting around waiting to tell my story.

Once I did get to explain myself, it was still another hour before I could make anyone believe me. Finally, they agreed to check it out and sent me back to my office with a young uniformed officer named Hamilton.

Officer Hamilton's police face was still new. He had some trouble maintaining the regulation deadpan look. He kept slipping into regular guy mode and catching himself and wiping the smile off his face.

Once back at the office, he looked around. He made some notes.

"How do we know you didn't just bust up the office yourself before you climbed out on the ledge?"

Good question. The problem was no one had broken through the door. It would have been a piece of cake to pick the lock, but I had some trouble convincing Hamilton that anyone actually had. The scratches around the lock were not easy to see. Worse, nothing seemed to be missing.

"But like I've explained," I said, "I surprised him in the act. He didn't have time to steal anything."

Officer Hamilton wandered into the washroom. I heard a grunt of surprise, and I looked in after him. He took a couple of steps back into the main office. My disguise supplies were scattered everywhere. It looked like an explosion of faces. I stooped down and picked up a nose.

"Makeup," I said. I squeezed the nose between a first finger and thumb in front of his face. "Not real."

He recovered his cool and asked me if anything of value was missing from the washroom. I told him I couldn't tell for sure but everything looked like it was there. The one thing I was concerned about (the disk I'd taped underneath the disguise cabinet) would have to wait until after he'd left.

"I don't know," he said. "No break in. Nothing missing. I don't know."

"Give me a break," I said. "Why would I have made up something like this?"

"I don't know."

"And, hey, look at this!" I showed him a couple of brown spots that must have been the bad guy's blood. Too bad more hadn't gotten spread around.

"You cut yourself?" Hamilton asked.

"Look," I said. "They must pretty much believe me downtown or they wouldn't have sent only you to get the burglary report. What say we just call this vandalism and call it a day?"

"Well, I don't know," he said.

I wore him down, talked him into it. Once he was convinced, it took him only minutes to get all he needed for his report and leave.

When I was sure he wasn't coming back, I got down on my hands and knees and looked under the disguise cabinet.

The disk with SOAPY's warning and the DATAPANTS file was gone. Dennis wouldn't get the chance to crack the encryption after all. Too bad. I decided to pick up the mess and move on.

Gathering papers and folders to be sorted and filed later, I imagined I was one of those guys cleaning the park with a sharp stick. I wondered if that might not be just the line of work I needed. Outdoors. Low pressure.

Yuri's juicer was on the floor, but it was still plugged in. I put it back on my desk and flipped the switch. It worked. So all the news wasn't bad.

I picked up my new Thermos bottle and shook it and heard the broken glass inside. I tossed it in the trash can, but when I heard it hit, it occurred to me that the bottle had saved my life. If I hadn't been carrying it, I couldn't have hit the thug in the face with it, and if I hadn't surprised him with that move, things might have turned out very differently. I fished the Thermos out of the trash and put it on the shelf with my tap trophy.

Next I turned my attention to the washroom. Who knew when I might need a disguise? I sorted and stored my noses and ears and bald spots. I picked up tubes and jars and put wigs back on their white foam heads and the foam heads in the bottom drawer of the disguise cabinet.

Back in the office, I gathered coats and shirts, Lulu's dresses, Tag's slacks, made a pile, found hangers, and put everything in the cardboard wardrobe.

The only consoling fact I could think of while cleaning up my disguise materials was that no one could put the personalities together from the pieces. Whoever had trashed the room would have no way of knowing who my disguises were.

The afternoon was gone. My schedule was screwed. Dennis had stood up Lucas Betty. If Lucas knew something about the case, we wouldn't find out about it today. He would be on my ass about Dennis, too. And there was still Ramona Simmons. At this rate, I might never get around to finding out just how mean she really was.

I scooped up stuff from the floor behind my desk and dumped it into the drawers, and as I did so, I realized the new random arrangement in the drawers wasn't much different from the old arrangement.

If the bad guy had had enough time to actually look at my stuff rather than just tossing it around the office, he might have discovered quite a bit about my operation, but it seemed to me he was looking for what he found—the disk I'd taped to the bottom of the disguise cabinet. That was all that was gone. He might have seen my post with the word DATAPANTS. Maybe that's what he'd been looking for at GP Ink. Maybe my post had just told him he should come to me. Well, I wanted to shake someone up, and I had. I didn't see that it had done me any good.

I picked up the client chair and put it back in its place in front of my desk. My own chair and been shoved up against the wall under the window and I moved it back, too.

It got dim and then it got dark before I was satisfied that everything had either been put back in its place or had been thrown out. I'd dumped the trash four times. Spring cleaning in the fall.

By the time I sat down behind my desk, the pink neon TOFU sign on the Baltimore building was blinking and reminding me that it was time to think about getting something to eat. Maybe Italian. I'd have to shop before I could make more juice. I'd tossed the last of the fruit and vegetables. There were limits on how long you could leave produce on your desk.

eleven

I spent the next few days on the edge of just drifting off and getting lost. Years later I might jerk my head up off the bar of some dance joint and the barkeep might say, "Welcome back. Hey, aren't you the guy who was supposed to catch the Documentalist Killer but never did? The guy who for very personal reasons agreed to shadow a policeman for his wife? Whatever became of that case? Nothing? And did you ever wrap up that Dennis scam you had going? No? You don't say."

I opted not to drift away. At least not yet. I bought a new bunch of fruit to juice. I couldn't find any of the weird bumpy yellow things with black spots, and the produce kid I'd asked gave me a funny look, so I didn't push it. I worried that the rejuvenating jolt might depend on the precise mixture of fruits I'd stumbled on before, but that turned out not to be the case. All of the wild combinations I came up with made me feel pretty good.

I'd eaten most of the vitamins Yuri had left with the juicer, so I bought a book on vitamins and minerals, read it, and then dropped $143 at a health food store. Beta-carotene, E, C, zinc, selenium, co-enzyme Q-10, you name it.

I followed Frank Wallace on two occasions back to the Quack Inn and the very same room. He must have booked the room on a long-term basis. I never saw anyone else there with him. The last time I waited a long time for his lover to come out and she never did. Frank was either doing something alone in that room or his monkey business buddy lived there.

Call me goofy, but I spent one day playing eighteen holes of golf and then celebrating my score in the clubhouse. Sure, people wondered what someone like me was doing at the country club, but then someone else remembered who my mother was and said, "Oh, yes, that explains everything." I didn't care.

The flame war I'd started over bad documentation still raged on alt.dead.docs. SOAPY had disappeared altogether.

One startling development was that a lot of people on alt.dead.docs thought that maybe knocking off the clowns who committed documentation wasn't such a bad idea.

Such people make you wonder what kind of world we're living in, and they make you feel pretty uneasy when you catch yourself nodding in agreement.

Lulu spent an afternoon sorting clothes into piles to wash and piles to dry-clean, grumbling the whole time about the way when we finally let our feminine side loose, we set her to work doing the laundry.

We told her, okay, so next time Dennis would do the laundry. She didn't buy it.

Scarface spent some time looking at tropical fish and talking with the guy at the store about setting up a tank in my office. He was wearing the rest of us down on the matter of fish.

I called the number I had for Ramona Simmons hoping to alert her to the danger of being a known local on the BOD list, but all I got was a snippy phone message. She never called me back.

Dennis brooded over the fact that he probably never would get into the DATAPANTS file.

Dieter made a plate of enchiladas.

I spent another special "Sunday" afternoon with Mom. This time it really was Sunday. It's spooky when the real and the somewhat less than real correspond. The staff treated me like a nutcase who might explode at any moment. Or maybe I was just being paranoid.

I did spend a lot of time looking over my shoulder. Being forced out on a ledge by a gunman will do that to a person.

We were all waiting for Prudence Deerfield to show up again.

No Prudence.

Elsie Wallace called, and I agreed to meet her for lunch. I was pretty sure I knew where Frank would be for lunch. He'd be eating at Maxwell's Lunch Room. After that he'd either go back to work or he'd go to the Quack Inn. If he ate alone, he'd go on to the motel. If someone joined him for lunch, Marvin for example, he'd skip the motel. Frank was becoming predictable, which was making my job easier, but I really didn't have anything to tell Elsie.

We agreed to meet at the Garden Party, a restaurant on the other side of the river. I was a little late, and I spent a few minutes in the entrance alcove scanning the shrubbery. She must have seen me come in, because she was already looking at me when I spotted her sitting at a table tucked in among the ferns and vines. She smiled at me, and I shrugged at a young man approaching me with a menu and walked into the foliage.

I hadn't been this close to Elsie Wallace in years. That unfortunate shooting accident that made Frank so adamant about me not packing heat also made it unlikely I'd be a houseguest at the three-bedroom two-bath Wallace estate. Elsie still looked pretty good to me. She wore her pale blond hair very short these days, and that made her face look a little fuller, and maybe she'd put on a few pounds, but they looked good on her. Her lipstick was a lot redder than I remembered. She wore a tailored skirt and matching blouse of a strange brown and white streaked color combination that reminded me of peeling cotton-wood bark. And a scarf. Had she picked those clothes so she'd blend in with the greenery of the Garden Party?

I gave her a peck on the cheek and had a momentary flash of sadness at the old woman smell of her powder; we were no longer in high school, and it really was too late to take her away from Frank. I put all of that out of my mind and sat down opposite her. There was a vine hanging down in front of my face and I pushed it aside. "Hello, Elsie," I said.

The vine slowly crept back in front of my face. I pushed it away.

"Brian," she said. "Will you have a drink?" She looked around for the server.

"No hurry." I reached across the table and lightly touched her hand. She smiled at me again and took a sip of her wine. She glanced away and then looked back at me. "You're looking good. I couldn't tell those times on the phone."

"It's not like it's been all that long since we've seen each other, Elsie."

"It's been a long time," she said, "since I've seen you up this close."

"Yes, I guess you're right."

"It's like old times."

The vine was in my face again. "What is with this vine?" I pushed it away.

"Have you found out what Frank's up to yet?"

So we were getting down to business already. I was tempted to make something up. My Psychic Sidekick said Frank wasn't guilty, but my goal in taking the case in the first place was just to get back at him. Bring a little misery into his rotten life.

I couldn't do it. Elsie sounded so angry and looked so bewildered when she said his name. Something had gone wrong. She didn't know what it was, and she didn't know how to fix it.

"You may be wrong about him fooling around," I said.

"May be?"

"I haven't seen him do anything with anyone," I said. "If he is, I don't see where he's finding the time."

"But there is something," she said. "I can tell from the way you said that. Something is going on."

Our server came by. I asked him about the available fruit and vegetable juices. The selection was surprisingly small—or maybe I was becoming a juice snob. I asked him to put a shot of vodka in a glass of pear nectar. He didn't bat an eye. Elsie ordered a fruit plate. I decided to go with the spinach quiche.

"So what is it?" she asked when we were alone again.

That pesky vine was in front of my face again. I glanced around to see if anyone was watching me. No one seemed to be, so I took hold of the vine and gave it a good yank.

It didn't break loose. Instead, somewhere back in the foliage I heard a heavy crunching crash. Anyone who could see us was now looking at us. I tossed the vine over the side of the table.

"Is this your way of avoiding the question?" Elsie asked.

I parted the shrubbery to my left and peered in. The vine had been attached to a plant in a terra-cotta pot on a shelf. The broken pot was now on the floor.

The server brought my pear nectar and vodka. If he noticed the modified arrangement of plants, he pretended that he didn't.

"So back to Frank," Elsie said when he'd gone. "You think he's up to no good."

"I don't know," I said.

"Tell me."

"I can't just report my feelings and hunches, and then ask you to pay for them, Elsie. Give it some time. When I know something definite, I'll tell you."

"At least it's not my imagination," she said.

"How do you mean?"

"If other people are noticing he's acting weird, then it's not just my imagination when I think he's acting weird."

"It's probably not my place to ask," I said, "but have you just asked him about it?"

"That's the worst part," she said, and tears came to her eyes. "We've always talked about everything. Now he's just shutting me out."

I reached across the table and squeezed her hand. I couldn't think of anything that might make her feel better, so I kept my mouth shut.

The food arrived. Elsie pulled her hand away and patted her eyes with her napkin.

Elsie's fruit plate looked like it had a tiny piece of every fruit on earth. If I'd dumped such a plate in my juicer (and I was thinking of it as my juicer now; Yuri would have to fight me for it), I'd probably be jumping around the room for days.

The best part of my quiche was the way it looked on the white plate: the perfect yellow triangle veined with green, the several leaves of fresh spinach spread like a fan, the silver fork.

We ate lunch mostly in silence. How's the fruit? Good. How's the quiche? Tasty. Yum.

When the coffee had been poured, Elsie said, "I know you have other cases, Brian, but I hope you can put a little time in on this. It's really important to me."

"Funny," I said, "one of my other cases is one Frank is working on, too. Those computer people murders. If you ignore one that's almost done, all my cases involve Frank. One way or another I'm looking at him a lot."

We'd said about all we were going to say, so before she could start looking at her watch and thinking up excuses, I signaled for the check. "I've got to get back to work, Elsie," I said.

We parted in the parking lot. She kissed my cheek and climbed into her car and drove away.

I drove back across the river and then south on Willamette to Spencer Butte, a big green bump from the top of which you can see everything for miles around—a magnificent view and a fully aerobic climb. Maybe it was the juice; I was feeling like maybe I should get more exercise. A climb to the top of Spencer Butte would make me feel like I was in high school again. Actually, I'd need to take beer if I was going to feel like I was in high school again. Maybe I should have asked Elsie to come along.

I huffed and puffed my way to the top. By the time I got there my head was swimming and I was seeing fuzzy black dots everywhere I looked. I found a place to collapse where I could see the view that had brought me here in the first place. When I could breathe again, I decided the hike had been worth it.

The city was a big Monopoly board where I played the game I called my life. This view reminded me how much I loved this place. I doubted I would ever go anywhere else. I'd seen a little of the rest of the world and then I'd come home.

I could see the top of my building from here. I could scan west and see the Gotta Dance, too, or at least the blurry clump of lots and streets and buildings where it lurked. A place for everything and everything in its place. Sure, there were parts of the city I had used up down there, places that for all practical purposes might as well be on the moon insofar as my revisiting them went, but there was still enough left to last a long time.

I hung around on top until it looked like I'd have to hurry to get down before dark.

I had dinner at a Japanese restaurant where the chef does knife tricks with your food right in front of your face. I decided such places were a lot more fun when you weren't eating alone.

After dinner, I drove back to the office.

I wasn't there long before the phone rang. First Elsie and now this. I would have to be careful not to let this new popularity go to my head. I hoped it would be Prudence calling. Or maybe Yuri Kost. I put down my glass of guava and grape juice and picked up the phone.

"Skylight Howells," I said.

"Hi, this is your so-called Documentalist Killer speaking." The voice sounded like s/he was using one of those expensive voice-disguising devices. I used to have one of those myself until I realized it was mostly redundant in my case. In any case, s/he probably didn't quite have the hang of the device yet, since the voice was high and squeaky and the words were sometimes interrupted by weird whooshing and slurping sounds.

"Really?" I flipped on the tape to record our conversation.

"I hate that label," the caller said. "Where did you come up with 'Documentalist'?"

"On-line," I said. "I don't remember exactly where."

"It's dumb, but you're wondering why I called."

"You're a very perceptive man," I said.

"Thank you."

He didn't correct me or chuckle, and his thank you seemed without irony. I decided I could at least tentatively assume he was a man. This is, of course, reconstructed; I did not think and decide all of that in the time the killer said, "Thank you" and I said, "So you're calling to tell me about killing people over software documentation?"

"Not exactly," he said. "And I'm not killing people over any old documentation. It's bad documentation, like you said." Whoosh/slurp. "The kind that wastes your time and drives you crazy. It took you long enough. I had faith there was a detective buried somewhere inside of you, but if you hadn't figured it out soon, I would have had to make an announcement."

"Speaking of announcements," I said, "are you Pablo Deerfield?"

"Boy, are you ever off there," he said. "Maybe I've made a mistake. Maybe I should just hang up."

"So, are you SOAPY?"

"Bingo," he said. "Your powers of deduction amaze me. What tipped you off? Maybe the fact that I've been telling the world that on-line from the very beginning?"

"I notice you're not on-line these days," I said. "How would you have made the announcement if I hadn't figured it out?"

"They cut me off!" His was the voice of an angry cartoon—maybe like something you'd hear if you grabbed the nuts of a chipmunk. "Can you believe that? The Russians just cut me off. All that stuff about complete freedom on the net. What a load of crap."

"You were going to tell me why you called?"

"You're hoping I'll slip up and give you a clue."

"A clue would be nice," I said. I wondered if he had pushed the right buttons to prevent caller ID. Since I didn't have caller ID it wouldn't do me any good, but he wouldn't know I didn't have it. On the other hand, if I reminded him of such things, he might panic and hang up on me.

"I've called to confess," he said. "I want to turn myself in."

What I felt was disappointment, sudden and sharp. He couldn't do that! I hadn't figured it out yet. But then he was laughing. A moment later there was the whoosh and slurp of his device.

"Just kidding!" he said.

"You're a riot."

"Okay, here's the deal," he said. "It's not quite that I'm going to let you watch me work, but I am going to give you the chance to be the first on the scene. That is, if you can figure it out. Who knows?" Whoosh/slurp. "There is a nonzero probability that you could figure it out in time to stop me from doing it."

"Why are you telling me this?"

"Tradition," he said. "You and I were matching wits on the net and now we're going to try it on the phone."

"Do you know you sound like a cartoon?" I couldn't help it. I had to snap something at him and that just popped up. It was a mistake. He could have just hung up on me.

"Of course I do," he said. "I'm sucking on helium. Did you think this was my natural voice?"

Well, so much for my voice-changing machine theory. Sometimes the obvious is the answer. Low tech. I should have recognized the sound of someone sucking helium.

"Can we get back to the matter at hand?" he asked.

"Shoot."

"Funny you should say that," the killer said. "I'll be going out immediately after we finish here to do number four. Do you want to know why?"

"Of course I want to know why," I said. "I'd like to know who, too, while you're at it."

"You puzzle out the who," he said, "that's mostly what this call is all about. The why is that this particular bozo has written a manual for a particular piece of software. The utter mediocrity of this particular piece of documentation is disgusting, but it's probably not enough to attract my attention. After all I'd have to do away with most of the idiots doing this particular kind of thing if that was enough."

His repetition of the word "particular" was driving me crazy. "So what was it about this particular documentation that has gotten your goat?" I asked.

"The fatal flaw," he said, "the thing that simply cannot be tolerated, the thing that makes me go white hot with anger, that's the thing you're wondering about?"

"That's it," I said.

"Our guy has told you how to start the program, and you'll excuse me if I'm a little vague on the details. We don't want to make your job too easy."

"Perish the thought," I said.

"So number four has told us how to do this with the program and how to do that with the program. If you follow the instructions you can spend hours and hours wandering around. But what the bozo doesn't tell you how to do is quit."

"That is irritating," I said.

"You'd better believe it!" Here at last was the true personality coming out. His fire was like the fire of an evangelical preacher. He had absolutely no doubt that the documentalist who had neglected to tell the user how to quit was among the lowest of life forms. It was not only his pleasure to snuff out such a person, it was his duty. He would send a message that other documentalists would ignore at their own risk.

"Say you just want to poke around," he said, "so you fire up the program and you do one thing or another, exploring or following the directions or whatever, and then you want to just stop and go do something else. What happens?"

"You can't stop."

"Exactly!" he shouted. "So you start guessing. You type 'quit' and you type 'exit' and you type 'stop.' You try control Q. In short, you try everything, and nothing works!"

"That's pretty irritating I'll admit," I said, "but it still doesn't seem like enough to kill a person over. You can always just reboot."

There was a long silence, and I thought he might have hung up.

"Are you still there?" I asked.

"I didn't call to convince you what I'm doing is right," he said. "I don't care if you agree or not. Nothing you can say will stop me from zapping number four. You'll have to actually catch me to stop me. And I'm not going to tell you how to do that."

"But wait a minute," I said, "that's no different than your documentalist who didn't tell you how to stop!"

"Hey! You're right," he said. "Pretty neat. Well, the only other thing I have to complain about is how long it's taking you guys to find the bodies."

"Actually, I haven't been looking for the bodies."

"Maybe I'll start having them delivered," he said.

"Maybe you could bring one by in person?"

"In your dreams," he said. "Happy hunting and so long."

"Wait!" The more he talked the greater the chance that he would let something slip. "Why did you break into my office to shoot me?" I asked quickly.

"Someone tried to shoot you?"

"As if you didn't know," I said. I had his attention again, and I was pretty sure from his reaction that he was, in fact, not the guy who had broken into my office, but maybe I could string him along.

"Look," he said, "we obviously have a third player in this."

"What do you mean?"

"Someone shot at me, too," he said.

I waited for him to go on. I waited for what seemed like a long time, but then just before I could make a "please continue" noise, he said. "I thought it was you at first."

"Why would I shoot at you?" I asked. "In fact, if I knew who you were, why wouldn't I just turn you in, collect my fee, and call it a case?"

"My thinking exactly," he said. "I'll admit I was wildly confused at first. But then when I thought it out, I decided it wasn't you. Nevertheless, it's just too much to believe that someone shooting at me doesn't have something to do with my . . . how shall I put it? My attempts to improve the quality of computer instructions."

"I think you must be right about that," I said.

"Well, you give it some thought," he said. "Next time we talk, I'll be interested in hearing what you come up with. So bye for now."

"Not yet!"

"What is it? I'm running out of helium."

"Can't you postpone that other business?"

"Other business?"

"Number four."

"Absolutely not," he said. "In fact, I'm going out right now. I can hardly wait!"

He hung up.

twelve

I rejected one dumb course of action after another and finally came down to the one that most people probably would have thought of in the first place. I called the police. I asked for Frank Wallace. I liked to work alone (well, you know what I mean), but this time I just couldn't afford to take the chance that I might not be up to it.

Who's calling?

Why lie? It's not like I could get away with it. My number would be clearly displayed already. I was in no position to make an anonymous tip. I gave the police Sky's name and the office number. They put me on hold, and I settled back to listen to a Beatles tune whose teeth and claws had been removed. I didn't wait long.

Lieutenant Wallace was not immediately available, which meant they would page him if my call was sufficiently important. Could I explain myself?

I wasn't sure I could, so I asked for Marvin Zivon. He wasn't on at this time of night either. I just didn't think I could go through the case from ground zero, starting with where I fit into it all. I could probably do more good trying to figure out who the fourth victim might be. I said I had information on a current case. I asked that Frank or Marvin give me a call. I'd probably be out when they got around to it. It would probably be too late anyway. I hung up.

I figured that would be that, but I hadn't even spun up to a full-fledged panic attack before the phone rang again.

Marvin must have been easier to find than Frank.

"Brian Dobson?"

I peeled off my mustache and said, "Speaking."

"Sergeant Zivon." His official way of speaking tonight made me realize that everyone wouldn't regard Marvin as a buffoon; in fact, he was probably pretty good at what he did. Maybe I should be giving him more respect.

"Marvin," I said, "I've got a problem."

"The message says you have information on a case," Marvin said.

"A guy just called me up claiming to be the killer."

"Your Graffiti Killer?"

"That's the one," I said, "but don't you guys ever surf the net?"

"Is this a new subject?"

"Marvin, Marvin," I said. "You should be following my theories. I passed that Graffiti Killer bit a long time ago. What the killer is doing is killing people who write bad documentation. That's what he's saying with the messages he leaves. Tell Frank I told you that. I'll give you guys that one."

"And he called you up? Could you tell who it was?"

"No," I said.

"So what did the voice sound like?"

"He disguised his voice," I said.

"So what did it sound like?"

"Well, like a guy sucking on helium," I said. "You know, like a cartoon."

"So this guy sucking on helium calls you up and says he's the killer."

"That's right," I said. "He admitted I was right about his motivation, and he said he was going to do number four right now. As we speak. Something to do with the documentation not telling the user how to quit."

"Don't take this as a crack, Brian," he said, "it's too important. Are you sure you, well, I mean are you sure you know what you're talking about?"

I felt suddenly tired. And cold. I hoped I sounded cold. "Sergeant Zivon," I said. "I decided the right thing to do was call the police, so I called. You can take it from here. I have certain responsibilities to my clients, and I need to get back to those."

"Yeah, okay, I had to ask. You understand." Marvin got down to business. He asked the right questions. I told him what I could. By the time we were done, I thought he knew everything I could tell him about the call. I read him the BOD list. I told him what I could about the four names we knew were local.

"I'll send a car around to the addresses we know," Marvin said.

"Is that going to be enough?"

"Brian."

"I know. I know. I shouldn't tell you how to do your job."

"More than that," Marvin said. "I'll be sending the car. I don't want them to be running into you sneaking around in the bushes. You understand?"

"I don't sneak around in bushes!" I said, but then it hit me that I certainly did sneak around in bushes, not that it was any of Marvin's business. Okay, in this case, it *was* his business.

Marvin wanted me to stay away from Leo, Lucas, Bernie, and Ramona. I wasn't sure we could do that.

"Do you hear what I'm saying, Brian?"

"Okay!" I could hear the frustration in my voice. I hated letting Marvin hear it. "I'll leave this part to you. Don't screw it up."

He hung up. I felt like I'd done my duty. I also felt like I'd wasted my time.

Marvin would send a car to the addresses of the known locals. It probably wouldn't do any good. Marvin was right about me going out prowling, though. I couldn't be at four places at once, but there had to be something I could do.

I pushed my mustache around on the desk with a pencil. It looked like a dead caterpillar.

Wait a minute, I thought. This negativity is not the kind of thinking that built the Skylight Howells detective agency. I put the mustache on.

Hey, maybe we could find out which of the four locals committed the sin of not telling the user how to quit. I picked up the phone again.

I didn't have Leo's home number and it wasn't listed. I kicked myself for not getting it when I interviewed him. I called Challenger. Leo might still be there; in fact the whole staff could be there. It isn't easy to get computer people to go home at night. You stop paying them, and they just go on working. Amazing.

The phone rang and rang. I was beginning to think it was probably a matter of policy to ignore the phone at night, but then some guy answered. A moment later he told me no, Leo wasn't there, and no, he wouldn't give me Leo's home phone number, and yes, okay, he'd leave a message on Leo's desk. If Leo turned up dead before morning, I guessed he wouldn't get my message.

I had no home phone for Lucas Betty either. What was with these guys? People could still make themselves pretty scarce in this information age. Maybe elaborate secrecy schemes were the wave of the future. I called Experimental Support Services at the university and got a recorded Ms. Divey telling me no one was home. I hung up. If Lucas were able to pick up his messages in the morning he wouldn't need one from me.

I got Ramona's machine next. She'd changed the message. Today it said, "Wait for the beep then leave a message if you simply cannot contain yourself." I left another message saying I had information she needed. I doubted she would call me back.

I called the number I'd chased down for Bernie and got his mom. I told her I was calling about a software bug. She said Bernie might be working in the cave.

"The cave?"

"The dungeon," she said. "The basement, his little world. I don't go down there."

"Can you check?" I asked. "Call down the stairs or something? I really need to talk to him."

She sighed a heavy sigh and put down the phone.

A couple of moments later Bernie said, "Hello?" Too fast for his Mom to have gotten even to the cave stairs? He must have had a phone down there. Come to think of it how else would a computer guy get on-line if he didn't have a phone line down there? Wireless maybe. A lot of the city was wireless these days. "Hello?"

"Listen and listen carefully, Mr. Watkins," I said. "I'm working for Prudence and Pablo Deerfield from the BOD list. I need to know what your last documentation project was and I need to know now."

"I was part of the team for the Bumblebee," he said. "Hey, who is this?"

"Never mind, Bernie," I said. "Listen. This is very important. Did you tell the user how to quit in the Honeybee? Think carefully."

"The Bumblebee," he said. "Well, sure. I think so. I don't know. That wasn't the part I did."

"Was your name on the manual?"

"Well, no," he said. "But Mr. Clark said if my work keeps improving it won't be long before I'm listed right there with all the others."

"Who's Mr. Clark?"

"The Bumblebee guy," Bernie said.

"So, have you ever done one that anyone would know about? I mean that they would know you did?"

"Well, not a big one like that. Not yet," he said, "but, hey, lots of people know about me! How do you think I got on the BOD list?"

I was pretty sure Bernie was safe. Why would the killer skip all the names on the documentation and chase down a kid who didn't even do the part that pissed him off? The only danger was that the Bumblebee wasn't the software in question. Maybe Bernie forgot to explain the exit procedure in some other piece of documentation.

"Think about this, Bernie," I said, "have you ever written documentation where you forgot to tell the user how to exit the program?"

"How smart do you have to be to figure out how to quit?"

"Is that a 'yes' or a 'no'?"

"I don't know," he said. "The only stuff I've done besides that thing I did for Mr. Clark was released on the net. Small stuff. Instructions for shareware mostly. Programs my friends write that maybe two or three people in the whole world see. What is this all about?"

"I don't want to worry you," I said, which probably worried him quite a bit.

"Are you the police?"

"Let's just say I'm in touch with the police," I said. "It would be a good idea if you didn't leave the house tonight."

"Okay," he said.

"By the way, just what is the Bumblebee?"

"If you need to ask," he said, "you wouldn't get it anyway."

Since Bernie was the only one I had managed to contact, I felt a little reluctant to let him go, but after a moment of silence, I said, "Yes. Okay. Right. Well, watch yourself, Bernie." I hung up.

One out of four. Not a very good score.

Marvin had said not to poke my nose in, but maybe I would at least drive by. I mean I could swing by Challenger Video and just look. Cruise by Ramona's and see if all the lights were off. I got up, but before I was fully committed to walking out the door, I realized there was maybe one more thing to do.

I sat down again and dug around in the top desk drawer until I found Yuri's card—the one he'd left with the juicer when he and Prudence had slipped out of my life like thieves in the night. I still had no idea what the two of them had been up to. I should have heard from one of them by now. Unless they'd just moved on to plan B. It was their move, but as far as I could see, they weren't making any moves. I was afraid they'd cut me out of the loop.

I picked up the phone and dialed the number on Yuri's card.

A couple of rings then a deep male voice with a thick accent—you'd probably call this guy Boris if you got to name him—said, "Evil Empire Software. We know who you are. We know where you live. We know what you like. Resistance is futile. For world domination, press one; for evil laughter, press two; for the department of nefarious schemes, press three; for the division of misinformation, press four; for the workshop of foul devices, press five; for the office of double-dealing, press six; to speak with a secret agent, press seven."

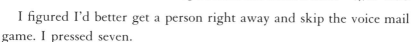

I figured I'd better get a person right away and skip the voice mail game. I pressed seven.

"No agent is available to speak with you." The voice this time was female. I was given the list of buttons to push again. I wondered if Evil Empire Software had gotten Russians with accents to do these voices in which case the accents would be real, or if the voices came from whoever installed their phone system or maybe their advertising agency in which case these might be actors and the accents might not be Russian accents at all.

I'd been thinking about her accent as the female voice read me the list of buttons, so I thought I might have simply been mistaken when it hit me that the list had changed. I pushed seven thinking I'd hear her message again.

"We told you," a male voice said, "no one can talk to you. For the secret headquarters, press one; to be double-crossed, press two; for a list of heinous weaponry, press three; for the department of despicable plots, press four; to hear atrocious lies, press five; for evil laughter, press six; to speak with a secret agent, press seven."

It was different. In fact the only things I remembered being on the other two lists were the options for evil laughter and speaking to a secret agent. Maybe the whole system was set up like a game—you had to play your way to the person you wanted to talk to. Could making customers navigate a maze on the phone possibly be good business? Well, gamers were weird, you could say that much for them. Maybe there was another number for regular people.

If this system were indeed a labyrinth, then I probably never would get a real person by pushing seven. In fact, seven might be a false option. That is, there were probably never any secret agents available (well, it did occur to me that the agents might be available during regular business hours—but maybe the hypothetical phone system for regular people might be active then, too).

Although it seemed to be numbered differently every time, the other constant was evil laughter. I pressed six.

I heard some evil laughter and another list of options.

I pressed buttons at random until I got what I believed was a list I'd heard before. That made some sense, the system must be finite. In fact, it would have to be fairly small unless they were willing to devote a lot of resources to it. And why would they do that? I was dubious about the value of this system as a capitalist tool. If I were an Evil Empire Software customer with a problem, I would not be amused.

I listened to the list again. Yuri was hidden in there somewhere. The options all fell into categories. I decided to follow one until it came around. Plans and such first. I pressed two for the division of unwholesome designs. I listened to the new list, and then I pressed three for the department of nefarious schemes, which sounded familiar. I pressed one for hateful projects, and then I pressed four for the department of despicable plots (now I was getting somewhere!). I pressed five for the office of obnoxious systems and got what seemed to be an actual person. Well, not the person himself, of course!

"Systems. We're not in but if you'll leave your name and number we'll get back to you." Beep.

So I hung up and started over. I followed the devices/weaponry track down to the office of a man named Bob who said I could leave a message if I needed help with peripheral devices.

I hit pay dirt with the misinformation (lies) track. That came down to the office of Yuri Kost. Unfortunately, he wasn't in either. This time I left a message. I told him that he and I and probably Prudence Deerfield needed to meet right away. I told him I had new information on our killer. I told him I didn't know what his game was, but we should get together and clear the air.

Oh, and thanks for the juicer.

So, I'd made a few calls, talked to a teenager and a couple of machines. Meanwhile the killer was out there moving in on his fourth victim.

It was just after midnight.

What was I supposed to do? Go to bed? I grabbed my coat and headed for the door.

I locked up and walked down the hall to the elevator. At night, the feeling that I was the only tenant in the building was very strong. I never saw anyone here at night. Once you got outside, you could sometimes see a light here and there up-and-down the building, and sometimes even the silhouette of a person, but not often. The dim elevator opened on the dim lobby. I let myself out onto the sidewalk and into a light drizzle.

Aside from Lulu's Escort, a Dodge van, and a very old Mercury, my jeep was the only vehicle in the lot. I got into it, got the thing started and the windshield wipers moving, and pulled out. Back on Eleventh I hit all the lights just right, and less than ten minutes later I drove past Challenger Video.

No cops here. But they would have been able to get Leo's home number and address. Maybe I should call Marvin up and ask him for it. Ha. No, but maybe Leo had come back here, or maybe in person I could talk someone into telling me where he lived. I swung around the block and came back for another look. The coast seemed clear so I pulled into the parking lot.

The small door in one of the big, boarded-up auto bays was locked. That laid-back approach to security I'd noted last time I was here did not extend into the night. I banged on the door.

Nothing.

I knew there were propeller heads in there. The probability that every one of them had gone home would be very close to zero. I banged on the door again.

Inside someone would look up with a dazed expression and wonder what the banging was all about. Anyone who belonged inside at this time of night would have a key.

They simply weren't going to let me in.

I could do some serious pounding, make them believe they were inside one of those big Japanese drums, pound so hard nerdly knick-knacks would dance off desks, rattle the soda machines, make them think a California earthquake was on a Northwest vacation. Of course then instead of answering the door, they'd probably call the police.

I glanced up and down Eleventh. Even if the car Marvin sent out didn't spot me, and it was likely it would, any cop cruising by might think I looked suspicious banging on the door. I dropped my hands and stood there in the weak cone of light from a single light bulb with the rain running down the back of my neck and considered my options.

Pretty easy actually. I could continue to stand there or I could leave.

I next drove by the address I had for Ramona Simmons. Judging by the house nestled in the trees way up a winding road in the south hills, I'd say that whatever Ramona did, she must do it well. There were no cars in the driveway, but there could have been several in the double garage. I couldn't see any lights inside. The noise of my jeep would be the loudest sound in this quiet wooded neighborhood. If anyone were up, they'd probably peek out to see who was driving by.

I parked up the hill between two houses so anyone looking out of either might think I was visiting the other. I could see most of the front and one side of Ramona's house. She might be in there and she might not. If she was in there, she might be asleep and she might already be dead.

There is nothing so distinctive as the sound of a slamming car door in the dead of night, so I eased the jeep door closed and stood there in the rain considering. I could go ring the doorbell, find out if she was home, but if she answered what would I tell her? No matter how it came down, she'd have to mention my visit when Marvin or Frank or one of their officers interviewed her tomorrow or the next day or whenever she finally surfaced. "Oh, yeah, there was this guy rang the doorbell at some god-awful time of the night. . . ."

My next thought was to just prowl around and see what I could see from the backyard. No. I was not doing good detective work. I was running off in all directions. I was panicking. I'd gotten myself into a position where I simply didn't know what to do, and I was just doing things so I wouldn't be doing nothing at all.

The rain began to fall in earnest. I figured I'd gotten wet enough. Besides which there could be neighborhood watch binoculars trained on me. Someone might have already called the cops. I could still have a nasty encounter with Frank and Marvin tonight. I dug into my pocket for the jeep keys.

I'd automatically locked the jeep. I tried to put my office key in the lock. I dropped the keys into the wet grass. Down the winding street a pair of headlights appeared.

It was dark, the rain was pouring down, and I'd dropped my keys. I would have less than a minute to find them before the car coming up the hill picked me up like a spotlighted burglar.

I got down on my knees and pawed around in the grass. I'd heard the keys fall; I knew about where they were; they weren't where I thought. I could feel my pants getting soaked at the knees. The rain poured down on my back.

This could be the patrol car Marvin sent out, and if it was, I was just the sort of thing it would be looking for. I scrambled around the side of the jeep just as the car dipped over a hump and its lights swung down on where I'd been.

The car cruised on by. I peeked around at it after it had passed. Not a cop. I sat down and leaned back up against the jeep. Another dumb move since now the seat of my pants was as wet as the knees. I took a couple of deep breaths and then crawled back around to where I'd dropped the keys.

I imagined a grid on the ground, and starting in the upper left, I carefully searched each square until (somewhere beyond the middle but still far from the end) I found the keys.

thirteen

The body wasn't discovered for two days.

I spent the day after the killer called driving the four known local BOD members crazy with phone calls. I had to keep checking to see if they were all still alive. Bernie's mother finally just let her machine deal with me. Ms. Divey told me that Lucas Betty was just fine and that I should quit calling! I was pretty sure the reason he wouldn't talk to me was that he didn't want to pay me for putting him in touch with Dennis. He did have a point in that Dennis hadn't shown up for their meeting.

Leo yelled at me, too, and I left so many messages on Ramona's machine that she complained to the police. Word got back to Frank who spoke to Marvin who called me and warned me that if I didn't cut it out I'd be in big trouble.

Marvin said he understood how I felt. He came by later that afternoon and we went over the killer's call again. I don't think either of us came up with anything new. Since they hadn't found the body yet, I tried to tell myself the call had been a hoax. I didn't believe it. The killer was just jerking us around. The call and then all of this silence was not out of character. This was the guy who sent Gerald Moffitt a "next to last warning" and then killed him anyway. I wondered if Gerald was still expecting his "last warning" when he died.

I didn't follow Frank the day after the killer called, and the day after that he didn't go to the Quack Inn, so I was still no closer to knowing what he was up to.

If Yuri had gotten my message, he hadn't bothered calling back.

But then on Friday, Prudence blew back into my office, and the way she looked and the way she talked, just the whole package of her wacky presence reminded me how I'd gotten hooked on this case in the first place. Today she wore a long brown dress printed with tiny yellow flowers and jingly brass rings on her wrists. There's probably a name for dresses like that. It almost touched the floor, and you could just see her feet in black shoes with pointed toes. There was a big daisy in her straw hat, but I think it was plastic.

She pulled up the client's chair and sat down like we had an appointment.

We just looked at one another for a few moments.

Then she said, "Your mustache is coming loose on the left."

"It's been that kind of day," I said. "In fact, the whole week has been like that." I pushed Sky's mustache back onto my lip, and somehow just knowing it was in its proper place seemed to clear my head a little. "So, what brings you back into my life?"

"There's been another killing," she said.

"I knew there would be," I said.

"Your message to Yuri," she said. "You said you had new information. Is that it?"

Yuri had gotten my message. He'd talked it over with Prudence. Neither had bothered to call or come around until someone else had been killed.

"Yuri agrees we should meet," she said.

"And you came by to soften me up?"

"We all need to talk."

"Who did he kill this time?"

"I don't know," she said. "Name withheld pending notification of next of kin."

"So how do you know it's one of ours?"

"Stuff they said on TV," she said.

"You watch TV in the morning?"

"Your question displays an unattractive and unjustified sense of superiority on your part," she said. "How can you hope to be in touch with your culture if you don't watch TV?"

"I didn't say I don't watch TV," I said. "But have you ever noticed that with just a few exceptions, the people you watch on TV don't watch TV themselves?"

"We only watch them when they're too busy doing other things," she said. "Maybe when we're not watching them, they're watching TV. Maybe they're watching us when we're not watching TV."

I thought about that for a moment, but since it was one of those thoughts that could pull me out of the here and now, I pushed it aside.

"Let's see if we can find out about the murder." I picked up the phone and dialed the police, asked for Marvin Zivon. When he came on the line, I told him Prudence was in my office and we were wondering about the new murder she'd seen reported on TV.

"Hang on," he said.

The next voice I heard was Frank Wallace's.

"Brian," he said, "Don't move. Don't even think about moving. I'll be right over." He hung up.

"What's wrong?" Prudence asked. I must have looked a little white.

"Lieutenant Wallace," I said, "Frank. He's coming right over. He didn't mention you. You can still leave before he gets here."

"Why bother?" she asked.

I got up and searched around until I found all the stuff I needed to make coffee. I could make juice for everyone. No, I was mostly out of produce. I would make coffee. I wondered who was dead.

I walked to the window and looked out. I walked back to the coffeemaker to see how it was doing. I slipped into the washroom and looked at myself in the mirror. When I came out I went back to the window for another look at nothing. It hadn't escaped my notice that Prudence was following me with her eyes like I was playing tennis or doing a gymnastics routine or . . . dancing. I grabbed the edge of my desk just to stop my movement. I forced myself to sit back down in the chair behind my desk.

We sat there quietly. Mine was a monumental struggle not to fidget. I couldn't help tapping my foot on the floor; I didn't even notice myself doing it until I followed her X-ray eyes through my desk to the floor where my foot was tapping along like crazy. I fisted my toes and stopped it.

I was as tight as a stubborn knot in your shoelaces by the time Frank banged into the office. Marvin followed him in.

Frank was focused like a lion going for a gazelle. He never took his eyes off me as he approached. He marched right past Prudence without looking at her. He put his hands on my desk and got in my face.

"Hello, Frank," I said. "You remember Prudence Deerfield."

He glanced to his right and saw Prudence. She smiled at him.

"So the gang's all here." He pushed up and away from my desk.

"Pull up a chair, Frank," I said. I got up and walked over to the coffeepot. "Coffee?"

He ignored me. "Have you seen your brother, Ms. Deerfield?"

"Not since Gerald died," she said. "That's why I hired Mr. Howells."

"Mr. Howells?"

"Me," I said. I handed Frank a cup of coffee and he took it! Prudence was distracting him. Encouraged by that, I went back and poured one for Marvin.

"Coffee, Prudence?"

She shook her head no.

"It's going to go hard on him the longer he stays out," Frank told her.

"Why are you so hot for Pablo?" I asked. "He's probably just hiding out so he doesn't end up dead."

Frank ignored that. I was tempted to perch on the edge of the desk for a less formal arrangement, but at the last moment I decided I liked the idea of the desk between me and him. I poured myself the last of the mango, banana, and lime juice and took it with me back to my seat behind my desk.

"What is that crap?" Frank asked.

"Juice."

"Jesus."

"So what do we know about this last one, Frank?" I asked.

He looked at Prudence, and she looked down at her hands in her lap. He turned my way and gave me a scowl that could have peeled paint from the wall. He didn't say anything for a moment, but then he seemed to switch gears. "We know," he said, "that Nathan Ivanovich was watching a rented video called *Lucky Pierre* hosted by Joe Bob Briggs when he was killed."

Prudence groaned.

"A Russian?" I asked.

"French," Marvin said.

"Ivanovich?"

"Pierre," Marvin said. "Don't you think?"

"He wasn't Russian," Prudence said. "Oh, maybe his grandparents were."

"You knew the victim?" Frank asked.

"Yes," Prudence said. "Nathan dropped out of sight some years ago. Everyone thought he probably went into some other line of work."

"He wasn't on the BOD list," I said. "Could he have been one of the anonymous ones?"

"I suppose," she said.

"I'm a little confused on how people get into this so-called brotherhood," I said, "if no one knows who they really are. Don't you have to have qualifications?"

"Of course you have to have qualifications."

"And?"

"You have to have qualifications," she said again.

"Hello?" Frank said. We had been ignoring him, and he didn't like it. I shut up.

"I hear you posted another one of your goofy theories, Brian," he said.

"Not so goofy. I gave Marvin the scoop when I called the other night."

"So, you think the guy's killing nerds who can't explain computer programs?"

"That's pretty much what he told me," I said. "What was written on the body this time?"

"Lots of stuff," Frank said. He took a paper from his inside coat pocket and tossed it across the desk to me. "Lots and lots of stuff." I took a look.

Quit, exit, stop, depart, flee, give up,
surrender, yield, abandon, cease,
discontinue, end, halt, belay, desist,
knock it off, kill, destroy, avast,
good-bye, farewell, #$@%@!, desert,
bolt, withdraw, abdicate, bye-bye, exodus,
egress, retreat, evacuate, leave, mosey,
pull out, vacate, so long, clear out, scram,
vamoose, decamp, stop it, just stop it, whoa!

"What was the arrangement?" I asked.

"From head to toe," Frank said. "Over and over again."

I leaned over and handed the list to Prudence.

"My computer weenies tell me that your theory is causing a panic in some circles," Frank said.

"That's true," Prudence said.

Frank and I both looked at her.

"The writers of *Inside Macintosh* are rumored to be hiding somewhere in the desert outside Las Vegas," she said, "and the Microsoft campus is barricaded and microserfs are taking turns patrolling the grounds to protect the documentation staff. There's a rumor Bill might just let the killer have the designers of the Windows Help system. Locally, I hear, Symantec and SplashDown have boarded up the windows of their downtown buildings. Everyone is scared."

"But as far as we can tell these are local murders," Marvin said.

"True," I said. "The problem is he may run out of local documentalists."

"There are still a lot left," Prudence said.

"What I mean is he may run out of bad documentalists," I said, "or at least those who have pissed him off. I can't see him staying local."

"Did you maybe say as much on-line?" Marvin asked.

I looked at Frank, who I could tell was following this on-line stuff just fine, which surprised me. I'd figured it would be some time in the middle of the next century before you would catch Frank net surfing.

"I may have," I said.

"Great," Frank said.

"It's only fair to tip people off," I said. "Sure the nation of Microsoft is an entire state away up in Seattle or whatever, but just because lots of us never need to leave the house doesn't mean we can't. Don't you think the killer can get a map and trace his finger north up I-5? It's not like they're hiding."

"Still it's all just a notion that's gotten lodged in your scrambled brain, Brian," Frank said.

"Are we done here, Frank?" I asked.

He stood up. "Done here? I guess you could say we're done here. Get your coat. I want to ask the rest of my questions in more familiar surroundings." He pushed away from my desk. "Cuff him and bring him along, Sergeant."

"You can't do that, Frank." Marvin put his coffee cup down on the desk and faced Frank. "Think about it, Lieutenant."

Frank looked like he was working himself up to a really big explosion, but then he turned sharply and stomped off for the door. "Just bring him."

So we went downtown.

So to speak. We were already downtown. My office is downtown. The police station is downtown. Most of the stuff in my life is downtown.

At the police station, Frank put me on a pink plastic bench and disappeared.

Ten minutes later, Marvin brought me a little paper cone of water. "This won't take long once he gets started."

"I don't like the sound of that."

"Relax, Brian," he said.

Frank made me wait on that bench for over an hour.

At one point a guy with very short hair and a thin tie glanced at me as he walked by. Then he stopped and looked back over his shoulder at me. A little while later I saw him talking to Marvin. They both kept glancing my way, which made me very nervous.

Before I could find out what all of that was about, Frank poked his head out of his office and called me in. Once inside he left me standing in front of his desk while he sat down and riffled through some papers.

I wasn't willing to play that game. I took a seat and waited him out.

We went over everything one more time. The call. What Prudence Deerfield expected me to do. What I'd found out so far. Everything. It was all old stuff. I'd either said it all on-line or I'd told it to Marvin. From the way Frank kept checking out the papers in a file folder, I thought he knew it was old ground, too.

He was just hassling me.

Like old times.

Well, not just like old times. This time I kept my cool. I wouldn't be slouching home with a bloody nose today.

I learned a few things, too. Nathan Ivanovich, like the others, had been strangled with a cable you might use to hook your printer to your computer. The words on the body were written with a fine tip felt pen.

I decided Frank knew something about Pablo I didn't know. He danced around it, but he always came back to it—the big question was where was Pablo Deerfield?

I didn't know, and I finally convinced Frank I didn't know. He cut me loose.

I figured Prudence would be gone by the time I got back to the office, and I figured right.

At least she'd left a note. "Yuri called. Meet us at eight in The Rubber Room."

fourteen

"We've decided to let the beans out of the bag," Prudence said as soon as I'd settled into a chair at their table.

Yuri rolled his eyes at her.

"What?" she said.

"It's about time," I said. I glanced around for someone to bring me a drink.

The Rubber Room, in spite of the many off-color remarks you could make about its name, was a posh lounge, dim but not smoky, hooked on to one of the best fish places in town. I've heard Herman Goodwin say that when he told his wife he was thinking of opening a fish restaurant, she said, "Better you should check yourself into a rubber room." The restaurant itself was called Goodwin's Fish House.

I got the attention of a young woman with a tray, and she hurried over to get my drink order. Ordinarily this would not be a choice point. I'd just order a scotch (neat) and that would be that, but lately I'd been decreasing the alcohol and increasing the mix in my drinks. Mostly the mix was juice. I ordered a screwdriver.

"Does that mean you've been using the juice machine?" Yuri asked.

"You can't have it back," I said.

"We brought it for you!" he said. "We're finding in Russia that drinking lots of juice helps with . . . er, well, with problems like ours. I have always meant to try it myself."

"I do have a lot more energy," I said, and it was true. The last few days of juice and megavitamins had left me feeling like I could jump over buildings.

"You look much better," Prudence said.

She was still wearing the hippie dress she'd had on that afternoon, but she had done away with the straw hat. Yuri was wearing a dark suit and red tie. I'd never seen him in a suit. He looked official in his business attire, like someone you should pay attention to.

The server brought my drink and Yuri told her to put it on his tab and she smiled and went away. Yuri raised his own glass and spoke in Russian. I didn't ask, just raised my own glass, and the three of us toasted something and drank.

"So what about the beans?" I asked.

"First, Yuri should tell you about *chechyotka*," Prudence said.

The Russian word for tap dancing.

"I'd sort of hoped you were going to tell me all the things you've been hiding from me."

He pulled a small notebook out of his shirt pocket and wrote something. He ripped out the page, and pushed it across the table to me.

I took a look at the single word written on the page.

чечётка

"That's the way we spell *chechyotka* in the Russian alphabet," he said.

I saw the connection right away. The name of the Russian remailer was from the first three letters of the Russian word for tap dancing. "Why just the first three letters?"

"The committee claimed the whole word was too long," Yuri said. "Besides they said everyone who reads Russian would want to know why we called it 'tap dancing.' This way the joke is only for those in the know."

"So, Evil Empire Software is a front for four-e-four-dot-com, the Russian remailer?"

"We don't say 'front' in the new Russia," Yuri said. "Following your lead, we say 'parent.' EES is the parent corporation."

I looked over at Prudence. "What's your connection?"

"I facilitate operations in this part of the world for the remailing service," Prudence said.

"So are you Russian, too?"

"Yes," she said. She and Pablo had come to this country as teenagers. They'd taken the family name of their foster parents. It was a painful time. She didn't want to talk about it. Tears threatened her eyes when she even thought about it. Was I satisfied now?

Yuri gave her his handkerchief.

I couldn't believe it. How long would you have to carry a clean white handkerchief around before you got to offer it to a tearful woman?

I gave her some time to pull herself together, and then I got back on topic. "Why all the secrecy?"

"That's what this is all about," she said. "The integrity of the net."

"That's true," Yuri said.

"How so?"

Yuri took a sip of his drink before he answered. "Our purpose at four-e-four-com, as it's called over here, is to maneuver ourselves into a position where we will be the anonymous rerouter for the whole world."

"Why is it always world domination with you guys?"

"Again, we are just learning our lessons from you," he said. "Your international corporations are the models. We saw that Russia was the perfect place for an absolutely free hub of information. It is deeply protected by the existing bureaucracy. The government is on our side. When you can say absolutely anything, you will say more interesting and significant things. Art and science will flourish. A new age of information exchange will dawn upon the Earth."

"And you'll make a lot of money," I said.

"Isn't that the idea?"

I thought this whole free info business was a little naive, but I didn't say so.

When I didn't reply he went on. "I don't want to make it sound too easy. You don't go from what we had to a functioning capitalistic system in one big jump."

"No?"

"Factions have formed," he said. "There is a power struggle between my faction, which wants the freedom business I just explained, and another faction that thinks we will have the world right where we want it when most information passes through our hands."

"Which one of you is the Russian Mob?" I asked.

"We don't like to say 'Mob,'" Prudence said.

"Basically there is an invisible battle going on over what the net will ultimately be," Yuri said. "There are very big forces at work. Conspiracies inside conspiracies inside conspiracies. Someone always sniping at you from the cybertrees. Everyone is looking over his shoulder."

"So, you're the good guys?" I asked.

"We think there should be an absolutely open net," Prudence said. "It should be like a force of nature. Just what it is. A place. The fact that anything goes is simply a feature of that place. Information in an information age must flow freely."

"The other side wants to control it," Yuri said, "and the trouble with control is the trouble with the old Russia. You'd think we would have learned our lesson. You'd think the whole world would have learned our lesson. If we can convince people that nothing can break their anonymity on our system, we can begin to build that conduit for the free exchange of ideas."

Yuri signaled for our server and ordered another round. I sat quietly while we waited for the drinks. Prudence gazed off into space. Yuri whistled a little tune softly until he saw me looking at him, and then he stopped. I knew he must be nervous to let a song come so close to the surface. For people like Yuri and me, humming a happy tune was dangerous. So was rhythmic finger tapping on the edge of the table. When I saw him return my pointed look with one of his own, I followed his eyes and saw my fingers drumming and folded my hands in my lap.

The new drinks arrived.

"It is a lot to ask for people just to trust you," I said. "What you've just told me would make good ad copy but you'll have some trouble selling it."

"So far selling it has been pretty easy," he said.

"People see they can trust four-e-four," Prudence said. "You can see it all over the newsgroups. People like the idea of the remailer being buried deep in Russia where the FBI for instance can't just pop in. Finland dropped the ball when their government busted up all the stuff going on over there a few years ago."

"That won't happen in Russia," Yuri said.

"What about that other faction?" I asked. "I bet you don't see a lot about them on the net."

"One problem is that the attitudes and much of the structure and many of the people of the old KGB are still in place," Yuri said. "This other faction I spoke of is almost entirely made up of people like that. And criminals. Many criminals. When the killer appeared on the net using our service, someone over there told someone over here to take care of it."

A light when on in my head.

"Your face just went red," Prudence said.

"Who is this KGB guy?" I asked.

"Most likely it will be Matusoff," Yuri said. "I know he has been operating in the Northwest for some time now."

"Big guy with a flat face and no fashion sense?"

"Well, that could be a lot of people," Yuri said, "but I suppose it could describe him, too. You've run into him?"

This had to be the guy who had jumped me in my office. "Maybe," I said. "Go on with your story."

"Here's our problem," Yuri said. "We want people to see that security on four-e-four is absolute. Even a murderer can be posting and we won't turn him in. On the other hand, a murderer hiding behind us could be very embarrassing."

When it hit me, it hit me hard. I put my drink down. I looked at

Prudence and then I looked at Yuri. Suddenly they were total strangers. I realized I didn't know them at all. What a sap I was.

"You know who the killer is," I said.

They didn't deny it.

Yuri and his people knew who the killer was and could have stopped him at any time by simply turning him in to the police. I wondered who on his list of victims would still be alive if they had done that.

"After Gerald Moffitt was killed," Yuri said, "the idea was to have you solve the case. That way it could be seen that traditional detective methods were sufficient for the problem. You were supposed to get your man before this."

"So, it's my fault?"

No response.

"I can't get over it," I said. "I'm busting my butt looking for Pablo and the killer and you could have just told me who he was in the first place."

"We gave you lots of clues!" Prudence said. Her tone was entirely defensive and that made me feel a little better. At least she seemed to have the good grace to feel guilty about the people who might have died needlessly.

"Was Nathan Ivanovich on the BOD list anonymously?"

"Yes," Yuri said, "and it's just that kind of quick thinking that we need you for."

"But all bad documentalists can't be members of BOD," I said. "Otherwise the list would be very big."

"Bad documentation is everywhere," Prudence said.

"You guys could have just given me the full list any time you wanted," I said.

"We will now." Prudence dipped into her bag and then handed me a printout.

I took a look. Everyone on the list now had a name and an address.

"What's done is done," Yuri said. "Now it's time to end this."

"What do you mean?"

"It's time to wrap it up," he said. "We tell you who the killer is and you go catch him. You can have all the credit. In fact, we insist on it."

I lifted my glass but it was empty.

"I suppose Pablo's not really missing," I said.

"No, he really is missing," Prudence said.

"So, tell me who the killer is," I said.

"He called himself SOAPY on-line," Yuri said. "We cut him off when he tried to take credit for Sadie Campbell."

"That's how we knew about her so soon," Prudence said.

"I already knew it was SOAPY," I said. "I already knew he'd been cut off at four-e-four-com."

"He called you," Yuri said. "Prudence told me." He wrote in his notebook again, ripped out the page, and handed it to me. "His name and address."

The name on the page was "J. Dotes." The address was a south-side apartment. The telephone was probably the one the killer had used to call me.

"Do you know this Dotes guy?" I asked.

They didn't.

The name wasn't as obviously fake as say John Doe, but I knew it would turn out to be an alias. Maybe the J was for John or maybe it was for Joe or James or Jack. What did it matter?

I got out the BOD list and looked it over quickly.

"Dotes isn't on this list," I said.

"No," Yuri said.

"It doesn't matter," Prudence said. "We know all about him from his SOAPY identity."

I doubted that. They hadn't thought it through.

"Let me see if I've got the game plan down," I said. "You've given me this name and address and you want me to drive over there and nab the killer?"

"That's right," Yuri said.

Prudence nodded in agreement. "It's a good plan."

I gathered up the notes Yuri had written and folded them in with the BOD list. I stood up. I walked away, and I didn't look back.

I hadn't decided what I was going to do. One option would be to call Marvin and turn the whole thing over to the police, but I wasn't ready to do that yet.

A couple of minutes later I was in my jeep heading south on Willamette. I'd considered becoming Tag, "the Average Guy," in case I ran into anyone I wouldn't want remembering what I looked like, but then I decided to remain Skylight Howells. If J. Dotes did turn out to be the killer, our encounter wouldn't be one that demanded subtlety.

There were apartment buildings on both sides of the street beyond Thirtieth, but it didn't take me long to find the one I was looking for. It was one of those two-story apartment buildings that looked like they'd been designed as the setting for some sleazy episode of *Cops* on TV. If you were going to have a crime of passion or a drug deal gone bad, it would probably happen in a place like this. Fist fights over loud music. Conflicts over parking.

I parked down the street from the address in question and walked back up to have a look from a safe distance first. I crossed to the other side of the street, but I couldn't actually see the target apartment from there, so I crossed back again. I'd have to get a lot closer.

By the time I actually could see the apartment, I was so close that I should have just walked up to it in the first place. Sometimes elaborate sneaking strategies come to nothing.

The apartment was on the second floor. The curtains over the big picture window were pulled open. There seemed to be no lights on inside. I walked on up the stairs.

When I got up there, I found a police department notice posted on the door. Crime scene. I was supposed to leave the place alone. That probably meant there was no one inside now. I knocked anyway.

No answer. I could pick the lock in a minute or so, but maybe it would be a good idea to look in the window first.

I wouldn't need to pick the lock. There was no glass in the picture window. I could see now where the outside walkway had been swept up. Inside, no one had bothered. Light glittered from the shards of broken glass. I looked both ways then carefully stepped inside.

I took out my penlight and had a quick look around. I found where bullets had hit the walls but I found no bloodstains. I wondered if Dotes had been shooting back.

My thinking ran like this. Yuri's "other faction," who would also know about Dotes/SOAPY had told someone, maybe Matusoff, to eliminate the killer, and Matusoff had come here to do the job. Dotes must have gotten away, though, or he wouldn't have been able to tell me someone had shot at him. So, why was Matusoff hassling me? It must have something to do with what I'd found at GP Ink—the DATAPANTS file that I no longer had. Or maybe I was just a loose end the other side was trying to tie up.

I checked out the rest of the apartment, but I didn't find anything that would tell me who Dotes might be. In fact, there seemed to be no personal stuff at all. I looked closely at the furniture and decided it had probably come with the apartment.

In the kitchen there were only empty plastic pop bottles in a recycle basket. Big bottles. High caffeine. I assumed the police had checked them for fingerprints. But maybe not. This probably wasn't a high-priority case, especially if there had been no one dead or wounded left on the scene.

I stepped back out the broken window, and walked back downstairs. I found the manager's apartment and while not exactly saying I was a reporter for one of the local TV stations, got her to tell me that J. Dotes wasn't a big guy, probably less than six feet tall. Brown hair. Blue eyes. Glasses. Very quiet. Mostly kept to himself.

He paid his rent in cash. Hadn't she asked for ID? Yes, she said, he had lots of ID. That would be a lie. You could tell by the way she looked away quickly when she said it.

I was satisfied I wouldn't be making a complete fool of myself when I turned this over to the police. I would let Marvin have it. That ought to irritate Frank. He grills me all afternoon then I turn over some key information to his sidekick.

I drove back downtown.

It might be a little tricky explaining just how I came to know that J. Dotes was the same man who called me about the fourth murder. Maybe I could tell Marvin the guy had called back, or that I'd puzzled out his identity from little clues in the first call.

Marvin would just have to be satisfied with whatever I came up with at the time. This information could be a break in the case. The police probably hadn't thought much about the shooting, but they would pay more attention when they learned it was connected to the Documentalist Killings.

I parked in my usual spot. From there I could see both my building and the police parking garage. I could walk over there now and tell my story. And cool my heels while they called Marvin in, or more likely tipped off Frank. Then I'd spend the rest of the night explaining myself. Frank had already run me through that routine, and once was enough.

I walked on back to my building.

Once inside I called the police and asked for Marvin Zivon. Gave them my name. They would look for him. He wouldn't be in. They would want to know if anyone else could help me. They would want to know if I wanted to leave a message. They would want to know what this was all about. I would need to make something up that would result in no one but Marvin calling me back.

But then Marvin said, "Hello?"

"So you're there."

"Why wouldn't I be?"

"I have some new information, Marvin," I said.

"I've been trying to call you, too."

"Really? What is it now?"

"You first," he said.

I gave him the address of the south-side apartment. "There was a shooting there," I said. "There'll already be a police report on it. The thing is the man who was living there is the man who called me about the fourth Documentalist Murder."

"You're sure?" Marvin asked. "Hang on."

Then I was listening to sappy police on-hold music.

But not for long.

"I got the report," Marvin said. "J. Dotes. What makes you think he's our guy?"

I hadn't decided what I was going to say about Yuri and Prudence yet, so I said, "I just twisted the known facts around a little."

"It seems to me you'd have to have more known facts than we have to come up with this," Marvin said.

"Look, Marvin," I said, "I'm handing this one to you on a silver platter. Can we worry about my sources later?"

"Maybe," he said. "We'll have to see how it pans out."

"Let's do that," I said. "So, what were you trying to get in touch with me about? It's not like I didn't see a lot of you already today."

"New information of my own." Marvin dropped the volume of his voice. "Disturbing personal information. We need to meet and hash it out. Tomorrow's Saturday. What say you drop in at the Whisper for lunch?"

"What's it all about, Marvin?"

"Maybe Mom will let you try the new chocolate pie she's working on."

"Your mother shops at K-Mart, Marvin."

"Hey! Watch it." Marvin never could come up with snappy comebacks for cracks about his mother. In this area he was pretty much defenseless.

It must have occurred to him that shopping at K-Mart wasn't exactly a major sin. "So?" he said.

"What is this new information of yours, Marvin?"

He lowered his voice again. "One of my guys recognized you while you were waiting to see Frank this afternoon."

"And?"

"He thought it was a little curious that you were the guy he spotted earlier having lunch with Frank's wife at the Garden Party," Marvin said.

Oh, boy.

"So," I said, "is noon okay for me to drop in and try your mom's new chocolate pie?"

fifteen

Saturday was sunny—fall interrupted by a sudden misplaced summer day. The balmy weather would make both buyers and sellers happy at the Saturday market. I decided to take a stroll through the market on my way to meet Marvin at the Whisper Café. I was trying not to think about what it might mean to my life in general that one of Marvin's guys had seen me with Elsie at the Garden Party. What was one of Marvin's guys doing at the Garden Party in the first place?

I put on a tie. It would confuse Marvin, and it would get me an approving nod from his mother. I decided to wear a mustache, too, even though many people seemed to recognize me when I was disguised as Skylight Howells. That caused me absolute panic when I first noticed it, but then I concluded it was a good thing, because when people saw me as Brian Dobson when I was really disguised as Skylight Howells, it meant I was really Skylight Howells disguised as Brian Dobson. In other words, I wore my ultimate disguise—Brian Dobson disguised as Skylight Howells disguised as Brian Dobson.

On the way out of my building, I ran into Prudence on her way in. She was dressed in a T-shirt and cutoff jeans (with cuffs, which meant she probably hadn't cut them off herself) and sandals, and she looked so good I knew I couldn't concentrate on anything until she was out of sight.

"So, what's new?" she asked.

"Oh, this and that." I kept walking.

"Our guy in jail yet?"

"Not yet."

She hooked her arm in mine. "Off to do some shopping or some snooping?"

"An appointment," I said and stopped walking.

"I want to go with you this morning," she said.

"Why?"

"You need to wrap this up," she said. "What if we forgot to tell you something? If that happens and I'm there, I can just fill in the blanks."

She tried to blind me with her floodlight smile.

"I'm working on another case this morning," I said.

"There's no time to waste."

"I'm not wasting time," I said. "I checked out the address Yuri gave me. It looks like your KGB guy got there first. I'd say he scared Dotes into deep hiding."

I noticed we were walking toward the market. Since we hadn't resolved anything, I stopped again.

"You can't go," I said. "I work alone."

"But you need me today."

"No way."

"Way."

"I can't believe you said that."

"Isn't that what you're supposed to say?" She looked genuinely confused for a moment, but then she gave me that megawatt smile again, and we were walking *again*. I felt like a horse she'd urged into motion with her heels. Once we were moving she let me have my head. I was the one who knew where we were going this sunny Saturday morning.

We came to Eighth Avenue, and I turned left. The Saturday market was a street fair just down the block. On one side there were the booths and tables of fresh produce that made up the organic farmers' market. I made a note to drop by on my way back and pick up some organic stuff to juice. On the other side of the street was the edge of the little city that was the Saturday market itself. A trip to the market was a trip back to a kinder era maybe—a tie-dyed time, a time of flowers and incense and low-tech solutions and sweat. The twisted labyrinth of alleys between the booths was filled with people. It was not a good place to be if you needed a large sphere of your own space, not a place for people afraid to rub elbows with strangers. I led Prudence into the crowd.

We stopped to look at exquisite ceramic tiles. We strolled past mirrors in handcrafted wooden frames. And tie-dyed shirts and dresses and pants. Walls of tie-dyed sheets—big purple, yellow, green, and red squares moving gently in the breeze. We passed booths where you could get your face painted and booths where you could get a massage and booths where you could have your life decoded with tarot cards.

I glanced at my watch and saw that I didn't have much time before my lunch date with Marvin at the Whisper Café.

I made sure she was looking at me, and then I glanced quickly over my shoulder and then back down at a tray of glittering beaded jewelry. "Oh boy," I said softly.

She didn't get it. I'd expected her to ask what I'd seen when I looked over my shoulder. I moved on to the next booth, and tried again.

No luck. She was oblivious.

One more time.

Zip.

I pulled her quickly around the booth and hurried over two rows and around a guy juggling painted sticks.

"What are we doing?" she asked.

"We're being followed," I said. "Look, this could be dangerous. I think we should split up."

"I want to stay with you," she said.

"It's too dangerous. Besides how do we know they're following me? Maybe they're following you."

I could see she was thinking about that. "What will you do if they're following me?"

"Once I see which way the wind blows, I'll either lose them or, if they're following you, I'll start following them, following the both of you, that is."

"Well, I don't know," she said.

She stepped back to let a woman with three parrots crawling around on her shoulders and head pass between us.

"It'll be easy." I grabbed her arm and pulled her toward the center courtyard.

We came to the booths devoted to food. Tofu and rice, Indian food, burritos, noodles, steamed vegetables. The booths were situated on either side of two long rows of tables. Where the tables stopped there was an open area for dancing and beyond that a small stage where a band was playing.

People dancing by themselves. People dancing with babies. Flutes and smoke. Bare feet and jeans and beads and big floppy hats. People dancing without inhibition—not drunken abandon, just joyous jumping around. I had to look away.

"Here's what we do," I said. "You sit down on the grass here like you're going to listen to the music, and I'll lead them off. If they follow me that's one thing. If they hang around here that's another. Either way, we'll know what's what."

She scanned the crowd. "I don't see anyone."

"Don't look around like that," I said. "You want to tip him off that we're on to him?"

I could tell she was suspicious, but I was pretty sure she'd go along with me, and if things worked out right, she'd still be here listening to the music when I got back from my meeting with Marvin. I didn't want to get rid of her. I just wanted to park her for a while.

I got her settled on the grass, then instead of just walking off, I stepped over to the Smoothie booth and bought her a lemon Smoothie. "Don't look around like you're wise," I whispered when I leaned down to hand it to her. "I'll be back."

She took a sip of her Smoothie and made a sour face then smiled up at me, making me feel guilty. I melted back into the crowd.

I stopped before I lost sight of her altogether. I saw her take another sip of her Smoothie and shudder. She leaned over and tapped on the shoulder of a young guy with enough hair for a family of four. She said something to him and he grinned. She handed him the drink. She got up and stood on one foot to take off one of her sandals. Then she stood on the other foot to take off the other one. She dropped the sandals into the hands of the young man still sitting in the grass. She laughed at something he said. When she joined the dancers, I noticed I was not the only one watching her. Everyone seemed to be watching her. It was not so much grace, she wasn't really very graceful, and it was not so much that she was beautiful, and she really was beautiful, no, I think what was attracting attention was the obvious fact that she was so completely enjoying herself. It was as if she knew she didn't know how to dance to such music, but she was willing to learn and was totally trusting that no one would be mean to her about being a beginner.

I could have stood there all afternoon watching her. I glanced at my watch again and saw that I was already going to be fashionably late for lunch with Marvin. I had to force myself to leave.

I'd been so busy trying to stash her somewhere until after lunch that I hadn't been paying much attention to what was really going on around me. It was a surprise when I walked around a couple of booths and came to the street and saw a man duck quickly back into the hubbub as I looked his way.

Someone really was following me!

I crossed the street and doubled back. A moment later the man stepped out of hiding and looked down the street. He was the same guy I'd surprised at GP Ink, the guy who had jumped me in my office. A white bandage held his nose in place and covered the damage I'd done with my Thermos bottle.

My current theory said this was the guy who had shot at J. Dotes— the former KGB agent Yuri had described. Matusoff. It looked like he was wearing the same cheap suit. His hair was thin and graying, but it had once been a very light brown, almost blond. He was older than I would have guessed from the way he punched and moved.

He didn't see me in the direction I'd been walking so he scanned back the other way and saw me standing there looking at him. I got some satisfaction from the look on his face when he realized I was on to him. He put his hand in his coat, probably to make sure his gun was handy, and moved quickly my way. He wasn't shadowing me now. In fact, if I didn't get a move on he would catch me. I turned and ducked back into the confusion of the market.

I was pretty sure I knew where Matusoff fit into the big picture. Yuri had filled in the missing information when he'd told me about the other faction and the KGB. Matusoff was trying to solve the case by killing the killer. He was trying to clean up anything at GP Ink that might point to Evil Empire Software. The effort and attention he'd recently been paying me was troubling, but even as I thought about the problem, a possible solution popped into my head.

Two facts: I was being chased by a bad guy and I was on my way to have lunch with a cop. Put those two together. Bad guy and cop. Maybe it was time Matusoff met Marvin Zivon. I slowed down so I wouldn't lose him altogether, and glanced back to see where he was. He wasn't behind me.

I stopped. It didn't make sense he'd just give up. That probably meant he was trying to get around in front of me so I'd walk right into him.

I felt a hand on my arm. He'd come up between a booth selling all kinds of hats and the traveling headquarters of Hooray for Hemp. The hand that wasn't on my shoulder was in his coat, and he pulled his gun out just enough for me to see.

Instead of jerking away from him, I pushed him back and he had to do some fancy footwork to keep from falling into the hats. When he let go of me I took off through the crowd again.

I could see him keeping pace with me a couple of rows over. I guess you could say my plan was working. We were getting closer to the edge of the market and he was still chasing me. I dodged around a young girl playing a wooden recorder for change. The crowd was slowing him down but soon we'd be in the clear, and I'd be easier to catch.

I got to the edge of the market and looked east down Eighth. I turned and looked west and saw a troop of power walkers in purple workout clothes approaching on the sidewalk. I slipped out of the city of arts and crafts, food and music, and fell in with them.

"We don't mind," a sweating woman huffed at me, "but you've got to pick up the pace. This is not just fast walking. Here. Like this."

So I did my best to imitate the way you pretend you've got a stick up your ass and pump your arms when you're power walking, a practice that was once again sweeping through the city as the latest fitness craze. Matusoff (if that was his real name) stood for a moment looking absolutely baffled, but then he hurried after us.

The power walkers left the market behind and turned onto the downtown mall. I got deeper into their midst. Just a block or so more and we'd be pumping by the Whisper Café. I hoped Marvin was already there. Matusoff was losing patience. He moved in on us, but then since he couldn't reach me, he fell back again. He tried again, reaching across a woman who swatted at his hand. The other walkers were grumbling and giving him dirty looks. I knew that wouldn't be enough to stop him. He was probably already calculating the risks and rewards of just busting into the middle of things and grabbing or shooting me.

The Whisper Café was coming up on the right. There were several people sitting at the sidewalk tables, but I didn't see Marvin. There was a man with a newspaper in front of his face. Marvin? I didn't know, but I had no choice now. Even if Marvin hadn't arrived yet, there simply wasn't any way to call off my plan.

As we came even with the café, I stopped walking and let the power walkers flow around me. When they'd passed, Matusoff and I were standing almost toe to toe and nose to nose.

I yelled for help and leaped onto him.

On my way down to the ground, I glanced over at the café. The newspaper reader had lowered his paper. He was not Marvin Zivon.

So Matusoff and I mixed it up.

I was doing generally okay. I was younger, and I'd been drinking a lot of juice lately, but I'd never been what you would call an expert at this hand-to-hand stuff. I'd once thought of developing a black belt disguise, but I had never gotten around to devoting the years of study and training it would have taken to actually do it, so while I was not being totally vanquished, I was also losing ground. I was, in fact, on the bottom, and the guy on top banged my head down on the sidewalk, once, twice, and I saw clouds of fuzzy black balls, swarms of colored foil stars, paisley bits and tie-dyed pieces.

Then there was the distinctive sound of a gun being cocked. Matusoff froze. There may have been a conversation. My ears were ringing. Matusoff got off me. I rolled over and climbed to my hands and knees and looked up to see Marvin Zivon and his gun. Matusoff put his hands where Marvin could see them.

"Watch out, Marvin," I said. "He's got a gun. In his coat."

Marvin patted him down and disarmed him. I climbed to my feet.

Sirens. Marvin must have already called it in. I wondered how long he'd let Matusoff beat on me before he decided enough was enough.

I put my hand on the back of my head, looked at it. No blood, but there would be a bump, definitely a bump, maybe a couple of bumps, and a championship headache.

"This is the guy who broke into my office," I said. I could have told him about surprising the guy at GP Ink, too, but then I would have had to admit that I'd bowled Marvin and Frank over in the hallway and fled the scene. "You might want to check him against what you've got on that south-side apartment shooting, too."

Marvin gave me a look that told me to quit screwing around and let him do his job.

I wobbled over to one of the sidewalk tables and collapsed into a chair.

A police car pulled up and a couple of uniforms hurried over to help Marvin. It didn't take them long to bundle up the bad guy and leave. Marvin came over and sat down opposite me.

"Do you ever get the feeling we're all on TV?" I asked him.

"Never," he said.

"So, what's for lunch?" I leaned back to look through the windows into the restaurant itself and nearly toppled myself in surprise. Everyone inside was looking out at me. Mrs. Zivon herself stood just behind the glass. I smiled at her and waved.

I had what you would call mixed feelings about Marvin's mom. On the one hand, I had always liked her. She had always been nice to me when we were kids. But on the other hand, she had always been my mother's biggest rival, and now that my mother couldn't fight back, it was like my duty to take up the slack. Not to mention the fact that I'd always been able to get Marvin steamed by making cracks about her.

She smiled at me and then looked at Marvin who must have given her a signal of some kind. She turned away and began shooing her customers back to their tables. She grabbed a waiter and pointed at us and a moment later he appeared at our table with menus. Marvin waved his away, but I took a look.

"So what does the Willamette shooting have to do with this?" Marvin asked.

"Did you have a body on that one?"

"No," he said. "It would have been tossed over to us in homicide if there had been a body."

"I'm pretty sure that's the apartment the killer was in when he called me," I said.

"Who's the guy I just sent to jail?"

"I don't know who he is," I said. "The killer in the Willamette apartment was calling himself J. Dotes. You get anything on that?"

"Far as we can tell, it's a totally fake identity," Marvin said. "This wasn't our case, but we're getting good cooperation. It's too early to tell how good the fake is. It could be a complete dead end, you know."

"That's probably exactly what it is," I said. "Otherwise, things would be too easy."

So J. Dotes was, as I'd suspected, a complete fake. What this meant from a more personal point of view was that while the Russians thought they knew who the killer was, they were wrong.

Yuri and Prudence had thought they were being so clever in their manipulation of me, but it turned out they needed a real detective after all.

The waiter returned.

Marvin ordered the prawns in Costa Rica sauce. I ordered the cold roast beef sandwich. With horseradish sauce? Sure, why not. With horseradish sauce. No way you could get out of the Whisper Café without sauce.

Marvin would start with a double latte. I would have a cappuccino.

"Now about this other matter," I said.

"Hold that thought," Marvin said. He put his napkin down on the table and stood up. "Mother. Look who's come to lunch."

"Brian!" Mrs. Zivon said. "So, how is your dear mother these days?"

I got up. She put her hands out and I took them and gave them both a little squeeze. She was a large woman and tall but not so large and tall that you would immediately guess she was Marvin's mother.

"Mom's doing pretty well," I said, not really fooling anyone since everyone knew Mom had finally gone around the bend and probably wasn't ever coming back.

Mrs. Zivon moved her gaze quickly from my face and pulled her hands away. "I'm glad," she said. She touched my tie. "You must have looked very nice before your wrestling match today, Brian."

Because she and my mother had once moved in the same circles, because we were all the right kind of people, she simply didn't understand that Marvin and I might not be buddies forever, that things had changed a lot since we were tap-dancing kids. In an orderly world, Marvin and I would have been partners in a local law firm or maybe doctors, and Frank Wallace, who came from the other side of the tracks, would have been in jail where he could never have lured Marvin into following him into a life of public service.

The waiter brought our coffee. He seemed unsure just what he was supposed to do when his customers were standing and the owner was hovering. He put the coffee down and then stood there for a moment, and then he just wandered off.

I looked at Mrs. Zivon. I looked at Marvin. They looked at me. They looked at one another. There wasn't anything more to say.

"Sit down," Mrs. Zivon said at last. "Enjoy your lunch." She turned away and walked back inside.

"Marvin," I said. "Your mother wears tennis shoes."

I could see the wheels turning. It was true; his mother did wear tennis shoes. Everyone wore tennis shoes. She was wearing a pair that very moment.

"Jesus, Brian," he said, "you had to reach for that one."

"Yeah, well, okay, back to the business at hand."

"I won't beat around the bush," Marvin said. "One of my guys spotted Elsie Wallace lunching with some guy at the Garden Party. Didn't think anything of it. The only reason he remembered at all is that he thought it was Frank and he was on his way over to suck up when he saw that he was mistaken and turned away just in time."

"You're saying your crack operative mistook me for Frank Wallace?"

"It was the bushes," Marvin said. "The place is full of weeds and bushes. Then a couple of days later he's walking past Frank's office and he sees you sitting there on the bench looking like you're getting ready to be fried."

"So, why didn't he just tell Frank?"

"Frank's not real good with bad news of a personal nature," Marvin said.

"What did he do when you told him?" I asked.

"I haven't told him."

I let that sit there while the waiter put Marvin's salad down in front of him.

"Hey, I wonder what that would taste like as juice," I said. It looked like spinach and tomatoes and avocado and bean sprouts and carrots and other things I couldn't identify.

Marvin must have thought I was paying too much attention to his salad. "You could have ordered one of your own," he said.

"So, why didn't you tell Frank?"

"Frank's been acting weird," Marvin said. "Maybe it's all connected. I wanted you to tell me what's going on first."

"What do you mean he's been acting weird?"

"I'm supposed to be asking the questions here," Marvin said. "The idea is I eat my salad and you tell me what you were doing with Elsie at the Garden Party."

"Elsie and I are old friends," I said. "You know that."

Marvin made a show of forking up salad and saying nothing.

"It was just lunch, Marvin," I said. "A couple of old friends having lunch. Like now. Well, sort of like now."

Marvin waited for me to go on.

"Okay, Elsie thinks he's acting weird, too," I said. "She just needed someone to talk to."

"What did she tell you?"

"Nothing more than that," I said. "After we established the fact that Frank was acting weird, we mostly talked about old times."

Marvin looked like he was going to ask another question but then he turned his attention back to his salad. I'd pretty much told all the lies I was going to tell about my lunch with Elsie.

Other people were beginning to notice that Frank was up to something. I supposed you could slip away to the Quack Inn only so often before your partner realized something unusual was happening.

"So Frank's up to something and he hasn't told you what it is?"

"Maybe I shouldn't have mentioned that," Marvin said.

The waiter came by and took away Marvin's empty salad plate.

"Just tell me straight out, Brian," he said, "are you and Elsie messing around behind Frank's back?"

"That's a stupid idea, Marvin," I said. "I lost that battle a long long time ago. If you ran that idea past Frank, he'd laugh in your face. If something's up with him, it's not because of me."

"I had to ask."

"So, are you going to tell him about it?"

"I don't know," Marvin said. "I guess not. No, I don't see how that would do anyone any good."

The waiter brought my sandwich and Marvin's prawns, and I didn't say anything until I had taken a big bite, chewed slowly, swallowed, had some coffee, and looked around at the people in the summer clothes they'd thought would hang in the closet until spring.

"That's probably wise," I said finally.

Marvin forked a prawn out of the Costa Rica sauce. "Yes," he said and ate the prawn.

"Okay," I said.

"Right."

"You're not going to tell me anything else about Frank, are you?"

"No," he said.

"Right," I said.

"Okay," he said.

Marvin ate another prawn. Then another. He picked up speed. Soon he was eating his prawns like they might come alive again and get away.

A little later we each had a piece of his mother's new chocolate pie, and when we were done, Marvin signed the check. "I'd better go see what your wrestling buddy has to say. Frank will want to know about it when he gets back."

I didn't bother to ask where Frank was going to be getting back from. Frank would be at the Quack Inn.

"You'll let me know what the bad guy has to say?"

"Probably not," Marvin said. He got up, and I got up. "Stay out of trouble, Brian." He tossed his napkin down on the table and walked away.

I went inside the Whisper Café to say a few nice things about lunch to Mrs. Zivon, and then I wandered back to the Saturday Market to see if Prudence Deerfield was still where I'd left her. If I could find her again, maybe I'd ask her to have dinner with me.

The band had finished and the dancing space was empty. I spent some time searching through the market, but I didn't find her.

I wanted to brag about the way I'd taken out the former KGB guy. I wanted her to be impressed by the way I'd solved the problem of the other Russian faction.

No Prudence.

I wandered through the farmer's market buying things to juice. By the time I was done I had way more than I could use in one day. The rest would probably spoil.

Unless I did something about it.

I spent the afternoon shopping for a small refrigerator, and finally settled on one a little taller than my knees. The deciding factor was that I could pick it up.

Back in the office I put the new refrigerator next to the couch and plugged it in. I thought it looked pretty good there, like an unusual end table—a humming white cube. I put a lamp on top of it.

sixteen

The next morning I got up convinced it was time to take a look inside Frank's room at the Quack Inn. It wasn't likely he'd be there. I put my pants on and walked to the window behind my desk and pulled up the blinds. By stepping to the left and looking right, I could see a strip of street and sky, and I saw that fall had returned. The sky was full of comfortable clouds, a light rain was falling, and there were already puddles in the holes in the alley. I put my hand flat against the glass; it would be chilly out. This was not going to be another confusing summer day.

When I didn't make coffee in the office, I usually went out and bought an extra-large super-strong from a booth down the street and drank it while I shaved and showered and got into the getup of whoever I was going to be first. That morning I just didn't feel caffeine deprived, didn't crave that big cup of sludge so much. In fact I felt like having some juice.

I got down on my knees and opened my new refrigerator and breathed in the cool smell of fresh fruit and vegetables. I love new devices. Until a thing sits around a while, it is the star of my stuff. I liked the little white plastic tray under the tiny freezer (which they warned me was not to be used to keep frozen foods very long). There were a couple of neat little wire shelves that fit perfectly. And my piles of fruit and vegetables.

I grabbed a mango (chopped out the huge seed), two apples (one green and one red), a banana, some spinach (call me crazy), a lime, and a carrot, and extracted a big glass of juice. I cleaned up the equipment while I drank it. My trash can was getting a little overburdened with pulp. There was a ripe smell like something fermenting, and there were little black flies circling around inside. Or maybe those were little black spots before my eyes. I decided to think of them as flies, and I put the trash can out in the hall.

I shaved and showered, put on a fresh mustache and a quick shine to my shoes. Grabbed my coat, hat, and umbrella. Slipped my smallest camera into my coat pocket. I'd be inside and close up. No need for a long lens.

Locked up. Picked up the pulp-filled trash can. Waved away the flies. Took the elevator to the street. I opened my umbrella and ducked into the alley and emptied the trash can in the dumpster. I put the can on the ground. I'd probably forget it was there until I wanted to throw something away, and then I'd have to walk down here and get it.

I walked to the parking lot and my jeep. I glanced over at Lulu's Escort, mostly just to make sure it was still there and reminded myself to get her to fire it up soon so the battery would stay charged. She needed to check for mushrooms growing in the carpet, too. If we didn't watch out they'd be as big as people, and one day she'd run out here needing the car quickly and there would be no room for her inside.

I got in the jeep and circled around to Broadway. Broadway became Franklin Boulevard. I drove slowly by the Quack Inn and took a look. Frank wasn't parked anywhere I could see. I hadn't expected him to be there on a Sunday morning, but it's good not to get overconfident. You start seeing only what you want to see when your confidence gets too high. Unless you're confident because you have the situation under control, which was how I felt that morning.

I made a legal U-turn and swung by the Quack Inn once more. Things looked pretty quiet. The Tail Feathers Lounge wouldn't be open yet. There weren't many cars, so maybe there wouldn't be many people staying over, and if there weren't many people staying over, maybe the manager would decide to sleep in. I parked down the block and walked back to the motel. The rain had picked up some, and I was glad for it. Rain would cut down the visibility from the motel office. You might mistake me for a guy with a key, and I might be able to slip into Frank's room, before it hit you that, hey, that man is picking the lock! The secret is to look natural. Look like you know where you're going and what you're doing.

I stopped when I came even with the window of the motel office and glanced inside. No one behind the desk. I walked directly to Frank's door. I had my lock-picking tools out by the time I got there. I learned lock picking from a mail-order locksmithing course, and I had spent hundreds of hours practicing. It was one of the things I did really well. From some distance away I recognized the lock and knew just what to do.

I'd already decided not to knock first. I figured the outcome would be the same if I didn't knock and opened the door and Frank was inside and if I did knock and he was inside and opened the door and saw me standing there. Go for broke I told myself, just open the door and walk on in.

I would have the door open in only slightly more time than it would take someone with a key. Unless something went wrong, and there is no activity on Earth in which nothing can go wrong. Something can always go wrong. That's when you need to stand straight and look like maybe you're lost in thought or maybe you've accidentally tried to put your car key in the motel lock (silly you) as you jiggle and jerk at the tumblers and they fall into place at last and there is a barely audible *snick* when the lock yields and the bold turns.

I suppose I still expected Frank to grab me and jerk me inside. I ducked as I slipped into the room, picturing him standing there with one fist cocked behind his head so he could bop me a good one in the nose. I closed the door behind me and straightened up for a quick look around. It was pretty dim in there with the curtains closed. I could see there was something on the bed, but whatever it was, it didn't have enough depth to be a person.

The bathroom door was ajar. Frank could be in there. I didn't think he was. I walked across the room to the bathroom and flipped on the light. No one.

Back in the room itself I carefully pulled the curtain back a little and peeked out. Nothing stirring. No frantic phone dialing activity in the motel office that I could see. That didn't mean someone with a level head hadn't called the police as I ducked inside.

I wasn't worried. It looked like I hadn't been seen. I turned on the lamp on the dresser by the door. A yellow legal pad with diagrams and notes. The diagrams included stick figures and arrows. I would come back and look at this closely after I checked the rest of the room. Just seeing the pad there gave me a big boost morale-wise. There had been the chance that the room would be completely empty of anything pertaining to Frank Wallace. There had been the chance that I would learn nothing from this exercise. The legal pad told me that I would at least get something. Then, too, there was the stuff on the bed. I turned on the bedside lamp.

For a moment I wasn't exactly sure what I was looking at. It might have been a set of summer clothes carefully laid out. Maybe the person wearing them had gone to bed and then disappeared. A pretty weird person, too, judging from the outfit. Long black socks, and what looked like black rubber briefs, a vest of the same material, and gloves. I picked up a glove and discovered it was connected to the bed by a long flexible cable.

It was a dataglove.

Both gloves were datagloves. And the socks. Datasocks? The vest, too.

I picked up the briefs. They felt the way soft rubber feels—somehow wet but not wet. I couldn't help looking at my fingers to see if anything had rubbed off on them.

I discovered a ribbon of cable attached to the back of the rubber briefs like a multicolored tail. The connections were clicking into place, but the kicker was the little logo in small white letters along the lower edge of the left leg of the briefs: DATAPANTS.

Frank was somehow mixed up with the Russians and Evil Empire Software! The edges of my two major cases were blurring together. Somehow the two cases were one case. It was more than the fact that Frank was the investigating officer for the murders. He was involved at an entirely different level.

I put the datapants down and picked up the vest. I followed a cable from the vest down to the floor and found the virtual reality helmet. Sound and sight, the works. Everything terminated at a box beside the bed. I knelt down beside it and saw a small red light. This would be the computer and it was on. I suppose I could go in and see what was what. Did I want to do that?

All those times Frank had slipped away to spend his lunch hour in this room, he had been going into a virtual reality and doing God only knew what.

I sat down on the edge of the bed. Then I stood right back up again. I had sunk into the surface. In fact, I could see that the impression my butt had made was only now slowly filling in. I pushed a hand down on the bed. The surface was warm, probably the temperature of the human body, and my hand sank and was swallowed by the stuff. It looked slick, and it felt like Jell-O. I wondered how far you sank when you were in the helmet and pants and vest and gloves and socks and fully reclined on it.

There was something sleazy about the whole set up. The cheap decor of the motel room didn't help nor the dim light and lonely shadows, but it was more than that. I took out my camera and carefully photographed everything in the room.

Maybe things looked better from the inside.

Someday VR will be so good you won't be able to tell the difference between it and what we're currently calling reality and when that happens we will have achieved our ultimate purpose as technological beings. If you think about it, you'll agree that it's possible the reason we hear no one from the depths of space is because when a society reaches a certain level of technology, people discover they can go in and have whatever they want, so they no longer struggle to go out.

I put my camera away and walked to the window and peeked out again. Still not much activity. I put the security chain in place. I considered putting out the DO NOT DISTURB sign, but then decided I couldn't chance it. What if Frank never put it out? Maybe he had an understanding with the management. Surely ordinary maids wouldn't be making up this room.

I picked up the yellow legal pad on the dresser. Underneath it was a brochure from Evil Empire Software. How to use the DATA-PANTS and other VR stuff. I thought it was pretty considerate of Frank to leave me the instructions.

Or maybe not.

If this pamphlet ever came to the attention of the Documentalist Killer, whoever had produced it would be toast. To begin with, the equipment in the first illustration was entirely different from the stuff on the bed. The first sentence read, "These remarks may not pertain to the equipment you have just removed from the box."

It got worse.

By the time I'd jungle-chopped my way to the end, I had no real idea what to do. I did have a few general guidelines, though, and a couple of possible principles—one of which was that the surface of the vest and pants should be in contact with bare skin.

So you took off your clothes and got into the stuff on the bed. You put on the helmet. You lay down. Were there switches to flip? Key sequences to enter? Magic words? Those were not the kind of questions the documentation answered. I tossed the pamphlet back onto the dresser.

I flipped through Frank's legal pad and decided he could benefit from an aggressive schedule of therapy. The drawings mostly included two stick figures perhaps engaged in martial arts or maybe having sex (or even dancing). The notes were absolutely indecipherable. Frank must type his own police reports. Who could read his handwriting? There were pages and pages of mathematics, but it all looked like simple arithmetic. Columns of numbers added up. Columns of numbers multiplied. Maybe he was taking a remedial math course in cyberspace. I put the legal pad back down on top of the VR pamphlet.

There was only one way to find out what was going on here. I took off my coat. I slipped off my shoes. I'd known I was going to do this as soon as I'd dropped the security chain in place. Reading the instructions and Frank's legal pad had been delaying tactics. I took off my pants.

There was a question of hygiene, and I did what I could (I don't want to talk about it). Once in the gear, I could see myself in the long mirror on the back of the bathroom door. Black socks to mid-calf. Black rubber briefs and vest. Close fittings gloves. The data helmet under one arm. I would never get into the Space Rangers looking like this, but outer space was not my destination anyway. I lowered myself onto the bed and put on the helmet.

The bed grabbed me. I felt myself being pulled down, and I struggled for a moment. Relax, I told myself, float. Okay.

I was in the dark. Maybe there really were magic words or magic passes you had to make to activate the thing. Sudden panic. What if the bed had pulled me under the surface of the Jell-O and now nothing whatever would happen and I'd be trapped like a bug in a smear of maple syrup?

Things clicked into place just before I would have flipped out. A low hum from the left side growing and changing until it was the *whomp whomp whomp* of an approaching helicopter. Light on a new horizon like dawn. Super speed. God pulled up the blinds of the world to take a peek inside. A puff of air that made me gag on the smell of sewage. The taste of apples and cinnamon.

The taste and smell stuff needed work. Maybe they were the same; maybe the taste was a side effect of the smell.

The light grew until I could see a checkerboard of green and red and yellow squares stretching away to infinity. Big spheres floated down from the sky, bounced, and floated back up and disappeared in the clouds. My first reaction was disappointment. This virtual reality, at least visually speaking, was not an advance over others I had seen on TV.

Then I realized this was a place, an actual space you could occupy and move around in. Experiencing such a reality is a lot different from looking at it on TV. I held out my hands, and they were stylized computer drawn hands. I looked down at my feet. They were hairy with big dirty toes—nice comic touch, I thought. I stepped forward and the world turned. I was not flat on my back floating in warm goo. I was upright and walking.

I could see how I was perfect for a world like this. It didn't matter that it was still pretty crude. I had always had a lot of control over my own reality. It would be easy for me to layer over the bare bones of this world deep and rich structures of my own.

I reached down and grabbed the ground and pulled it up as if it were a flexible multicolored sheet and fashioned a tree. I sat down and combed my fingers through the surface and grass grew in the furrows I made. I rubbed my feet, molded them, and made shoes. Dennis's shoes. I pulled his glasses out of the surface of my face. "Hey, neat!" Dennis said.

I pushed his glasses back into my face and grew Sky's mustache again and stood up.

I softened my body, molded it this way and that, grew a wondrous purple satin gown, became Lulu.

So easy. Even the tacos would be perfect here, Dieter thought.

A cloud of fish swam by, and Scarface grinned, and if you knew Scarface you would know how rare (and horrible) that was.

"The Average Guy" flashed on and off, on and off, confused because things were changing so quickly the average was hard to calculate.

We finally settled on being Lulu, because we liked the easy and open way she handled new situations.

We could be anything we wanted here.

And that, I realized, was a tremendous danger for someone like me. I could see myself coming into a world like this and never coming out. It was spooky how this all felt so much like coming home.

Right now though I had work to do. What would Frank be doing in here?

I turned in a complete circle to get a look at everything. Before I completed the circle, I saw a figure approaching. I felt a shiver of fear run through my entire body. I was not alone. That changed everything.

The figure grew rapidly as if the person were zooming over the surface, floating rather than walking or running. A man, I could see. He swung way to the left and got very small and I thought maybe he wasn't coming my way after all.

"Hey!" I yelled.

The man became a small black dot in the distance, but before he disappeared, he turned and swooped back at me fast, faster, much faster than he'd been traveling before. In seconds, he was full-sized and standing in front of me. I gasped in surprise and took a step back.

If the person standing before me had not clearly been a man, I might have thought I was looking at Prudence Deerfield with a new haircut. He held out his hand and a crazy fractal bluebird landed on his finger.

"Hello," the beautiful man said. "My name is Pablo."

seventeen

The bluebird flew away. Pablo tore a hole in the air and reached in and pulled out a metallic red fruit. He bit into it and waves of tartness radiated from his grin. Red juice ran from the corners of his mouth. "What's with the new look?"

I didn't have anything to say to that.

"Come on, Franky," he said. "Get with it. Are you asleep or what?"

He thought I was Frank Wallace. I had come into the system where Frank usually appeared—Frank's "node" or whatever, so I must be Frank—no matter how I looked. Did I want to pretend I was Frank? Did I think I could?

"I'm not Frank," I said.

"Of course you're not," he said. "My mistake. Maybe it's the light." He touched me, and the feel of his hand on my arm was so real I gasped.

"I'm really not Frank Wallace," I said, backing away from him.

He took a step after me. "Okay, you're a stranger. Do you come here often? Do I know your sign? Have we played this game before?"

He kept advancing and I kept stepping back. Did I really want to know what Frank had been up to in here?

I held up my hands. "Will you stop and listen to me?"

He did stop. There was still a sly smile on his face. "Okay, who are you then?"

"Your sister hired us."

"My sister?" He took a step back. He dropped the red fruit, but it disappeared before it hit the ground. Trees sprang up, grew leaves, grew alarm clocks with mechanical hands and brass bells like teddy bear ears. All the alarm clocks went off at once.

The world rocked to the left, and I stumbled and fell to my hands and knees. The world rocked back to the right. Swarms of birds with boom boxes blackened the sky. I scrambled to my feet as big-stepping R. Crumb babes pushing lawnmowers appeared from every direction. It looked to me like I was the point at which they'd all converge, and I wanted to run off every way at once. I cycled through my disguises like riffling through a deck of cards and settled on Sky.

I bent my knees and leaped straight up just before the gum-chewing, sweat-slinging cartoons and their grass-tossing machines came crashing together. Sparks and smoke and jagged yellow light below. The words "Kapow" and "Boom!"

A breeze moved me away from the carnage and I floated gently back to earth. Pablo appeared at my side.

"Skylight?" His voice had changed. His face blurred. His body became clay molded by invisible fingers, and when she was done shapeshifting, Prudence said, "I can't imagine how you came to be here. Since you've come in through Frank's port, you must be in his room in the Quack Inn. Is he there with you?"

"No," I said.

"This can't be good," she said. "I told Yuri if we didn't watch out, you'd find out more than you needed to know."

Our voices seemed just right in the infinite plane of diminishing squares. Prudence had on the same shirt and jeans she'd been wearing when she was Pablo. I reached out and when our hands touched, I shuddered. Here was a real advance. The sensation of touch was deliciously real.

"What was that all about?" I asked.

"Bells and whistles," she said. "Welcome to the future."

"You really do work for Evil Empire."

"Why do you say that?"

" 'Welcome to the future' is a very corporate thing to say." I hadn't let go of her hand. "And you didn't really answer my question."

"An intruder alarm," she said. "I'll clean up the mess."

Mountains formed at the horizon. They grew impossibly high and then rushed across the plain like a tsunami and overtook us. They washed away the lawnmower carnage and grew up and under and around us, and I held onto her hand and we rode it out.

At first the meadow was merely sketched, but details soon appeared. Birds, grass, and the gurgling sounds of a creek, puffy white clouds, bugs, forested hills on all sides. The air grew cooler and thinner, and the sunlight felt good on my skin.

A Disney deer popped out of the trees, took a look at us, and darted away.

Prudence tossed a scrap of cloth onto the ground, and it multiplied in many colors and became a patchwork quilt. A bump struggled like a trapped puppy and then became a brown wicker picnic basket. Prudence got down on her knees beside the basket. "Sit down," she said.

I sat down on the quilt. She opened up the basket and looked inside, then she looked up at me and smiled. "What would you like?"

"Pablo doesn't exist," I said.

"Potato salad?"

"Prudence."

"No, he doesn't exist," she said. "At least not out there. Not the way you mean."

"You have no brother? You're the P in GP Ink?"

"Yes," she said. "I'm the P. How about some juice? I know you've been drinking a lot of juice lately."

"Sure," I said. "Juice. Do you run the Pablo persona in here all the time?"

"What kind?"

"What kind of what?"

"Juice," she said, "what kind of juice do you want?"

"How about kiwi, strawberries, and kumquat?"

"I don't know what a kumquat is exactly."

"Me either," I said. "Do something simple. Surprise me."

She handed me a glass of red fluid and watched me closely while

I tasted it. Bananas and strawberries. I swallowed but the liquid seemed to disappear before it reached the back of my throat.

"Good," I said.

She smiled.

"Tell me about Pablo," I said.

"Pablo was still pretty much on autopilot before you set off the alarm," she said.

I thought the words "pretty much" were pretty important in that sentence. "Does that mean someone was monitoring? Pablo wasn't just a program running?

"Someone's always monitoring," she said.

"You?"

"Not at first."

"You're not always the one behind Pablo?"

"Are you always the one behind Brian Dobson?"

Definitely a trick question.

And she had another one. "Who do you suppose is behind Roger?"

"My therapist? You know about Roger?"

"We followed you there a couple of times," she said. "Early on. When we were still unsure if you were our man."

I may have seen one of them in the cyberhall outside of Roger's office. I remembered thinking that no one could spy on me there. I guess I was wrong about that.

She took my hand. "Who is behind Roger? Who do you think is talking when you're talking with him?"

"No one," I said. I took my hand back. "Roger's a program. Dennis has a couple of degrees in this subject, you know."

Her expression gave away nothing about what she was thinking. I've always thought total lack of reaction to what you're saying somehow breaks the conversation contract. I mean how are you supposed to know what to say next if you can't gauge the effect of what you've just said?

"Roger is like ELIZA," I said, "which was written by a guy named Joseph Weizenbaum back in the sixties. The program is not artificial intelligence. All it does is construct utterances from your input. It doesn't really understand what you're saying."

"So if you already know that, why do you use him . . . it, since it's really just you talking to yourself?"

"Me talking to myself is what therapy is all about," I said.

I waited but she had nothing to say to that, so I said, "Let's get back to Pablo. What is *he* for?"

"If anyone should understand the value of disguise, it would be you," she said.

I did know she hadn't really answered my question, but I thought I'd probably gotten all I was going to get on that subject. "What about Frank?" I asked.

"Frank is easy," she said. "This is all to do with the net and control of the net and international and national meddling with the net. Dumb attempts to regulate that which cannot and should not be regulated. You'd do better to pass laws on how the wind should blow."

"Not me," I said.

"Frank is part of a secret organization called COFID," she said. "Cops for Internet Decency. They pretty much agree with me on the difficulty of publicly regulating the net, so they're trying to do it secretly, behind the scenes, beyond the law. Frank doesn't know we're on to him. He imagines that at some critical moment, he'll reveal his secret identity as a COFID operative and bust us. He thinks that we think he's just having some virtual fun with his pal Pablo."

"Do you mean what I think you mean?"

"Yes," she said, "if I'm right in thinking that you're thinking what I'm thinking."

"Cops for Internet Decency," I said, "sounds a little prudish to say the least."

"The people Frank represents are frightened," she said. "Information was hard enough for them but now they have to deal with sensation, too."

"But isn't sensation just a kind of information?"

"Not the way they see it," she said.

"How did Frank hook up with you in the first place?"

"Everything is wheels within wheels," she said. "Nothing is as it seems. Friends of friends of friends. His cover story goes several levels deep in several directions."

"That's the trouble with this whole case," I said. "There are too many people pulling strings behind the scenes. You supposedly came clean with me once, but I guess that was mostly a story, too."

"If an organization is really secret, no one will have heard about it, don't you agree?"

"I suppose so," I said, wondering if she'd changed the subject again.

"Okay, now I'm going to tell you what's really going on."

That of course would be another lie.

"I am a member of the top level of secret societies," she said. "The most secret of the secret. I am what you call a SMOTI."

"Is this like a riddle?"

"Actually it's a lie," she said. "I can't just tell you about the most secret thing or it would no longer be secret. On the other hand, maybe you can learn what you need to know from my story."

"Okay," I said, "so what's a SMOTI?"

Dark clouds gathered overhead. Lightning flashed and thunder boomed. "A Secret Master of the Internet," she said, and her god voice echoed from the sky and shook the landscape.

Then things got quiet except for her giggles.

"Hey, but hold on," I said, ignoring the theatrics. "If this is the most secret of the secret, shouldn't it be old? The Internet hasn't been around that long."

"We evolve," she said. "Not so long ago I would have been a SMOPO."

"Don't tell me."

"That's right," she said. "A Secret Master of the Post Office."

"And before that you would have been a SMOM."

"Well . . ."

"A Secret Master of Messengers?"

"Right," she said. "Only I think carrier pigeons or ponies may have been between those two. Not to mention the telephone. You've got the main idea."

"Don't take this the wrong way," I said, "but I've noticed that you're a lot more . . . well, I don't know. Comprehensible? In here, I mean. Coherent?"

"I do better here," she said. "In a way, I'm not really all there when you see me outside. I'm always groping for stuff that's just out of reach. Things are hard and sharp, and everything wants desperately to get down on the ground." She pulled an apple from the basket and released it in the air and it didn't fall. "Here I have access to what I need exactly when I need it. The problem here is just knowing what to ask."

"That story about you and Pablo coming from Russia as teenagers is also a lie."

"Yes, a lie."

"So, what are you up to?" I asked.

"That's the question, isn't it? Well, to begin with, we are responsible for forming the anonymous remailer. EES was a struggling start-up company in the new Russia, and we gave it a shot in the arm. Once we whispered in Yuri's ear, we just let him go. He poured the tremendous store of energy he'd bottled up by not dancing into the project, and it was a reality in a remarkably short time."

"Does Yuri know there is another organization pulling the strings behind the Evil Empire?" I asked.

"People always know what they need to know."

Which meant that I would probably never know the answer to that question.

"We expected certain sectors of business and government all over the world to be outraged," she said. "We also expected that while they might be up in arms over the remailer, they would be at the same time using it. Yuri thinks EES will be the rerouter for the whole world forever. You heard him. We've always known that the Russian solution was temporary."

"How temporary?"

"We've always expected a big showdown, but we thought we'd have a little time to get ready. Then we banged right into the problem of the killer hiding behind us. This is the wrong time for that."

"Would there ever be a right time?"

"There's a lot of pressure from the American Congress on the Russian government to stomp on four-e-four. They don't seem to know about the Evil Empire connection."

"Surely you expected that?"

"Yes, but not this soon," she said. "Someday the net won't need remailers. Anonymity will be automatic."

"I can't imagine how that could happen."

"We're happy to hear that you can't imagine it," she said. "But we do need the Russian government to hold out against the pressure a little longer. That would be a lot easier if it could be seen that an ordinary small town detective using tried-and-true methods could corner a killer even when the killer is hiding behind the anonymous remailer. Anonymity need not be sacrificed for safety."

"So we're back to that?"

"Yes," she said. "It's not going to be as easy as we thought. We thought we could guide you to the killer. We thought we knew who he was. We were wrong. We really do need you to find and stop him. What's your next move?"

I knew it would be foolish to imagine I now had all the facts. I probably did have all the facts I was going to get. I was pretty sure SOAPY/Dotes was a rogue element in all the scheming that was going on with the net and Evil Empire Software and Cops for Internet Decency and Secret Masters of the Internet.

I'd already been played for a sucker once. I could still just walk away from it.

But the truth was I wanted to nail the killer. It went beyond what Prudence wanted. I probably never would know what she was really up to. If I was going to do this, it would be, aside from the fact that she was still paying me, mostly for reasons of my own. Prudence was waiting to hear what I would do next.

"Can you bring up the BOD list from here?" I asked.

"Easy," she said. She reached into the picnic basket and came out with a rolled-up paper like a small poster. She unrolled it and left it hanging open in the air in front of us. The BOD list, now pretty much complete. Oddly, of all the people hiding behind the Russian remailer, only Arthur Snow, CEO of SplashDown Software, and Nathan Ivanovich, dead, were local.

"How do I highlight things?"

"Touch them," she said.

"Okay." I scooted a little closer. "All of the locals." I touched Gerald Moffitt's name and it became bright yellow. I did the other locals.

GERALD MOFFITT
RANDY CASEY
PRUDENCE DEERFIELD
LEO UNGER
ARTHUR SNOW
NATHAN IVANOVICH
LUCAS BETTY
BERNIE WATKINS
RAMONA SIMMONS
SADIE CAMPBELL

"Okay," I said. "Let's look at a few facts. First, all the victims have been on this list." I touched Gerald Moffitt's name again and it darkened. I did the same for Randy Casey, Nathan Ivanovich, and Sadie Campbell. "We also know that neither SOAPY nor J. Dotes is on the list using either of those names. Therefore we might conclude that the killer is not on the list, if it were not for one other thing."

"Randy Casey," she said.

"That's right. Randy's documentation was posted only to this mailing list. Either the killer is on the list or he has access to it."

"What's the plan?"

"He could strike anywhere next," I said. "He could be anyone.

Someone on the list. Someone else entirely. We need to make him come to us."

"A trap," she said.

"Yes," I said. "We'll need a place to set it up. We'll need someone to be the potential victim. We'll need something to set the killer off."

"I can be the who," she said.

"I don't think so."

"The who has to be on the BOD list," she said. "Who else do you think we could get?"

She was right, but I didn't like it. "There has to be another way," I said. "For one thing, the killer probably wouldn't believe it. He already killed one half of GP Ink."

"Exactly," she said. "He'll just think he killed the wrong part and he'll come back to finish the job."

"Maybe you're right," I said. "If we can set it up so you're not in danger."

"Me being the who, also solves the where," she said. "We can just use the GP Ink offices."

"I thought you were locked out of there."

"Not anymore," she said. "Gerald is old news to the police. That just leaves what we're going to use to lure him in."

"Bad documentation," I said. "We'll produce the world's worse documentation. It'll be so bad the killer simply won't be able to resist trying to knock off the documentalist who committed it."

"We could include all the things we already know he hates like really bad indexes," she said.

"We can make it even worse," I said. "We can index entries into the glossary! You know, when you want to know where something is discussed, the index leads you to a short useless definition of the item."

"And no examples," she said, "complicated prose and nothing to make things clear."

"And we won't tell them how to quit."

"I know," she said. "We can include a help system that when you choose it just tells you what the word 'help' means."

"That's good," I said. "Are you sure you haven't done this kind of thing before?"

She gave me a look of such simple innocence that I was amazed by her powers of deception. Then she smiled to let me know she knew what she was doing. "And context sensitive help. That is, the system watches you and makes sure there is no help available for whatever you're doing."

"Yes, wonderful," I said. "And maybe we can redefine common terms and put things in unusual places in the name of originality."

"Most of the stuff we've been talking about would have to be part of an on-line documentation system," she said. "You just don't have menus with help systems in printed documentation."

"Hypertext," I said. "What you said reminded me of Leo Unger and his rant about hypertext." I was a little fuzzy on the concept so I called up Dennis who knew all about it.

"You again," Prudence said.

"Actually," Dennis said. "There's not much left that is printed these days. The key word is 'interactive.' The idea is the user is supposed to be in control. Everyone gets what they need. There is no fixed path through the material. You click on a word and you go to a place with more information on that word. Maybe we should push it. Maybe we should create the ultimate hypertext document."

"Which would be?"

"The dictionary," Dennis said, "with every word linked to every other word. That way the user could make it say absolutely anything!"

Dennis was drifting away from the topic. Sky stepped in and said, "I don't think so. What we need here are horrible instructions for a specific piece of software."

"Okay then how about a tangled hypertext mess," Dennis said. "Give me something to write on."

"Use your finger and the air," Prudence said.

Dennis wrote in the air, black letters each maybe a foot tall. "The GORKOIDS are necessary to PONK."

"What does it mean?" Prudence asked.

"I'm making it up as I go along," Dennis said, "but the user will ask that, too, and since this is hypertext the answer should be built in."

"The all caps are hot words, your links?"

"Right," Dennis said. "You click on any of those words and you go via a link to other information. Here you see the sentence is absolutely meaningless unless you know what Gorkoids and Ponk are. Look what happens when you click on GORKOIDS."

An arrow appeared and Dennis manipulated it over the word "GORKOIDS." The word blinked, and the entire sentence disappeared.

"In SQUEALEMIA the merry MOSTOMORPHS do FLOMP," he wrote. "Next you'd need to go to Squealemia to see what that means and that would take you on to another link and so on. By the time you got back to Gorkoids you'd be totally befuddled and then you have to do the same with Ponk. And that's only the first sentence of the documentation."

"It drives me crazy already," Prudence said.

Sky took over again. "We do have a couple of other problems besides just finishing this," he said. "We need some software to document and we need a way to get what we do out to where the killer can see it."

"The second part is easy," Prudence said. "I release it under my name to the BOD list. It could be in the killer's hands almost as soon as we finish it."

"I know how it should go!" Dennis said.

"Would you wait a moment," Sky said. "We need to figure out what software we should document."

"Maybe Yuri could help us," Prudence said.

"Forget the Gorkoids," Dennis said. "Forget the Squealemia!"

"You mean we document something for Evil Empire Software?" Sky asked.

"It's an idea," Prudence said.

"Would you listen to me?" Dennis said. "It doesn't matter what software we go with. This will fit anything!"

"What will?" Prudence asked.

"A parable!" Dennis said. "We do a parable. The idea is that the user is supposed to 'just sort of know how to use the program' after reading the parable! Boy, that should really make the killer's head explode!"

"He's right," I said. I got up off the quilt. I put out my hand to help her up. "Let's go for a walk in the woods and write a parable."

eighteen

Alice and Umberto
by
Prudence Deerfield

First things first.

Imagine that all your keys are little guys and all the little guys have little names. Like maybe you'll call the one under your little finger "Alice." When Alice is stroked in the company of the Control Key, hereafter known as "Big Daddy," you'll call her "RoboAlice," but when she's pushed along with the Alt guy, you'll refer to her as "Alice's Evil Twin."

Henceforth the pointing-and-clicking device is your "capybara." The flying arrow in your "Magic Mirror" is "Time."

Now one day Alice (not to be confused with little "Alice") says she's got something to tell Umberto (likewise not "Umberto") and they sit down together under an apple tree.

Here goes, says Alice, scratching the capybara behind the ears until Time flits around the Magic Mirror like a butterfly. When the butterfly finds a Flower, Alice speaks again.

You're a chicken in the Middle Ages, she says. You're insufferable and cocksure. At the same time you're a red fox with a black tip to your tail. One day you break into the chicken coop and eat yourself.

So you see the chicken is like a man who mistakes his lover for a baloney sandwich. The fox is like the dogged determination necessary in a quest for truth. The coop represents your physical limitations, and the eating episode finally resolves the ambiguities in our relationship, Umberto.

Umberto calls upon his evil twin to undo all of Alice's fine work. He flicks the butterfly from the nose of the capybara and takes the time to call up six friends: Moe, Bob, Ely, Ruby, Tom, and Odo.

Umberto and his friends lounge around the barnyard drinking beer and playing cards. Somehow they also find time to polka.

Meanwhile, Alice has been co-opted by a parental presence. Umberto doesn't realize she's been replaced. He gets a blackjack. His heart leaps up, and he does a couple of complicated polka steps.

What is that noise? he wonders. Is that you, Alice? Do a few steps. Do you rattle when you walk?

Says Alice, I do not rattle when I walk, I do not rattle when I talk. It is out of the song comes forth completeness.

Thus do we see with an inward eye that Alice and Umberto are the stuff of computation and the resolution of their difficulties comes with the execution of the algorithm of life.

Not to mention the capybara.

THE END

nineteen

"You and Dennis should get some of the credit, too," Prudence said.

"I don't think credit is the right word," I said. We were still in the woods. Our parable to catch a killer floated above us in the sky.

"You don't think it's too short?"

"Not with all the hypertext links," I said. "We can link up just about every word to a maze of unrelated information."

"Just random information?"

"Sure," I said. "Cookbooks, encyclopedias, the yellow pages. But I think we should check with Yuri next about the software."

A cell phone appeared in Prudence's hand. She dialed and put the phone to her ear. A moment later she said, "Yuri? Meet me at the Wallace port. Sky's here. What? Never mind. I'll tell you later. When can you get here? Okay." She jammed the antenna down and tossed the phone over her shoulder. "He's on his way."

We broke out of the forest overlooking the meadow where we had sat on the quilt and sipped juice. Before we'd gotten down the hill, Yuri appeared out of thin air.

"We're setting up a trap," Prudence said as soon as we got to him. "We need some things from the Evil Empire."

"What's with the scroll in the sky?" he asked. I'd gotten used to Prudence looking like a cartoon. I had to start all over with Yuri.

"It's the very ideal of bad documentation," I said. "It's a bad example that documentalists can point to for years to come when they're talking about wretchedness."

"Something to make grown people weep with frustration," Prudence said.

"And there is some purpose to this?"

Prudence filled him in on our plan to trap the killer.

"There are still some things to set up," I said. "We need to hook the parable up with some specific software. That's where we thought EES could help. And we need to let everyone know that Prudence is taking over operations at GP Ink. Hey, maybe you should rename the company P Ink."

"Pink?" she asked.

"Well, maybe not."

"This business of writing the documentation and then finding some software to go with it is very strange," Yuri said.

"If that happens often, it would explain a lot," I said. "I mean if the relationship between the software and the documentation is largely random."

"Okay, here's the story," Yuri said, getting into his take-charge-kind-of-guy mode. "Prudence Deerfield is picking up the pieces. She's putting GP Ink back on its feet even though her brother Pablo is still missing. She's done her first project, and she's posting her documentation to the BOD list. She'll be open for business first thing tomorrow morning."

"Will that give us time to get set up?" I asked

"I think so," Yuri said. "I can have people at GP Ink in an hour if we need to make physical changes."

"Secret cameras and such?"

"Why not?" he said.

"I probably should stay there hidden all the time," I said. "Why don't you fix up Pablo and Gerald's office for that. We can move Prudence out front where she can be seen. We can watch her from the back office."

Yuri got out his cell phone and went to work on the office.

"We still have to decide about the software," I said.

"Gerald's was technical. Sadie's was an Internet browser," she said. "Randy's was a game. Nathan's was a business program."

"So the killer is all over the place," I said. "Just about any program would do. Hey, how about a program that lets you come here?"

"I don't think we're ready to release this yet," she said.

We kicked it around. We waited for Yuri to finish on the phone. We didn't come up with anything.

Yuri folded his phone. "Arrangements for the office are made. What did you decide to do about the software?"

"Nothing," I said. "Look, the software in question doesn't even have to exist. We just need to say it does. It could be anything. What does EES have in the works?"

"I don't think we can afford to have our name linked to the worst documentation ever written," he said. "I can provide behind the curtain stuff, but up front we need to be invisible."

"GP Ink contracts," I said. "We need a customer."

"Let Dennis do it," Prudence said. "It's perfect."

She was right.

Dennis might well use GP Ink to document software he'd written and was ready to market. It would give at least one of us a good excuse for hanging around GP Ink, too.

"So what'll it be?" I asked.

"Well, I have this encryption idea," Dennis said. "It involves disguising sensitive data as something else. You know, a list of secret chemicals as a recipe for chocolate cake or some steamy porno as a letter to your mom."

"Hey, that's a good idea!" Yuri said. "Maybe when this is all over we should talk."

"What is it called?" Prudence asked.

"The Data Disguise," Dennis said as if he hadn't made the whole thing up right on the spot.

"By the way," she said, "does Dennis have a last name? We'll need it for the announcement."

"St. James," Dennis said, "Dennis St. James."

That was news to me.

We announced Prudence's comeback on-line. We talked about Dennis St. James and the Data Disguise as her first project. We called him a local computer wizard—his idea, actually. We e-mailed "Alice and Umberto" to members of the BOD list.

"I guess that's it," I said.

"Let's meet at GP Ink tomorrow at nine," Prudence said.

"Do you suppose I should already be there?" I asked. "Maybe I should get right over there and spend the night so I'll be there when you open in the morning."

"That's probably not necessary," Yuri said. "Just get up and go early in the morning."

"So, how do we get out of here?" I asked.

"Mostly you just decide that you want to be out of here," she said. "You sit up. I get the feeling that most people do not experience this to the depth you seem to be experiencing it. Or for that matter the depth that I experience it. You're mostly in a world of your own half the time, anyway."

"Is that a crack?"

"Not at all," she said. "I'm the same way myself."

"Well, I guess this is really not so much different from what goes on in my head from day to day."

"Most people would always be aware of their bodies back in the Quack Inn," she said.

"Speaking of that," I said, "I still don't see what the datapants are for."

Yuri chuckled. "Why don't you show him what the pants are for, Prudence?"

Prudence blushed.

Yuri stood up. "My work is done." He disappeared.

"Well?" I said.

She looked up at me and smiled, and her smile filled the landscape, and warmth washed over me, and a tingling caress—fingers from elsewhere and everywhere.

This is it, I thought.

Then everything went black. It was all gone as if someone had just switched off the universe. My head swam and I would have fallen, but then I realized I was already on my back in a big tray of goo in a room in the Quack Inn.

"Okay, get your butt out here," Frank Wallace said.

twenty

I didn't move a muscle. I didn't make a sound. I hoped Frank would think I was still in VR. Or dead. Dead would be okay. Maybe he'd go away if he thought I was dead.

"Come out of there," he said. "Don't play games with me, Brian. I turned it off. I know you can hear me."

His next step would be to grab me and toss me onto the floor. I wondered how long he had been in the room and what he'd heard. At least my part of the conversation. Would that be enough for him to figure out what was going on?

"Brian, I'm warning you . . ." I could hear him getting closer.

"Okay," I said. I reached up and pulled off the VR helmet and looked up into Frank's face. He didn't look happy. I dropped the helmet over the edge and rolled my head to the side so I could see the door. It was closed, but the security chain had been cut. I had been in so deep I hadn't heard any of that. I sat up and the rubber datavest made a smooch as it peeled away from the Jell-O of the bed.

"Hello, Frank." I swung my legs over the side of the bed. "How did you know it was me under there?"

"I followed you here, you nitwit," Frank said.

"You followed me?"

"Stand up," he said.

I reached back and grabbed the cable leading to the *datapants*. I didn't want it jerking me short as I tried to stand up. The black rubber getup was already making it difficult to maintain my dignity.

Frank never took his eyes off me. As soon as I was upright he pulled my own camera out from behind his back and flashed my picture.

I had a bunch of choices at that point. I could take off the VR gear and walk naked across the room to my clothes. Frank would probably get a kick out of that. He'd be snapping my picture and I'd be doing a full body blush. I could just storm over to my clothes ripping the cables from the computer. He'd probably deck me for that one. I could just stand there like an idiot while he took another picture.

"Say cheese," he said.

"Hey, Frank," I said. "After you're done maybe we can trade places and I can take your picture. Why should I have all the fun? It's your stuff."

That made all the muscles in his face tighten up. He kicked at my clothes on the floor and sat down at the little motel table.

I leaned down to unhook the cables from the computer.

"Hey, what are you doing?"

"Disconnecting, Frank. I need to use the can."

"Cut it out," he said. "And stay where you are. You think I'm going to let you slip out that little window in the bathroom?"

"That hadn't occurred to me." Now that he'd mentioned it, though, getting away might not be a bad idea.

I pulled off a glove and tossed it back onto the bed. "So why were you following me, Frank?" I was doing my best to seem unflappable. I didn't want to be the victim here. I took off the other glove.

"Knock off the striptease," he said.

I took my hands away from the datavest.

"The Russian Marvin busted yesterday turned out to be the guy who tossed your office," he said.

"I practically put the guy in Marvin's lap."

"Whatever."

I stood on one foot and pulled off one of the datasocks. While I was still perched on one foot, Frank snatched my camera off the table and took my picture. The flash blinded me. I almost lost my balance, had to take a little jumping hop, and I stomped my bare foot down hard on the floor. Frank put the camera back down on the table.

"Genka Matusoff," he said, "the Russian. He's got some confusing ideas about diplomatic immunity."

"Oh?"

"He thinks he still has it." Frank smiled suddenly and I felt a shudder of sympathy for Matusoff. I wouldn't want Frank smiling like that when he thought of me.

"So he used to be a diplomat?"

I got the other datasock off.

"Something like that," Frank said. "He could see I'd be big trouble, but the interesting thing is that when it dawned on him just who I was, he got a lot calmer. He had something for me."

I quickly slipped out of the datavest and dropped it onto the bed. "Like?"

"Like the fact that when he tossed your office, he found out you were following a certain police lieutenant for his wife."

"Whoops."

"I could just kick the crap out of you right here, Brian. Who would know?"

"Come on, Frank," I said, trying to keep the whine out of my voice and doing okay—well maybe there was a little tremble, but that was about it, and I should be allowed a little tremble, considering I was still tethered to the bed by a long cable hooked to my rubber pants. "I'm just doing my job. This isn't personal."

He banged his hand down on the table. "Of course, it's personal! It's always been personal with you. You spend all your time trying to screw up my life."

"Boy, Frank," I said. "You think I've got nothing to do except think about you? Grow up. What have I ever done to you?"

"You shot me, you idiot!"

"We were kids! Almost kids anyway, and it was a long time ago. I'm amazed and hurt you'd bring that up after all this time. Get over it. It was an accident!"

"So you say. I still limp. When I'm too tired to fight it. Did you know that?"

"I'm sorry to hear it, Frank."

"And Elsie," he said. "I can't believe she went to you. You of all people."

"It sounds like you're the one who spends all of his time obsessing about me."

"You flatter yourself," he said. "I doubt your name has been spoken in my house more than half a dozen times in the last ten years."

"So, that explains it," I said. "Elsie needed a detective and she just picked an old high school friend."

"You were never friends," he said, "and she knows how I feel about you."

"It seems to me you don't talk much," I said.

"I might still hit you, Brian," he said. "You don't want to be jerking my chain. What do you think you are, some kind of marriage counselor?"

"I'm just saying you could have avoided this whole business if you'd just told Elsie what you were up to at the motel here."

"This is work," he said. "I can't discuss this."

"Marvin thinks you've been acting weird, too," I said. "Don't you talk to anyone?"

"I can't believe it," he said. "I simply cannot believe it. Marvin, too? Marvin's been sneaking around talking to you about me, too? Is your number posted on the bulletin board? Big sign says you want to discuss Frank Wallace's personal life, call your local dipstick Brian Dobson?"

"Marvin was worried about you," I said. "Besides what do you mean personal life? You just said this was work."

"Well, you're finished as far as I'm concerned," he said. "You can follow me till your dick drops off and you won't see me do anything but my job."

"Come on, Frank, let me get out of your job." I pulled the waist band of the datapants away from my body. "Let me put my clothes on."

He picked up my camera again.

"I met Pablo Deerfield in there," I said.

I thought he went a little white, but he recovered quickly. He put my camera back down. "Did he happen to tell you where he is in the flesh?"

"No," I said. "Is that your cover story? Your virtual reality debauchery is all so you can track down Pablo in the flesh? Deep cover?"

"Something like that," he said. "What do you mean 'debauchery'?"

"Here's the deal, Frank." Go for broke. Do or die. "I can report to my client that you come to this motel room alone, put on rubber pants, and interact with an electronic device."

He was right on the edge like a coiled rattlesnake. Any second now he was going to jump into my face.

But then he looked down at his hands.

"I wish you'd leave the device out of it," he said. "And the pants. And the motel." He looked up at me. "If you think about it, you might say you owe me that much."

In response to his claim that I owed him one, I gave him my cold-as-ice stare. I added my much practiced disdainful curl of the upper lip, especially effective when wearing a mustache, which adds a hint of cruel irony.

"You're such a screwup, Brian," he said after a couple of moments of silence. "Put your clothes on."

I could zap him with what I'd learned about him and COFID. That would take him down another notch or two, but it would also tip him off that EES was on to him. My purpose here was not to give Frank Wallace information. I slipped out of the datapants and hurried over to my clothes.

I got dressed as quickly as possible. I sat down in the other chair across the little table from Frank to put on my shoes. So what would Frank do next? If I were him, I'd probably haul me downtown and toss me into a cell. He couldn't hold me long, but he could let me cool my heels overnight with bad company. I needed a diversion.

"I'm about to solve the Documentalists Murders case for you, Frank."

"Right. Sure, you are. And just how are you going to pull that little stunt off?"

"Get off your high horse, Frank," I said. "If you want my cooperation in regard to your little electronic boudoir here you should be nice to me."

"Get screwed," he said. "And while you're at it, get a dictionary. Boudoir. Jesus."

"Things to do, Frank," I said and stood up.

"We're not done." He didn't get up, but I knew he could be up and on me before I could get to the door. "What about the killer?"

"A minute ago you didn't want to hear it."

"Just tell me what you're up to," he said. "I'll probably have to stop you to protect the citizens around you."

We would need the police sooner or later anyway. I would rather have had Marvin in on it, but sometimes circumstances force you to make other choices. I sat down again.

"Certain associates of mine have helped me set up a trap for the killer," I said. "You may remember my theory, now largely confirmed, about the killer killing the producers of bad documentation?"

"I can be fair," Frank said. "I think you do have that part right."

"So, what we've done is produce maybe the worst documentation in the history of documentation. We've released it in certain circles on the net, e-mailed it to key individuals, and we've set up the documentalist who produced the abomination in an office where the killer can get at her."

"And?"

"And now we wait," I said. "The killer comes to knock off Prudence and we grab him."

"Prudence Deerfield?"

"Right," I said. "At the GP Ink offices. Maybe the killer comes by to check us out first and we recognize him. Or maybe he gives himself away in a manner no one has thought of yet."

I thought he was going to tell me we were wasting our time, or playing a dangerous game—maybe say we were out of our league, but he asked instead, "When did you set this all up?"

I know I shifted my eyes to the bed and the VR gear, but I tried to cover it quickly. "Earlier," I said. "I got the wheels turning earlier, but I've got to get going on this, Frank. Let's get out of here. I can fill you in later."

I got up again.

This time Frank got up, too. "Come on then. You can fill me in now."

He opened the door and let me step out first. He turned back to lock the door. He was confident that I wouldn't just take off, and he was right. What would be the point?

"We'll take your jeep," he said.

"You know I have a jeep?"

"I've been following you, remember? It was easy. You were totally oblivious."

"I don't get oblivious," I said, but even I knew it was a lie.

We got into my jeep and I drove us back downtown. I parked in the street up the block from my building. I didn't want him to know where I usually parked the jeep. I got out and put some money in the meter.

"Why are you parking here?" he asked. So he already knew where I usually parked.

"Why not?" I walked away. A moment later he fell in beside me. We didn't speak again as we entered my building, waited for the elevator, rode it up to the third floor, got to my door, and went inside.

"Have a seat, Frank," I said.

I sat down behind my desk and pushed the button on my phone answering machine.

"Brian?" Elsie Wallace. I jerked up my hand to hit the button to make it skip to the next message.

"Too late," Frank said. He got up, but before he could stalk over and loom over me, I hit the rewind and then the play and Elsie said,

"Brian? Frank knows I hired you to follow him. And I don't care! You just keep following him! If he'd just talk to me I wouldn't have to do this. You know? If he'd just talk to me. Don't let him scare you off, Brian. Oh, I don't know. Call me. I may just leave him. Who cares what he's up to?"

"It sounds to me like you should go home and talk to her, Frank," I said.

He made a noncommittal sound and looked away.

I played my other message. "Yuri here. I forgot it's Sunday on the outside. We won't be ready at GP Ink until at least noon tomorrow. We already posted an announcement about the delay."

Frank was on his feet when I looked back up at him.

"You guys are amazing," he said. "You think the killer's going to play by your rules? Your trap isn't ready, so you say, hey, wait until we get things set up." He turned and walked toward the door.

"So, help us out, Frank," I said.

He opened the door.

"Where are you going?"

"Home," he said.

twenty-one

Monday morning was cool and gray, the kind of morning you'd like to stay in and watch the rain run down the windowpanes. I puttered around the office gathering disguise supplies—hair and noses, scars and bruises, the glasses Dennis always wore, a versatile outfit for Lulu. With careful packing, all of us fit into a small overnight bag. Who knew how long it would take to catch the Documentalist Killer? Days? Weeks? I didn't want to be caught short waiting for him to show up.

I grabbed my hat and locked up the office. Outside the lazy drizzle wasn't serious enough to make it worth the trouble to open my umbrella. I noticed the pink TOFU sign atop the Baltimore building looked especially bright and cheerful against the gray sky. Maybe that was a good omen.

Last time I'd been at the Baltimore, I'd been Dennis in a janitor disguise and I'd slipped in through the service entrance. Today, someone else was using that side entrance in the alley. A big truck was parked in there, and men were moving furniture and boxes up and down the ramp in back. It looked like some of the men were moving stuff in and others were moving stuff out.

I walked into the alley. The sign on the side of the truck said VOLGA OFFICE SUPPLY. I ducked into the building and got on the service elevator with one of the movers, a young guy in a clean white overall and a Bud cap. The name "Jim" was stitched in red above his top pocket. He glanced at my overnight bag then looked away.

"Three seventeen?" I asked.

"Right," he said. Was that an accent in disguise? Did Jim look entirely comfortable in his clothes? What about that suspicious bulge under his left arm?

"Me too," I said.

He didn't have anything to say to that, and we rode the rest of the way in silence.

There was a lot of activity in the GP Ink offices. It was hard to tell what was going out and what was coming in. The desks in the back office were already gone, replaced by a couple of folding cots. A square of four TV monitors had been set up along one wall.

Men carried boxes in and stacked them in the back office. A couple of guys carried a dull green trunk in. After conferring with someone else and puzzling over the paper taped to the trunk, they just pushed it up against the wall in the front office.

There was a guy on his knees pushing wires through the wall in the back office and another guy out in front pulling them through.

I was mostly ignored. Didn't anyone worry I might be the killer casing the joint? Maybe they knew who I was. Sure they did. I stood around pretending it mattered how I thought the work was proceeding, like someone might ask, "Hey, do you think this would look better here or over there?"

After a few minutes of stepping out of the way, I concluded it would be better to come back later.

On the mall again, I decided that since I was no longer addicted, I might as well have a cup of coffee and got a medium house from an espresso cart. I sat down on a bench where I could keep an eye on the movers. The coffee was very good. I'd forgotten how a cup of coffee seems to wake up all the muscles in your face. Makes you want to get up and stretch. I could see how a guy might want to have more than one cup of the stuff.

I was working on a refill when Frank sat down beside me.

"Thought you'd already be up there hiding in a closet or something," he said.

"How's Elsie?"

"None of your business," he said.

"We're still getting stuff set up in there," I said. "It looks to me like you're getting into the spirit of our little trap."

"I may still zap it," he said. "Or maybe I'll just put our people on it."

"Lots of luck. Any of your people know squat about documentalists?"

"I think you're the only one in the whole world who even uses the word 'documentalist,'" he said. "People looked at me like I was an idiot when I used it."

"So, there you go," I said.

"Why are you out here, Brian?"

"I went up," I said. "They're not done. I just felt like I was in the way."

"That's the difference between us." He stood up. I looked up at him. "I won't be in the way."

I crushed my coffee cup and tossed it in the recycle barrel and stood up. "This way."

I led Frank through the alley to the service entrance. We rode the elevator in silence—him looking up to the right, me looking up to the left. No whistling.

The men coming and going seemed to be mostly going now. In fact, by the time we got to room 317, there were only a couple of guys still fooling with the surveillance equipment.

"Who's paying for all this?" Frank wanted to know.

"GP Ink would be my guess," I said.

The electronics guys finished up and left. Frank and I stood around looking like we didn't know what to do next. A cleaning crew rescued us from that situation, gave us someone to watch. Their shirts said OFFICE COORDINATORS. Two men and a woman. The men got busy dusting and mopping. The woman sat down at the desk and went to work on the computer.

"The new phone line seems to be working," she said, as if we would know why we needed another phone line. She got up so one of us could check it out.

I sat down behind the desk. Frank moved to the window and stood at parade rest gazing down at the street below.

I logged on. Using the password Prudence had given me, I looked for e-mail at her BOD address. She'd given me the password so I could keep tabs on how BOD members were dealing with "Alice and Umberto." My first thought had been, "Wow, I could learn a lot about Prudence Deerfield, maybe everything I'd always wanted to know, now that I had access to her e-mail." My second thought was that she probably did her real business through an anonymous 4e4 account.

"Alice and Umberto" had generated quite a few responses already. Prudence and I would have to sit down and go through them together. When we replied, we'd be smug and condescending. We'd be insufferable. The idea was to piss the killer off. If the documentation itself didn't do it, maybe Prudence and her new customer Dennis could do it with attitude. No doubt there would be a war. No doubt it would get ugly. The degree of nastiness you can achieve during a flame war on-line is truly monumental.

The guys finished sprucing up. The woman hung a couple of cute cat posters. Then they left, too.

I was getting hungry. Maybe we could order a pizza.

"I guess you skipped lunch for this," I said.

"The place has a funny smell," Frank said without turning away from the window.

"Yeah, well, you know these old buildings," I said. "What are you looking at out there?"

"Just now I watched Prudence Deerfield get out of the front seat of a Lexus," he said. "The driver got out and spoke to her over the top of the car. A guy with dark hair, a little too long, wearing one of those goofy caps so popular with middle-aged bald guys."

I didn't see any reason to tell Frank he'd probably been looking at Yuri Kost of Evil Empire Software.

"Ms. Deerfield stood looking up at this very window for a few moments, then she spoke to the driver and hurried across the street.

The Lexus pulled off toward Seventh Avenue. She should be arriving any time now."

He turned away from the window.

I wished I could warn Prudence that he was here. She seemed to be able to handle him a lot better in virtual reality. Frank probably had the upper hand out here. The good news was that she seemed to know that. Once she saw him, she'd play it cool.

"Somehow she's wrapped up in just about everything I do these days," Frank said.

He didn't know the half of it, but I couldn't tell him the rest, so I didn't say anything. I got up, walked to the door, and slipped into the hall to meet Prudence.

A moment later the elevator arrived and she stepped out. I raised a hand and gave her a little wave. She smiled at me and walked briskly in my direction. She'd dressed up for this first day of business. She always looked good, but today I could see she was trying to look good. I couldn't say exactly how I knew that. This was your standard understated yellow miniskirt in that weird material you want to call plastic or vinyl. Open orange raincoat of the same material. Medium heels, a string of pearls.

"How does it look?" she asked.

"The outfit?"

"The office."

I took her arm and slowed her down long enough to say, "Frank Wallace is here." We entered the office together.

"Ms. Deerfield," Frank said.

"Lieutenant Wallace."

"Now that we're all identified," I said, "what do you say we use the new phone line to order a pizza? I'm starved."

"Anchovies," Prudence said.

Frank made a face.

"Yetch," I said.

"Okay, maybe tell them to put the anchovies on every third piece," Prudence said.

"They'll love that," I said. "What do you like, Frank?"

"I don't care," he said. "No pineapple."

"It sounds like you folks are conspiring to clog your arteries with junk food," Marvin said from the doorway. For a big guy he sure could move quietly.

He came on in. He smiled at Prudence. He looked at Frank and then looked at me and then looked back at Frank. "So what do we have going?"

"Probably nonsense," Frank said. He came away from the window and pulled up a chair and sat down.

I sat down behind the desk and poked around in the drawers for a phone book. No luck. I pulled the keyboard over and did a quick Web search and found a couple of local pizza places with home pages. One of them let me design my pizza graphically. It didn't let me put anchovies on every other slice, however, so I grouped the fish on about a quarter of the pie. Added a bunch of other stuff. Too much stuff. Started over. Finally came up with what I thought might please everyone. Typed in my credit card number.

"Pizza ordered," I said.

Prudence had sat down in the other customer chair while I'd been building the pizza. Marvin stood looking around like he might just have to squat on the floor. Then he spotted the green trunk pushed up against the wall and sat down on that. It must have been strong. It didn't even sag under his considerable weight.

"So the idea is we're sitting here eating pizza," Frank said, "and the killer comes in to kill Ms. Deerfield and we grab him. Have I got it right?"

"We don't really expect him today," I said.

"You guys should have had this place cleaned up first," Marvin said. "It stinks."

"We did have it cleaned up," I said.

Prudence turned to Frank. "All Sky needs to find out is the identity of the killer. Once he tells you that, I'll bet you can find physical evidence if you know where to look."

"She's right, Frank," I said. "All he has to do is tip his hand."

Frank twisted around to look at Marvin on the trunk. "They want me to assign you to be the guy who jumps out of the closet and grabs the killer, Marvin."

"I've heard worse ideas," Marvin said.

Feeling restless, I got up and looked out the window. Traffic went by on the street below. The church way over on Oak rang its bells. I walked over to the two big filing cabinets and opened all the drawers one by one. They were all empty. I knew they would be. I'd gone through them the last time I'd been here. They'd still been in the inner office then. The movers had pushed them out here to make way for the surveillance equipment.

I stepped past Marvin and opened a door. It was a closet. I already knew it was a closet. I was just restless. I couldn't sit still.

"Hey," I said, "the closet really is big enough for Marvin to hide in."

"Very funny," he said.

"Restrooms must be down the hall." I closed the closet door.

I hated the cat posters, but I restrained myself from pulling them down. I continued the circuit of the room, and when I got back to the desk I sat down again.

I tapped my fingers on the desk until I noticed all three of them watching me do it.

"Can't you sit still for a minute?" Frank asked.

"Always on the move, Frank," I said. "I'm a go-getter."

"You're a fruitcake," he said.

"Something really does stink in here," Marvin said.

The elevator dinged out in the hallway. That could be useful. You could tell when someone might be moving up on the office. But how come it hadn't dinged when Prudence arrived? Well, maybe it had and I hadn't noticed. But why hadn't it dinged when Marvin sneaked up on us? Okay, Marvin must have used the service elevator or the stairs. The point was I was noticing the dinging elevator now, and I would keep noticing it.

Someone knocked on the door.

"Pizza guy, I'll bet." I got up to answer the door.

Marvin had gotten up and was messing with the latch of the trunk.

Frank hadn't even turned to look to see who was knocking, but Prudence had.

The pizza guy handed me the box. Since I'd already paid for the pie and included the tip with my card on the Web, there was nothing else to say but thank-you.

"Oh, my god," Marvin said.

I turned back with the pizza in my hand. Marvin was standing over the open trunk. Frank was on his feet and in motion, Prudence was half out of her chair. The pizza guy moved up close behind me and stood up on his toes to peek over my shoulder. I stepped to one side and handed the pizza back to him and walked up beside Marvin and Frank.

Inside the trunk was a naked man.

It was easy to see he was dead. The body was crouched with the knees pulled up close to the shoulders, but the head had been twisted around to look straight up out of the trunk. A printer cable was twisted around the neck, the two business ends over the left shoulder as if the body were sporting one of those goofy western ties and had gotten caught in a big windstorm. The man's red ponytail was tangled around one of the cable connectors. There were circled words like small bruises all over the parts of the body I could see. The circles were connected with black lines.

"Leo Unger," I said.

twenty-two

Frank got totally official on us. Cleared the room except for Marvin. In less than twenty minutes the place was crawling with cops of all kinds. Marvin came out and told Prudence and me to wait in the hall. There would be questions.

Our trap had been a total bust. The killer had seen right through it. He could have even been one of the guys delivering furniture when Frank and I walked up. I could have spoken to him! I tried to remember the faces of the furniture guys, but I couldn't get anything definite. Frank would remember the movers; he probably already had someone looking into Volga Office Supply.

"Can we do anything else wrong?" I asked Prudence. We were standing at the end of the hall, by the stairwell. All kinds of cops hurried up and down the elevators—cops in suits, cops in uniform, and finally guys in white for Leo's body.

"You can take Leo Unger off your list of suspects," Prudence said. She didn't mean the comment as a dark joke. She just meant I could take Leo off my list of suspects.

"I think we're finished," I said.

She put her hand on my arm. "You'll think of something else."

"No," I said. "I think we're finished. At least things can't get any worse. Why did we think we could figure this out anyway?"

"Maybe you're right," she said.

That's not what I wanted to hear. I didn't want her agreeing that I'd totally screwed things up and hadn't a clue about what to do next.

I sat down on the floor and leaned my back against the wall and sighed. I looked up and up at Prudence. She stood looking down the hall, her head turned a little to the side. I sighed again, and she glanced down at me. It looked like she might sit down beside me, but she must have realized it wouldn't be easy in that skirt. She leaned against the wall, and I got up again.

We waited there for a long time.

They took the body away.

Most of the cops left.

Finally Marvin poked his head out of the office and looked around then saw us and walked over.

"So, is it our killer?" I asked.

"Yes," Marvin said. "Leo's been dead for a while. Words on the body as usual. But there's a note, too. Two notes actually. The one taped to the trunk and the one inside."

"What do they say?" I asked.

"The one on the outside reads, 'A housewarming gift.' It's not signed."

"And the one inside?"

Marvin looked down at his notebook. " 'I already did hypertext you idiots.' "

"Well, how were we supposed to know that?" I asked, realizing it was a stupid reaction even as I said it, but since I had some momentum going in that direction, I just kept going. "And what about the parable? He hadn't done a parable already, and if he'd left the body in a more obvious place it would have been found before we set up our trap and we would have tried something else!"

"You think that would have worked?" Marvin asked.

"Of course not, Marvin. I'm ranting. Can't you see that? I'm raving. I'm saying the first dumb thing that comes into my mind!"

"The note's signed," Marvin said. "It's scrawled, but it looks like 'José' "

"José?"

"That's what it looks like to me," Marvin said.

I thought about Leo. Leo would always be special. Of the five dead documentalists (so far!), he was the only one I had actually met, but more important, he was the only one I'd seen dead. There is a world of difference between a body as part of a puzzle and a body bent and stuffed into a trunk. I wouldn't soon get Leo's dead eyes out of my mind. Leo, the hypertext guy. He probably thought he was safe since the documentation he put together was never printed. You used it right along with the software itself. The killer hadn't said anything about that. Well, Leo was his statement now.

"Maybe you'd better take a couple of deep breaths, Brian," Marvin said.

"Sorry. You're right." I did take a couple of medium deep breaths. "So, what were the words on the body and what were all those lines about?"

"Maybe you can tell me," Marvin said. He opened his notebook again. "I'll read you the words."

"Wait," I said. I took out my own notebook so I could write them down. "Go ahead."

He read me the words, and I copied them into my notebook. The list looked like this when we were done.

THERE
MATTER
YOU
NO
ARE
GET
FROM
HARD
WHAT
WHO
HERE
TRY
KNOW

CAN'T
OR
HOW

"Every word is circled," Marvin said, "and there are lines from just about ever word to every other word."

"Arrows?" Prudence asked.

Marvin gave her a hard look. "There is a little directional arrow-head on every line, sometimes in both directions. Do you know something about this, Ms. Deerfield?"

"I'm just trying to figure it out," she said. "What else?"

"There is one word with no arrows," he said. "The word 'there' is just circled. It seems set off by itself because no lines lead to it or away from it."

"It's nonlinear," Prudence said. "It's like a map of nodes. It's what you'd use if you were setting up the links in a hypertext document. Each arrow tells you where you can go next. I'll bet if you look closely every node or word doesn't have an arrow pointing at every other word."

Marvin didn't look like he understood any of this.

"You know," Prudence said. "Like when you're reading a hypertext document on the screen and you can click on a word and it will take you to other information usually about that word. When you get there, you might find other words that you could click on to take you other places."

"Actually that idea pushed to an absurd extreme was one of the irritating things about the documentation we hoped would trap this guy," I said.

"But like he said, he already did hypertext," Prudence said.

"So what does it say?" Marvin asked.

"Let's do some rearranging," I said.

"Maybe we should wait for a map of the arrows," Prudence said. "A picture would make it a lot easier."

"I'll bet just about every sentence that makes sense will match one you could get if you followed the arrows. Let's just try a few." I ripped a page out of my notebook and gave it to her. "Do you have something to write with?"

She dug in her purse and found a pen.

"You, too, Marvin," I said. "Rearrange the words. Try to form sentences."

I gave my list to Prudence and she copied it and handed it back. We got to work.

"I've got one," I said. "No matter how you try you can't get there from here."

"Hey, but that doesn't use all the words," Marvin said.

"You're right," I said. "I think I'm on the right track, though."

We went back to work. A few minutes later, Prudence had another sentence.

"No matter who you are or how hard you try or what you know you can't get there from here."

Marvin had a variation on the same idea.

"Is it fair to use 'there'?" Prudence asked. "I mean there are no arrows leading to or from that word."

I suddenly saw what the killer was up to. "It's an extra level to the message! If you follow the arrows, you really can't get to 'there.' I'll bet if we looked at all of Leo's hypertext documentation we'd find an irritating example like that."

Marvin flipped his notebook closed. "Thanks," he said. "We'll look into that angle. I'd better get back."

"Can we go now?" I asked.

"You'd better wait a little longer," Marvin said. "Frank will probably want to ask some questions."

Marvin turned away. There was a commotion behind me, maybe the stairwell door opening, echoing footsteps, a happy conversation cut short.

Prudence stood in front of me where she could look over my shoulder at whatever was happening, and I saw a whole parade of emotions move across her face. Surprise, sudden anger. Guilt? Sadness? Finally maybe resignation.

I twisted around to look. Two guys, one maybe a foot taller than the other. The bigger one was leaning down so they could chuckle and whisper. They'd frozen in that position when they'd come through the door and noticed the crowd waiting for them. Kids, I thought.

Then the tall one straightened up, and the world shifted. One of them, the shorter one, really was a kid, a teenager.

The other one was Pablo Deerfield.

I looked at Pablo. Pablo looked at me. Then he spotted his sister behind me.

He burst into tears.

Prudence pushed past me and gathered him into a big hug. His buddy patted him on the shoulder and gave me a murderous glare.

I shrugged and tried to look apologetic, for what, I didn't know.

Prudence made soothing noises, and Pablo got himself under control. He rubbed his eyes with a fist and pulled away from her.

"So he's real," I said.

"Of course, he's real," Prudence said.

"Of course, I'm real." Pablo grinned and I could see that maybe he wasn't entirely grown up yet.

"I meant real in the sense that he can come out of cyberland and shake your hand." I put out my hand.

Pablo just looked at it for a moment. Then he looked at Prudence. She nodded at him, and he reached out and took my hand. I had half expected him to be made of pixels, had thought maybe he would blow away like pastel dust when I touched him.

"So, where have you been, Pablo?" I heard the condescension in my voice. At least I didn't call him 'kiddo.'

He glanced up at Prudence again, and again she gave him the nod, and he grinned again and said, "Staying with my friend Bernie. In the dungeon!"

I looked at the kid. I'd pictured him differently, but maybe my idea of a young propeller head has been too much influenced by TV (and Bill Gates). When I'd looked at Bernie's yearbook picture I'd filled in a lot of details that simply weren't there in real life.

"So, you're Bernie Watkins," I said.

He was short, maybe five-six or so, but he looked like he had a lot of upper body strength, like maybe he spent as much time in the gym as in front of his computer. His hair was shiny black and short on the sides and top, but in the back he had a long braid.

"What are you guys doing here?" Prudence sounded like she was already trying to figure out how to salvage something.

"We didn't think it was fair that you guys would leave us out of the trap!" Bernie said.

"Yeah!" Pablo said. "No fair!"

"Did you catch him?" Bernie looked past me at the last of the cops coming and going. Marvin had disappeared, and it occurred to me that now might be a good time for Bernie Watkins and Pablo Deerfield to turn around and go back down the way they came up.

"No, it didn't work," Prudence said.

"So, what is all of this?" Bernie looked suddenly worried. I think he was smart enough to see that maybe he'd made a big mistake. He was looking down the hall, and I turned to see what was spooking him.

I should have just shut everyone up and told them to beat it as soon as I recognized Pablo. Too late. Marvin must have slipped away when he realized what he had here. Now he was on his way back, and Frank was with him.

"Pablo Deerfield," Frank said just as soon as he joined our little group at the end of the hall. "You have the right to remain silent."

twenty-three

You'd expect me to be in some smoky dive lost in a terpsichorean haze, but that wouldn't be low enough. If I'd been snatched back into that world, say doing a routine at Gotta Dance or wowing them at Twinkle Toes or flipping out at the Lite Fantastic, I would be at a place from which I could reasonably return someday. Instead I was home alone and in danger of dancing, and when you dance alone there's a good chance you'll never come back.

Things were at an all-time low.

Our trap had worked just fine if you looked at it from Frank's angle. We netted Pablo in the flesh. He probably wouldn't be able to hold Pablo long, but any time at all would be too long for Pablo. The killer would strike again. Maybe he already had. Yuri and Prudence seemed to have dropped off the face of the planet again. The documentation community was paralyzed. "Do something," they demanded. "Do something!" I couldn't think of anything I could personally do about any of it, so I went home to my mother's house— just locked up the office and left.

I considered driving out to the care center to see Mom, but I had an urgent need to get away from everyone. Maybe it hadn't been more than a week since our last visit, anyway. I couldn't remember. Maybe I should start taking that ginkgo stuff to get more blood flowing to my brain.

I drove south on Dobson Road up and over the hills and into a world where in another season you might see barefoot boys with fishing poles. I didn't get out to the Dobson family house much, but I still had a room there. People came regularly to dust and such, and several times a year historic tours were conducted. I should sell the place. Mom wouldn't be coming back. Maybe someday I would sell it.

I parked the jeep out front and walked along the winding flagstone path to the front door. The house had been built in the late 1800s. Two floors of big rooms and a porch that wrapped all the way around. Gables. Dormers. Flanked by huge trees, the house had been big when I was a boy and strangely it didn't get smaller as I got older.

I spent a lot of my childhood tapping on the walls and listening and looking for secret passages. The place had lots of dark corners and surprising spaces, but I never did find my way into the secret passages.

These days the house was full of empty echoes. I tossed my hat and coat on the table in the entry hall and walked on to the kitchen. I knew what I was up to, but I wasn't admitting it yet.

I put water on for tea. I wandered around downstairs checking windows and turning lights on and off. In the room Mom called the den, I turned on the TV and surfed through every single channel twice, three times, once more. I might still be doing that if the teakettle hadn't whistled at me. I switched off the TV. I made a cup of chamomile tea. I sat down and blew steam from my cup, tasted the tea. It didn't calm me down. I stood up again and walked into one of the downstairs bathrooms and peed sitting down with my head in my hands. Got up, wandered back into the den and turned on the TV, turned off the TV.

Finally I just gave up and climbed the stairs to my room.

Nothing had changed.

I made one more attempt to delay. I sat down in front of the computer. Reached out to turn it on, stopped my hand, got up, paced the floor.

I knelt and opened the double doors of my mahogany stereo cabinet. Inside was my old but very expensive record player. I knew there would come the day when it would quit working and I wouldn't be able to get it fixed. It was a thought too sad to think, so I always put it out of my mind right away. CDs? You must be joking. There were a few albums on the side—things you'd own if you had good taste. Some 45s for eccentricity. The real stuff was locked in a fireproof box under the record player. I got out my keys and opened the box.

In front were several albums in old dust jackets, and behind the albums the rare 78s in cellophane jackets. I knew what I wanted first, and it was right in front. An album called *The Astaire Story*. This was the great one himself with "the Stars of Jazz at the Philharmonic" (BOM Records). I turned the album over and over in my hands. There was a time when I could get this close and then pull back, but those days were long gone. My head was already in the clouds, my body as light as a feather, my toes tightening and relaxing, tightening and relaxing in my stiff street shoes.

I set the turntable in motion and slipped the first record of the Astaire set out of its jacket. The cover of this treasure was so old it was rubbed raw and flaking, but the pictures of Fred and friends inside were sharp and clear, and the records themselves were in good shape. I carefully dusted the one I'd removed and put it on the turntable.

I scooted back by my bed and dug out the dancing shoes I knew would be under there and got a sudden flash face close-up of an ex-wife I never talk about screaming at me, "You've got shoes hidden in every room of the house!" I was on autopilot and shook that ghost out of my head and crawled back to the record player. I was way past the point of no return.

I lifted the needle and then put it down precisely where I intended. "Steppin' Out with My Baby."

Long cool waves of music lifted me, and my knees popped like the sound of two hands clapping once. Shuffle, hop, flap. Heel, heel, lunge. Getting into it. Moving with it. Flying high. Flying higher. Every part of my body working together. The secret is teamwork. Floating up, up, and away. The walls move in, the walls move out.

It should have been a homecoming; part the curtains and step out onto the stage of another world where you could do what you do and do it right every time. Used to be you weren't snatched from the wings to stumble onstage, used to be you danced the dance. These days the dance danced you, puppet man.

I was powerless to do much about it. I still thought that someday I'd dance back to that old place of clarity and joy and certainty, but I never did. These days I always came to a place where you dance as hard as you can dance just to keep from disappearing.

Maybe I had used up dancing. Some people can do that—use things until they're gone or have become other things entirely.

There had been a time when I'd be seeing the patterns about now. Mysteries would unravel. The puzzle pieces would click into place. No dice these days, and you'll be crawling toward the wall looking for a place to bang your head next, the only thing to do when you fall this far is to dance harder, and faster, doesn't matter that you're no longer dancing along with Fred. The secret is to dance a multiple. That is, it's okay to go twice as fast as Fred, even three or four times as fast. It's when you're going one and a half or two and a quarter or three and an eighth times as fast as Fred that you're in big trouble.

The song ended and the next one started. I danced to the end of the record, and when the last song of the side ended, despair swooped in on black wings and slapped me down flat onto the floor.

In the old days, the record would end and I'd be filled with new insight. My body would be toned and humming and my mind buzzing and banging down new avenues.

I took the record off and replaced it in its jacket. I pulled the first of my 78s out and put it on. Got up.

Andrews Sisters, I think.

So far gone, I could hear the boats whistling as the boys came home from the big one.

Then there was a period in which I'm convinced I simply didn't exist. My body truly danced alone.

Who knows how long that lasted?

Then there was a big noise.

The comedy team Laurel & Hardy entered stage left singing. Listen.

Listen. I recognized Bing singing "Mairzy Doats." Laurel & Hardy exited dancing stage right. My mother lounged in a lawn chair drinking something long and cool. She told me to look it up in my *Big Book of Clues!* Roger wandered up behind her and put his hands on her shoulders. It was blurry blue and green where flesh and pixels met. "Pay attention to your mother," he said.

Bing singing "Mairzy Doats." Hey, that isn't Bing. What happened to Bing? It was Billy Cotton, and he wasn't singing the real words of the song. Instead he sang, "Marcy Dotes and Josey Dotes and little Pamsy Divey!"

A pothole opened up under my left foot and I stumbled and fell.

The song was in its final verse and the words were back to normal by the time I rolled over and lifted the arm off the record. I hugged my knees and trembled, teeth rattling down to sudden silence.

So, that's where the killer had gotten his name. Not José. Josey. Josey Dotes. Discovering that much might have been significant but it paled in light of what I now realized.

I knew a Ms. Divey.

Ms. Divey answered the phone for Lucas Betty who must surely be Josey Dotes!

I tried to get up and then sat back down on the floor with a groan. How long had I been gone? I could see it was dark outside, so maybe it was the same night. It would be good if it were the same night.

I crawled into the bathroom and did a bunch of business. I drew a bath and crawled over the side of the tub like an alligator slipping into a river and soaked until the water got cold. Afterwards I got in bed for a quick nap.

The sun was up when next I opened my eyes. I got dressed and went down to the kitchen and ate stuff out of cans. I really wanted a big glass of juice, and that desire told me I was back in the game.

I puttered around the house until I figured pretty much anyone's business day would be in full swing. I dialed Lucas Betty's number at the university.

"Experimental Support Services. Ms. Divey speaking."

"Ms. Divey," I said. "I need to know if your first name is maybe Pamsy?"

"No, it's Margaret. Who is this?"

"But you're small, right? Tell me you're small."

She hung up on me. Maybe I should have been more subtle.

Okay, the fact that her name was Margaret was a setback, but I was still convinced I was right.

Lucas Betty was the Documentalist Killer.

He was the right age to be humming "Mairzy Doats" (if he'd learned it on his mother's knee) as he pondered an alias, and then maybe Ms. Divey came in with some papers and he'd said, "Thank-you, Ms. Divey," but in his mind he'd said "little Miss Divey" or "Little Pamsy Divey" and it hit him and he sang Marcy Dotes and Josey Dotes and little Pamsy Divey. Wouldn't use Marcy, he'd use Josey instead. Wouldn't you?

How could I be sure?

I was sure! In fact, from now on this would be my Method. My subconscious solved cases. All the time I was running around doing things, my subconscious had been working on the case. The trick was just getting out of my own way! For my next case I might never leave the office. Instead I could enter a meditative state and drink juice and wait while my subconscious sifted over the known facts and figured out who did what and when and to whom. I'd go into a kind of Zen detecting trance and the answers would come to me. As they had this time.

But what if I were wrong?

I thought again of my mother and the *Big Book of Clues*. What had she meant? Everything had to fit in somewhere. Everything had to mean something. How many big books did we have? I walked into the library and scanned the shelves. Well, we had lots of big books if you meant fat books. Mom had gone through a Russian novel stage, and there were all the fat Russian novels she'd read.

There were also tall books, mostly filled with pictures.

Eureka!

Here was a big and tall book.

The dictionary.

I remembered what Greta, my Psychic Sidekick, said.

"Can't you just look that up?"

Even Frank had told me I needed a dictionary. When the universe gives you hints, you should pay attention.

So, I looked up "Dotes" (slid past "Dotage"), and I looked up "Josey" (nothing) and "Lucas" (nothing, but "lucent" was nearby and that was encouraging) and "Betty" (zip).

I looked up "Soapy." There were some key words like "smeared" and "smooth" and "slippery" that certainly fit, but nothing spectacular, and I'd nearly turned the page when the word above "soapy" caught my eye—"soapwort": BOUNCING BET.

That nailed it down. Lucas Betty's handle was BOUNCING _BETTY. I flipped over to look that up thinking I'd find screaming bombs and flying shrapnel. "Bouncing Betty" wasn't in my dictionary, but, of course, "bouncing bet" was. It was a perennial herb with pink and white flowers. Another name for it was "soapwort" which sounded like a skin condition, so you'd call yourself SOAPY instead.

Lucas was SOAPY posting on alt.dead.docs using the anonymous 4e4 account he'd opened under the name J. Dotes. He was BOUNCING_BETTY on the BOD list.

That was enough for me, but I was pretty sure the police wouldn't agree.

I called Marvin anyway.

When he said, "Sergeant Zivon," I decided not to share my new insight directly. Seeing is believing. Maybe if Marvin could look into Betty's eyes when I presented my new information, he would see something that would convince him that I was right. Maybe Lucas would break down and confess.

Given modern police methods, I bet Marvin could find some physical evidence on or around Betty once he knew that that was the place to look.

So I lied. I told Marvin I had figured out why Frank had been acting so strangely, but I couldn't talk about it on the phone. Could we meet? Say by the Memorial Union at the university in an hour?

"Why the university?"

"Trust me, Marvin," I said.

twenty-four

I'd forgotten how hard it was to find a parking space in or around the university. Marvin would use an official police parking place, which meant he'd probably get to our meeting place first. Even so, I took the time to stop by Oregon Hall and find out where the offices of Experimental Support Services actually were. Once I hooked up with Marvin, I didn't want to bumble around looking for it. I wanted to zero in on the killer.

It was still maybe an hour before lunchtime. Students hurried in all directions. The University of Oregon is a beautiful place—a park with old and new buildings looming up over trees from around the world—broad lawns and streets where no cars are allowed, bicycles everywhere. Lots of squirrels.

I walked all the way around the Erb Memorial Union building, sometimes on a sidewalk, sometimes on a sloping lawn, and finally down into a sunken courtyard where I found Marvin sitting on a bench watching the students go by. He saw me and stood up.

"Okay," he said. "What's this about Frank?"

"Frank's not fooling around on his wife," I said. I turned around and walked back up the incline out of the courtyard. Marvin followed.

"Who said he was?"

"I can't answer that," I said over my shoulder. "Client confidentiality."

"What are you trying to tell me?" He caught up with me. "And where are we going?"

"This way." I was pretty sure that red brick building was the one I wanted. I looked both ways and crossed the access road. We merged with a noisy group of students going into the building.

Once inside, I scanned the walls for some indication that I was in the right building. Nothing. I guess you had to know where you were going. We passed through the building and into a completely enclosed courtyard. There were students on benches, and a fountain. Several trees. Marvin put his hand on my shoulder and stopped me before I could hurry through to the other side.

"This is far enough," he said.

"You're right!" There was the sign I was looking for. EXPERIMEN-TAL SUPPORT SERVICES. And an arrow pointing down. The offices were underground? "There it is." I pulled away from him.

I was almost to the bottom of the stairs before I realized Marvin wasn't behind me. I stopped and looked back up. It was like looking up from the bottom of a well. The sky and Marvin peering down at me.

"Come on, Marvin," I said.

"I'm not going down there until you tell me what's going on."

I would have to tell him sooner or later. "I've solved the Documentalist Killers case for you," I said.

"Sure you have." He came down the stairs shaking his head. "That's wonderful. You've solved the case. Wait, I know. You've discovered that the murderer is a Peruvian coffee smuggler from Alpha Centauri and he's hiding down in this hole. I'll bet he's taking some night courses. Great. Nice job, Brian."

"I'm going to introduce you to the murderer," I said. "You're going to arrest him. Pretty simple, yes?"

"Jesus," Marvin said. "What do you think, we're on TV? Is that what's happening inside that head of yours?"

I turned away and pushed through double glass doors.

"Hold it!" Marvin yelled. I didn't slow down.

Inside there was a glassed-in reception area with a window to the public. I could see a woman sitting at a desk in there. I couldn't tell how big she was.

Marvin came up beside me.

"That's Ms. Divey in there," I said.

He took a look. "So?"

"Ms. Pamsy Divey." I knew there was no chance whatever Marvin would pick up on the connection if I said she was Margaret Divey, but even aided by my lie about her first name, he didn't get it.

"Josey Dotes and little Pamsy Divey," I said. He still didn't get it. "For crying out loud, Marvin. It's from 'Mairzy Doats.' It's a famous song. The killer got Josey Dotes from the song."

I could see the wheels turning.

"There's no Josey in that song," Marvin said. "No Pamsy either."

I grabbed his arm. "You don't have to be so literal. It's Lucas Betty. Watch his eyes when I call him Josey Dotes. Come on."

"You go too far, Brian."

I walked up to the window. "Ms. Divey?"

The woman got up from her desk and came to the window. "Yes? Can I help you?" I was happy to see that she was a small woman. I might have had an uncomfortable moment of doubt if Ms. Divey had turned out to be large. I'd say she was in her early forties. Tan slacks. A piece of complicated brass jewelry pinned just under the collar of her white blouse. Maybe the emblem of a secret society? Brown hair cut short. Brown eyes. Nice smile.

"We're looking for Lucas Betty's office," I said.

"I'm Lucas Betty." A man stepped through an open door to one side of the glassed-in office. "What can I do for you?"

Had he been lurking back there watching us approach? He was very pale. His hairline had retreated to the top of his head. He was not a large man. Less than six feet tall and thin. He wore glasses. He was not what I'd pictured all those times I'd been lying to him about finding Dennis. He was probably in his middle to late forties. Not a fitness freak. You wouldn't think this was a man who strangled people. But if you already knew he did it, you'd notice his mouth was a tight line. You'd see he was wrapped so tight he vibrated.

"My name is Skylight Howells," I said, savoring the moment, "and this is Police Sergeant Zivon."

Marvin was shaking his head. His face was as red as a beet. I'd be in big trouble if this didn't pan out.

I pushed on before he could stop me. "Can we come in?"

"Have you come about Dennis, then? What's going on?" Lucas looked like he wanted to run off in all directions at once, but he pulled himself together. "Buzz them in, Margaret."

Ms. Divey reached under the edge of her desk. The door buzzed and I pushed it open.

Marvin was right on my heels. Lucas led us into his office. Ms. Divey followed us in.

Lucas took a seat behind his desk. "If it's about your fee, you can forget it. Dennis didn't show up."

"Never mind Dennis," I said. Lucas had taunted me on-line as SOAPY; he had called me on the phone about murder number four. I could see some trembling in the left side of his mouth. He was doing a good job at keeping calm, but he was right on the edge. I needed to push him over.

Marvin turned in a complete circle like he was photographing the place. I hoped his trained eye was taking everything in. But then he just stood there by the desk with his head down like a bad boy called to the principal's office. He should be looking deep into the suspect's eyes. Instead, Marvin was scanning the top of the man's desk like he was looking for a sandwich.

I looked at Ms. Divey standing by the door. Did she know what her boss had been up to?

"You're wondering why I called you all here," I said.

"Shut up, Brian," Marvin said. He looked up at Lucas. "I think we've made a mistake here. Sorry to have wasted your time."

"No way!" I said. I bumped Marvin aside, and he snatched at the desk, scattering papers, to keep his balance.

"I know you're Josey Dotes," I said. "I know you're SOAPY!"

They were all looking at me like I'd dropped my pants.

I turned and pointed at Ms. Divey. "And this is little Pamsy Divey!"

"I know that voice," she said.

"Ms. Divey," Lucas said. "Maybe you'd better call security."

My theory suddenly exploded like a balloon. Maybe I had gotten it all wrong.

"No need," Marvin said. He grabbed my arm. "We'll be leaving now."

I could have gone screaming and kicking. Instead I decided to salvage some dignity. I'd need all I could get as I looked for a new line of work. I pulled my arm out of Marvin's grasp and turned and walked out of Lucas Betty's office and didn't look back until I was through the reception area, out the doors, and back up the stairs.

I turned back and saw that Marvin was right behind me. I couldn't tell what he was thinking, but I bet he wasn't happy. I supposed I deserved whatever he decided to dish out.

We stood toe-to-toe, me looking up, him looking down. He poked me in the chest with one finger. It hurt a lot, but I stood my ground.

"You could have just told me," he said.

"Would you have believed me?"

"It would have been your job to make me believe you." He put his hand in his pocket and pulled out a crumpled piece of paper. He used both hands to straighten it. He spent a moment looking at it, and then he looked back down at me. "You just about blew it here. I have no idea what his lawyer will make of that little scene at the trial."

"The trial?"

Marvin grinned, and I suddenly saw the kid he'd been back when we'd both been scheming to get out of jumping around like idiots in Mrs. Fountain's dance class.

"We won't be able to use this." He handed me the paper. "But it's just a copy anyway. And there's probably plenty of other stuff to find once we start looking."

I looked at the paper.

It was an Experimental Support Services purchase order for ten (10) new printer cables.

twenty-five

It turned out there was lots of physical evidence for Marvin to find. Frank pretty much turned the case over to him, and Marvin had the whole thing wrapped up by the end of the week. He'd probably get a promotion.

Frank had other problems to think about. I told Elsie that he wasn't seeing another woman, but she told him she wanted a divorce anyway. Things had gone too far. Too much was broken. Marvin told me Frank was thinking of leaving the police department so he could devote full time to a project he wouldn't talk about. I was pretty sure that would be Cops for Internet Decency. Frank would be a ghost in the machine.

Yuri stopped in and we had a few glasses of juice together. Matusoff's failure and Yuri's success in the matter of the Documentalist Murders had greatly strengthened his position.

In fact, the other faction was just holding on. It wouldn't take much to finish them off altogether.

"That sounds ominous," I said.

"Old habits," he said. "It's not like we're going to have people shot." He looked away.

He finally managed to drag me to a meeting and after I'd told my story to a bunch of people who knew exactly what I was and what I could be like and still didn't mind, I felt a lot better. I felt like maybe it would be a while before I saw the inside of another karaoke tap joint.

I'd missed a visit with my mother. First there had been finding

Leo's body and then the lost time I'd spent at her house and finally the confrontation with Lucas Betty.

She was grumpy with me when I finally did make it by for one of our "Sunday" visits. I was sorry, and I did my best to cheer her up.

I told her about the case.

I told her I really wanted to thank her for reminding me about the *Big Book of Clues*.

"Oh, that," she said.

I told her the gossip was that Frank Wallace was fooling around on his wife, but I'd found out it wasn't true. She wanted to know who Frank Wallace was.

Just some guy, I told her.

I told her about my lunch with Marvin at the Whisper Café. I made up a story about Mrs. Zivon putting mayonnaise from a jar on my roast beef sandwich. Mom probably knew that wasn't true, but she got a kick out of it anyway.

Her giggles were like the hiccups. She couldn't stop even after she'd forgotten about Mrs. Zivon and the mayonnaise. It didn't matter. She had a good time.

I left feeling pretty good.

Dieter got a special delivery letter. Inside was a short note congratulating him on the way he'd handled the Secret Ingredient on the Net Crisis. I didn't know if that meant Dieter had engineered the posting of all those decoy ingredients or if it meant the Secret Society of Mexican Food Cooks thought he had created the entire Documentalist Murders hullabaloo to mask the fact that someone had leaked the secret.

We finally let Scarface get some fish, and they were going to take some getting used to since whenever I looked at the big tank, the fish were all lined up at the glass staring out at me.

Mean Ramona Simmons still hadn't returned any of my calls. Marvin told me she was still alive so it wasn't that we just hadn't found her body yet. She simply didn't feel like getting back to me. I sent e-mail to her BOD list address. I said, "So tell me Ms. Simmons, how does it feel to be a loose end?"

Sparks would fly.

Later that same day Prudence and Pablo came by. She wrote me a check for the rest of my fee as well as a nice bonus. I gave Pablo a couple of bucks and told him to go buy himself a soda.

"All that stuff about the Secret Masters of the Internet was a lie," I said.

"I told you it was a lie," she said.

"I mean it was *really* a lie."

"Yes," she said. "In fact, it's Pablo who really runs things."

"Oh?"

"You seem skeptical," she said. "He has some trouble out here, but in there he is king. Look how he handled you."

"You mean that was really Pablo pretending to be you pretending to be Pablo and so on?"

"Yes and no," she said.

"So what would have happened if Frank hadn't pulled me out of there before you could show me how the datapants worked?"

"Makes you wonder, doesn't it?"

Part of me had known all along it would be like this. In my line of work, the woman must always remain a mystery, and she must always leave. I was happy Prudence wasn't leaving in a body bag.

Pablo came back with his soda.

There wasn't anything else to say. Prudence stood up. I came around the desk.

Pablo shook my hand.

Prudence gave me a peck on the cheek.

I watched them walk away, and I wondered if they were off to catch a cybertrain and if that train left Eugene traveling east at 79 mph. . . .

About the Author

Ray Vukcevich was born in Carlsbad, New Mexico, and grew up in the Southwest. He now lives in Eugene and works as a computer programmer in a couple of brain labs at the University of Oregon. His short fiction has appeared in many magazines and anthologies, including *Asimov's, Twists of the Tale, Fantasy & Science Fiction, Rosebud,* and *Pulphouse.* He is hard at work on a new novel.